IN A TAVERN BETWEEN WORLDS

"The ring I have led me here tonight," Prince Rupert responded. "Its brilliance blossomed high as we approached that steam train which we seized and drove from Yorkshire to Wales."

"Now wait a little," Holger protested. "I know something about the English Civil War of 1644—but steam trains?"

Valeria whirled. Her finger stabbed at Rupert. "Hold it! You talked about Hamlet and Macbeth as if they were both real. Well, did Romeo and Juliet ever live? . . . Was Richard III really a hunchbacked monster? Did Bohemia ever have a seacoast?"

To each flung question, Rupert nodded.

Valeria tensed. "Do you know the name William Shakespeare?"

"Of course," Rupert said. "He was the Great Historian!"

A Midsummer Tempest

Poul Anderson

BALLANTINE BOOKS • NEW YORK

The poem in Chapter XXI beginning "There will be other times" was originally published under that title in *Smörgåsbord*. Copyright © 1959 by Poul Anderson, and used by a permission which was not especially difficult to obtain.

Library of Congress Catalog Card Number: 73-11696

SBN 345-24404-4-150

This edition published by arrangement with Doubleday & Company, Inc.

First Printing: March, 1975

Cover painting by Darrell Sweet

PRINTED IN CANADA

BALLANTINE BOOKS
A Division of Random House, Inc.
201 East 50th Street, New York, N.Y. 10022
Simultaneously published by
Ballantine Books, Ltd., Toronto, Canada

To Karen
with thanks for twenty years of love

A
Midsummer
Tempest

i

THUNDER AND LIGHTNING. A HEATH ABOUT TO BE BLASTED.

THROUGHOUT that sullen day, cannon had spoken from time to time between the confronting armies. Otherwise there was no move of war. First Rupert waited for the Yorkshiremen; afterward he waited for morning, aware that meanwhile hunger, and memory of the defeats he had already dealt them, would gnaw his enemies for him.

But as evening drew in, clouds massed blue-black across heaven. A wind hooted bleak beneath, snickering in the whins. The gloom flared and banged. *Now God lets loose His own artillery,* went through Rupert. Across its noise came a sound nearly as deep and more harsh. *The drumfire of a Roundhead hymn replies. They seem to think the storm's a sign to them.*

He touched spurs to horse and trotted along the ranks of his cavalry and musketeers till he found the man he wanted. "This breeze is full of battle smells. Hoy, chaplain!" he called; the wind fretted his words. "Let prayers be said." On the way back, he added wryly, "We've done what else we can."

As he took station again, his dog snuffed his boot and offered him a somehow forlorn tail-wagging. He leaned over to rumple the great white head. "So, Boye," he murmured, "so, so, be easy, good old friend. Three years of strife have not yet seen us beaten." An inner pain touched him. *Although at Aylesbury I dared not attack, and in withdrawing lost four hundred men to snow and flood—foul weather, then and now.*

The service began. He rested helmet on saddlebow. Its white plume, his emblem, fluttered dimly in murk, vivid when lightning spurted. He barely made out the text of the brief sermon. ". . . *the Lord God of gods, He knoweth and Israel shall know; if it be in rebellion,*

1

or if in transgression against the Lord, save us not this day."—words from the book of warrior Joshua. Most of his mind prowled the field of coming combat.

He personally headed the Life-Guards on the far left, his flank warded by hedges and a ditch. Goring's riders poised on his right. Breastplates gleamed in a fitful glow, manes tossed, lances and muskets lifted stark. Beyond, cannon crouched like long beasts, slow-matches whipped well-nigh to torches in the hands of their masters. Further on, the white garb of the Yorkshire Lambs made a cloudy-faint mass beneath their pikes. Byron's and the Irish horse, and reserves to rearward, were formless bulks.

Rupert's gaze sought from them to his foes. They occupied a gently rising hill, planted in rye that had been almost ready for the sickle when Englishman came trampling to make war on Englishman. Along with rebel rode Covenanting Scot; Rupert himself faced the Presbyterian cavalry. To their left were Fairfax's foot, and left of those the Independent horse. Spies had reported that there the anchor of the Puritan line was a troop led by one Oliver Cromwell. . . . Rupert could see little through the murk. That fewer rebels than Royalists owned armor made them doubly hard to number. Against what sunset glimmer remained, the roofs of Marston village were limned more clear than they.

He shivered. "This waiting ought to suit the Roundhead well," he muttered unthinkingly: "cold game for colder soul."

"You'll dwarm 'em up," drawled a South country voice.

Turning, Rupert recognized the scarecrow figure hunched on an equally lank steed. "Hush, Will, attend the service," he warned. All at once he realized: "No, 'tis done."

The dragoon chuckled. "Zo now you can heat tha shot at pleasure, my loard—theirs, I mean, for thoase ball-pates 'ull glow red from tha breath o' Hot Rupert, tha Dragon Prince, as I hear their scribblers ha' named ye in their landlubbers' broadzides."

In both armies cannon flashed and boomed, muskets winked and cracked. Through the whistling chill Rupert caught drifts of bitter smoke, shouts of officers, oaths of men, sometimes a jagged scream out of a wounded animal. "Thou talkest overmuch," he said. "I know not why I tolerate thee near me, save that thou'rt good with my pets."

The soldier shrugged. "Tha guns talk moare an' louder, my loard. How they do argue, an' what a harsh logic they chop! I dwould I could zay, instead, they're ballin' each other; but no, that'd bring forth pieces on earth 'gainst men like good Will, an' mesim we been a-pistoled enough." He unslung a leather bottle from his belt and reached it over. "If you do want dwarmth, your Highness, heare, stoke yourzelf from a Puritan househoald where lately zome of us made requisition. Fear not, 'tis indeed a hellfiere preachment, but zafely decanted; for we'd hard ridin' ahead of us, an' thought that whilst tha spirits war for swillin', tha flasks war weak."

"No," Rupert said. "To thy post, clown."

A moment longer the commoner leaned toward his general, as if to memorize those features before too late.

Though tall, he must look upward, for Rupert stood six feet four inches in height, with breadth in an athlete's proportion. Bared, the prince's black locks fell past a weather-beaten face to the shoulders. He did not also follow the Cavalier fashion in beards but went clean-shaven. That made him look older than he was, the sternness became so clear to see. Otherwise his countenance was brown eyes beneath level brows, straight high-bridged nose, full mouth, cleft chin. A tinge of Dutch accent roughened his speech.

Impatiently, he lifted his helmet and coif and buckled them back on. The soldier withdrew into the dusk. Rupert glanced down at his dog. "See well to Boye," he called.

Heaven opened bombardment. For minutes rain cataracted, hail rattled on iron and skittered across ground, lightning etched the armies in molten white and thunder roared damnations on drowned guns.

The squall passed. It had ripped the clouds apart. A weird greenish half-light seeped from sky and horizon. And the men were moving.

Rupert's saber flew free. He raised his chosen war

cry, "For God and for the King!" and heard it echoed many thousandfold. In a surf of shouts and hoofbeats, he and the Life-Guards charged.

Through rye that flowed like water—up the hill—at the rain-wet riders ahead! As he galloped, he flickered an eye to the right. He saw a dash paralleling his, and the enemy's lumbering trot downward to meet it. Dismay flashed: *Byron, that fool, has left our strongest point and gone to call upon a willing host*— He shocked against the Scots.

Pistols spat. He paid no heed, nor did his followers. Swords sparked on armor, ripped flesh and half-seen tartans. Mass shoved at him, around him; braced in the stirrups, he crammed on into it. Steel dinned, men yelled, beasts snorted and neighed, now and then a trumpet rang. Bloody swayed the pennons of King and Parliament.

Here Rupert could not oversee the action. Yet between helmets and maddened faces he glimpsed signs he know how to read. *To rightward, Goring's men thrust on like mine. At times like this, that lame and boastful scoundrel shines forth in such a way that I could love him as if he were my brother . . . O Maurice, are you alike at war this very night?*

Through and through the Covenanters scorched the Royalists. For an instant, as they met the reserves beyond, they paused.

A white shape bounded baying past Rupert's left foot. "Boye!" he shouted. "Thou'st 'scaped the grooms? Come here, Boye, Boye!" From the dour array before him, little fire-tongues uttered spite. His dog leaped once, writhed in falling, struck trampled mire, and lay still. The attack passed over the body.

Tears ran with sweat across Rupert's cheekbones. His blade raged reaping. The Scots broke; the Life-Guards harried them off the hill and across the moor; a hundred lay dead at the feet of Boye.

Rupert reined in on the crest to see how the battle went elsewhere.

He stared at wreck.

Swart waves, wherein steel flashed like sea-fire, struggled howling and hammering. Artillery blared; muskets went off point-blank; never did the Puritan drums stop thuttering, and ever their own slogans tolled forth. While his mount shuddered with need of air, Rupert peered through sulfurous twilight and tried to understand what was happening.

The Roundhead left's destroyed the Royal right, he said at last, in a clenched mind, *clapped hands upon our guns and made them Judas to kiss our center, where the Lambs now bleed upon the altar of their loyalty—*

"We've heavy blows ahead when we be breathed." The voice near him was hoarse with weariness.

Rupert twisted around in his seat. "Be still," he gasped, "Who can't so much as keep a hound!" He choked on half a sob.

Will edged his horse away, though not far. "I'll leave off quackin', Highness; best I duck."

Rupert forgot him in the frenzy of re-gathering his men. It went slowly and ill. Many had scattered across miles in pursuit of the Scots. Those he could find were shaken to their bones by what they saw beneath a rising moon.

They were old comrades to slaughter, even of their fellows. New and terrible to them was the advance of the Independent riders. Their own chief had taught them to spill no time in stopping for a pistol volley. Their way was to charge straight into the thick of the foe, and always they had carried him before them.

Tonight the onset was his. He came in his plain buff jerkin, not at a gallop but a close-knit relentless trot, not hallooing but boulder-silent, no wind band of brothers but the machine which Cromwell had forged.

"For God and for the King!" Rupert clamored. The sound went lonely among cannon. A few followers answered, a few rallied around him.

The Independents broke his line and went to work with sword and ax, killing Cavaliers.

Rupert cut a man from the saddle, and another. He found himself surrounded and slashed his way clear. Across the heath, by hastening icy light, he saw his troop in rout. Their plate glinted like drops from a splash of quicksilver. The enemy sought after him. He skittered off to put together a fresh band, harangue it, and lead it back to fight on.

Again. Again. And then no more.

Over churned mud, smashed gun carriages, sprawling gaping dead, pleading wounded, lifted the thanksgiving chant of the Puritans. The Royal force was broken and the North was theirs.

The moon flew in gray-blue heaven through ragged whitecaps of cloud. Shadows scythed the world. Rupert and Will sat among the fallen of their last affray. Several hundred yards distant, but aimed toward them across the ruined cropland, came a squadron of Roundhead riders.

"Mesim 'twar wise we haul our skins from heare," panted the dragoon, "while still they may hold wine."

"And while I yet may hope to bring together men enough that they can cover their retreat . . . and mine," Rupert said.

Nearby stood a high wooden fence. Between its posts and rails he spied a beanfield reaching wan. Past this was a darkling, diminishing confusion which must be Royalists in flight, and past them a maze of hedges and narrow lanes where they could dismount and repel their pursuers by close fire—if first a leader overtook them. He brought his horse around and struck in spurs. "Once more, thou valiant beast! I wish thee wings!"

The exhausted animal moved forward. There was no spring in the gallop it finally achieved. The fence loomed; Rupert spurred deep; he soared.

He crashed and fell.

In mid-air he kicked free of his stirrups. He hit the ground and rolled among the bean-stakes. Muscles took up more shock than did armor. Bouncing back to his feet, he saw his horse flail about and scream. One leg flopped hideously, snapped across.

His companion's mount had balked at the barrier. The Puritans came on with unwonted speed. Did they know the white plume? An earthquake booming went under hoofs. Metal flashed glacier cold.

Will jumped down. A cloud, briefly covering the moon, made him invisible at a short remove. This close, one could barely see him rip off the King's tokens and sidle away into night.

"Thou'st left thy blade forgotten, in my back!" Rupert cried after him. "I thought at least thou wert as good a dog, if not as bright, as Boye that thou let die! Farewell, Will Fairweather—fairweather friend—"

He stooped, to draw his dagger and give his charger the last mercy. Thereafter he took forth his sword.

The Roundheads overleaped the fence and ringed him in. He looked from saber to saber, pistol to pistol. A craggy-visaged man who must be their captain squinted at him. "This is indeed Prince Rupert of the Rhine," he breathed.

He straightened. His steel snapped upward in salute. "Your Highness, you will not remember me," he said. "I was a humble knight you met at court, that time in youth when you from Holland came to guest his royal Majesty your uncle—who's still our King, and we his loving subjects who only fight his evil counselors—"

"You are so long of wind you ran me down," Rupert replied.

"I beg of you, your Highness, that you yield. You shall receive all honor due to you."

Rupert bit his lip. "Else lie a corpse, or piglike stunned and trussed?" Within their casques, the faces above him and around him strove to hold glee in seemly place. His sword sank, until he handed it hilt foremost up to the captain. "Well, have this of me, then, Sir What's-Your-Name, until another day." His head lifted. "For after all, 'tis no disgrace to fall to such as Cromwell. Beneath your buff, you men are Ironsides."

ii

A MANOR, SOME THREE MILES UP THE RIVER
AIRE FROM LEEDS.

THOUGH lately built, of modern brick and tile, it seemed
to belong to an earlier age. Twin battlemented towers
flanked its gauntness, and cannon the drawbridge across
a moat. Clearly, the owner had foreseen trouble return-
ing to England. Not far away on the right, well pre-
served but deserted, blurred by time and ivy, Kirkstall
Abbey was another remembrance, more peaceful and
more sad.

Both stood forth sharp upon a tamed terrain. Lawns,
arbors, and flowerbeds encompassed the manor, down
to the stream in whose sparkle yew and willow mirrored
themselves. Behind the house went that row of sheds,
stables, mews, and cottages which pertained to the estate
of any gentleman. The country around was mostly
farmed; besmocked hinds, their wives and children,
horses and oxen belonging to the master, could be seen
at work in several distant fields. One deserted steading
had not yet been torn down, for it was not so very long
ago that the last bankrupted yeoman was brought out,
the last tenant made into a hired hand, and the common
enclosed. Remotely to north, where hills rolled skyward,
blue haziness veiled a remnant of wildwood.

In that setting, the future made a deeper mark than
the past. From the largest of the sheds a railway ran
straight to a stone bridge across the river, and thence
vanished southward. Skeletal semaphores, spaced in
sight of each other, stood guard along the tracks. To
left, Leeds was a cluster of steeples, walls, and roofs,
blurred less by the miles between than by the smoke from
a dozen tall stacks which begrimed them. A grayness of
factories and tenements had begun to sprawl around the
old city. The wind bore a hint of iron in motion, stamp-

ing and grinding. On the western horizon, trails of fume
and soot marked where Bradford lay.

Here, however, July was pure. The morning sun
touched small wandering clouds with brilliance and
called a thousand different greens out of grass and
leaves, golds out of cornfields. The air carried odors of
blossom, earth, and growth. All trees were full of birdsong.

As the front door of the manor opened, two mastiffs,
chained near the guns, broke into furious noise. They
quieted when Sir Malachi Shelgrave stepped forth,
though they still bared teeth and growled at Rupert, the
stranger by his side. Behind came four halberdiers in
helmet and corselet, two-handed swords slung across
their backs, pistols in their belts. The drawbridge
boomed hollowly under their tread.

The captive was unarmed and unarmored. The
clothes he had worn beneath his mail—linsey-woolsey
shirt, leather doublet, coarse hose of blue wadmal,
knee-length flare-topped boots—had undergone a hasty
cleaning which left faintly visible stains of grass, soil,
sweat, and blood. His head was combed and barbered
but hatless.

His companion, who was of medium height, must
crane neck backward to meet Rupert's eyes. He smiled,
a stiff little twitch, and said in his precise voice: "I do
regret your Highness must go thus, as plain as any yo-
kel, for the nonce. You're such an unawaited guest, you
see. This house holds naught that's near to fitting you."

"No matter," Rupert answered indifferently.

"Oh, it is, if but to me. Sir Malachi Shelgrave's honor
makes demand that he show proper hospitality"—he
drew breath—"to Rupert, Prince and nephew of the
King, by birth Count of the Rhine Palatinate, Duke of
Bavaria and Cumberland, the Earl of Holderness, a
Knight o' the Garter, and, over all such titles from the
blood or from King Charles, his Captain-General."

For an instant, Rupert's set calm broke. He halted
and half raised a fist. Lips drew back from teeth, brows
down above stare. The guards gripped fast their weapons.

Shelgrave stood his ground, spread palms wide and

exclaimed: "I pray your pardon, did I seem to mock! I merely wish to show with what great care I've studied you, our glorious opponent."

Rupert let fingers unclench and fall. Again there was nothing to read on his face. The Roundheads looked relieved.

"This day a master tailor comes from Leeds," Shelgrave proceeded rapidly. "He'll measure you, drop every other work, and sleep will be a stranger to his shop till you are suited as becomes a prince in velvet, silk and cramoisie."

"No need," said Rupert. "I am a soldier, not a popinjay."

His gaze probed the other man. Shelgrave met it, and for a minute they stood locked.

At fifty years of age, the master of the land was still trim and erect. The hair had departed his high-domed skull, save for a brown fringe cut short around the ears; the grayish eyes were forever blinking; skin sagged beneath the chin of an otherwise cleanly molded sallow countenance; but those were almost the only physical scars which time had thus far dealt him. His clothes were of Puritan austerity in color and cut, though a glow in the dark hues bespoke rich material. A rapier hung at his waist, together with a large wallet.

"At least your Highness needs a change or three," he said. "I think you'll grace this house—perhaps a month."

Rupert failed to keep surprise quite out of his tone. "That long a while?"

"I pray my lord, consider." Shelgrave resumed strolling. Rupert fell into step, as well as such long legs were able. The Parliamentarian glanced sideways at him before going on: "They say you are a most blunt-spoken man. Have I your leave to use frank words?"

"Aye, do. I'm surfeited with two-tongued courtliness —" Rupert broke off.

Shelgrave nodded knowingly. "Well, then," he began, "your Highness—and Maurice, your brother, but you the foremost ever, these three years—you've been the very spearhead of our foes. Your name's as dread as Lucifer's in London. Without that living lightning bolt,

yourself, the armies of unrighteousness—forgive me—
would long be scattered from around the King like tempest clouds before a cleansing wind."

"In his sight," Rupert snapped, "you're the rude and
ugly winter."

"He is misled."

"Continue what you'd say."

"May I indulge my curiosity?" (Rupert gave a
brusque nod.) "Although I am no soldier born like you,
I did see service under Buckingham in younger days,
and was therefore made knight. Sithence a scholar of the
art of war, among much else, I've read not only Caesar
and other ancients, but the chronicles of later strategists
like great Gustavus. I've thus had knowledge to admire
your skill as it deserves. They call you overbold—but
nearly always, lord, you've won the day. And still so
young: a score of years and four!" Shelgrave blinked at
his prisoner, who did not act like a man tickled by flat-
tery. "The fight on Marston Moor thus strikes me
strange. When faring north to lift the siege of York, you
found your opposition ill-supplied, disheartened, split in
squabbling sects and factions, and in no favor with most
Northerners. You could have chivvied them as wolves
do kine until they broke, 'Tis what I feared you'd do.
Instead you forced a battle on a ground ill-chosen for
your side. I wonder why."

"I had mine orders," Rupert rasped. "More I will not
say."

" 'Tis honorable of your Highness, that—yet useless,
for it surely is no secret what envies and intrigues have
seethed around the youthful foreigner who sought the
King when war broke loose, and was at once raised
high. Which rival engineered those orders, Prince? No
Puritan would undermine—"

"Have done!" Again Rupert stopped as if in menace.

Shelgrave bowed to him. "Of course. Mine object's
only to explain why I've the pleasure of your company.
You see, you're priceless to our enemies, and hence to
us. Your capture was God's mercy, which brings in sight
an ending of this war. Yet still the Royalists retain some
strength. Their court's at Oxford, not so far from London. A massive raid by, let us say, Maurice might still

regain you for that high command which soon your
fiercest rival won't begrudge. It must not happen. Fairfax
saw this too. Accordingly, he had you carried hither in
deepest secrecy, here to abide until the East is absolute-
ly cleared. Then, without fear of any rescuers, you can
be brought to London."

"To what end?"

"That lies with Parliament."

The furrows tautened around Rupert's mouth. "I
thought as much."

Shelgrave took his elbow in companionable wise and
guided him on along the path. Roses stood tall on either
side, above a shyness of pansies; the breeze was full of
their fragrance. Sunbeams slanted through trees to dapple the lawn. Gravel scrunched underfoot.

"Your Highness, cast your melancholy off," Shelgrave urged. "You'll find enjoyment and surcease from
strife. The household staff and others you may meet are
under oath to breathe no word of you, and known to me
for their trustworthiness. And thus by day, though
guarded, wander free about these grounds." He gave an
apologetic sigh. "I dare not let you ride. I would I did.
I'm eager in the hunt, and you will like my horses and
my hounds."

Briefly, Rupert's fists knotted.

"But you can fish, play ball, do what you wish," Shelgrave promised. "I hear you are of philosophic bent.
Well, so am I. Make use of any books. Do you play
chess? I'm not so bad at that. At night, I fear, you must
be locked away in your apartment, high in yonder
tower. But 'twill be furnished with the tools of art—they
say you draw and etch delightfully—and you'll have ac-
cess likewise to the roof. There often I beguile a sleepless night by tracking moon and stars across the sky.
Come too! I'll show you mysteries in heaven"—his
voice trembled a little, ardor leaped behind his eyes—
"and maybe they'll convert you to the truth."

Rupert shook his head violently. "That lies not in
your sour and canting creed."

Shelgrave flushed but kept his words level. "Were you
not reared a Calvinist, my lord?"

"I try to be a proper Protestant, yet not cast off

what's good from olden time. I'd liefer hear a service than a rant; I do not think my Romish friends are damned, nor that 'tis right to persecute the Jews; I'd hang no helpless granny for a witch." Bitterly: "That day we captured Lichfield, I was glad to let its staunch defenders leave with honors. But then we entered the cathedral close and saw what desecration had been wrought on ancient lovely halidoms——" Rupert hewed air with the edge of his hand. "Enough."

"There goes a daybreak wide across the world," Shelgrave said, "which forces pretty stars to flee our sight. But oh, those stars were shining infamous within that chamber which a tyrant kept! 'Tis pity that you fight for fading night."

"I grant that James was not the best of kings——"

"He was the worst . . . and followed Gloriana. Harsh taxes to maintain a wastrel court, oppression of a rising merchant class in whom the seeds of England's greatness lie, and rural rule by backward-looking squires: such was the legacy that Charles disowned not. And worse, his queen herself is Catholic; the Papists get an easy tolerance; the Church of England stays unpurified. Small wonder, then, that free-souled men demand, through Parliament, long-overdue reform."

"I am no judge of that," said Rupert; "I'm merely loyal. And yet—you people prate so much of freedom ——" He waved toward the hireling workers in the fields. "How free are they? No lord looks after them. *You're* free to let them go in beggary across the gashed and smoky land you'd make."

The men paced on awhile in silence, bringing their tempers under control. At length Shelgrave said, his tone mild once more:

"I thought your Highness a philosopher who also cultivates mechanic arts."

"Well, that I do," Rupert admitted. "I like a good machine."

"What think you of our late-invented cars which run by steam and draw a train behind?"

"They've been too rare for me to more than glimpse, and railway builders all seem Puritan. We captured one such . . . locomotive, is it? . . . near Shrewsbury, upon that single line which leads into the West. I did admire it, but had no time from war to really look." Rupert's glance went as if compelled along the tracks to the biggest shed. Smoke drifted out of a chimney on its roof.

"I love them as I do my hunting horses," Shelgrave said softly. "The morrow is the truest freight they bear. To date they are but small, as well as few, scarce faster than a beast although untiring. They mainly carry wagonloads of coal to feed the hungry engines in the mills and manufactures of cloth and hardware which men like me are building ever more of—" With rising enthusiasm: "You may not understand what we are doing from such few glimpses as you got by chance. But you —but men now live who'll see the day when this whole island is enwebbed with rails and locomotives like Behemoth's self haul every freight, plus civil passengers, and troops and guns in time of war—a day when power does not grow from birth or sword, but out of mills and furnaces."

"Perhaps." However clipped his answer, Rupert's look kept straying to the shed.

The other observed, smiled the least bit, once more cupped the prince's elbow, and said with a gesture, "This is a spur of track for mine own use. I've ordered stoking, as you've doubtless guessed, because I hoped 'twould lift your Highness's mood to see a train in action, even drive it."

"You are most kind, Sir Malachi." The eagerness in Rupert's body would not stay altogether out of his voice.

"Then come," proposed Shelgrave.

A workman let them and the guards into the gloom beyond the doors.

A moment later, a coach and four rattled up a drive which curved to meet the Bradford road. As it halted, a footman in somber livery sprang off the back to open it up and offer a supporting hand. Jennifer Alayne didn't notice. She jumped straight out, looked around her, and cried in joy: "Oh, home!"

The footman bowed. His smile was genuine, as was that of the coachman. "Be welcome, Mistress Jennifer," he said.

"I thank you." She squeezed his shoulder—he was

taken pleasantly aback—and ran across the gravel onto the lawn. A lilac bush stood man-high, still wet from the heavy dew which had followed the stormy weather of the past few days. She seized its blossoms to her, buried herself in purple and fragrance.

Her maidservant, who had left the carriage more sedately, hurried after. "Mistress Jennifer!" she called. "Take care! You'll drench your gown—" She stopped. "Oh dear, the thing is done."

"'Tis best that thou'rt named Prudence, and not I." Laughing, her garb soaked indeed, the girl turned. "Forgive thy giddy jenny wren, I pray, and I'll try not to be a willful ass."

Prudence pinched lips together and walked stiff-legged to join her.

Aside from black garments demurely trimmed in white, the young woman and her bony elder might have belonged to two different races. Jennifer was tall, reed-slender save for her bosom but bouncy of gait. The hood had fallen back on her traveling cloak to show amber-colored hair coiled in heavy braids. Between them were big green eyes, thick-lashed under arching dark brows; slightly tilted nose; mouth whose width and softness stood at odds with the rake of chin and jawline.

"I'm but your humble maid and chaperone," Prudence said, bending her neck as if she were in church ordering Jehovah to the battlefront, "yet old in service of Sir Malachi and of his wife, who bade me tend you well. My duty is to help you learn behavior."

"I'm grateful." Jennifer's flat utterance drew such a look that she hastened to add: "Now I feel that this is home. Thou know'st I've missed mine erstwhile sea and hills, have often chafed in London and then here; but that was ere we spent those weeks in Bradford"—her words began to tumble forth of themselves—"those years, eternities!—of dinginess, of reeking air and racketing machines and workers shuffling past like broken beasts and joyless, wizened children at the looms . . . and rich men feeling smug about their works—"

"Be careful, child," Prudence broke in, "and speak no ill of progress."

"I'm sorry. I forgot. And, well, of course I've watched the same in Leeds." The rebuke faded from Jennifer's mind. She whirled about so fast that skirts lifted over ankles, flung her arms wide and cried: "Here's radiance! Each petal is a pane upon a lantern, a robin redbreast makes a meteor, a spider's captured diamonds in his web—" She danced from bush to tree to flowerbed, caressing them and singing:

> *"A weary age*
> *That felt the rage*
> *Of rain has won a pardon.*
> *Be done with gloom!*
> *The sun's in bloom*
> *And all the world's a garden.*
> > *"Highdy, heighdy, ring-a-ding-dady,*
> > *Seek the greenwood with thy lady!"*

"Hush, mistress. This is downright libertine," Prudence warned. Jennifer did not hear her.

> *"The bees, the trees,*
> *A gypsy breeze*
> *That skips along before us,*
> *The birds that sing,*
> *The brooks that ring,*
> *Say all the world's a chorus.*
> > *"Highdy, heighdy, ring-a-ding-dady,*
> > *Seek the greenwood with thy lady!"*

"She's seventeen," Prudence explained to God while striving to overtake the girl without an indecorous sprint, "a time to tax her elders, when Satan's dangled bait smells savory."

> *"The air is fleet*
> *And strong and sweet,*
> *And high the lark's at hover.*
> *Then let a maid*
> *Go unafraid,*
> *For all the world's a lover.*
> > *"Highdy, heighdy—"*

An explosive *chuff* broke across the little tune. Jennifer checked herself. Prudence caught up. Together they regarded the shed. Steam billowed from it and vanished.

A workman in oily shirt and breeches appeared to fling doors wide. Snorting, clicking, a locomotive rolled forth.

Its boiler, some ten feet long, sat black above great red-painted wheels. The stack, half as tall as that, belched smoke, sparks, and cinders. Motion made a brass bell jingle. On the open platform stood four men. Jennifer knew Sir Malachi Shelgrave, the driver, and the stoker who shoveled fuel into firebox—but not the dark, outsize young fellow whose gaze dwelt like a falcon's on everything the driver did, nor the soldiers perched precariously on timbers laid across the sides of the tender. As well as this, the locomotive drew a peak-roofed oaken carriage. Through its leaded windows one could see an interior furnished like an office chamber.

"Oh, uncle, art thou going for a ride?" Again Jennifer ran. "Can I come too?"

Shelgrave tapped the driver on the back. "Make halt, abide awhile." The engine gushed steam and clanked to a stop. The stoker sat down and wiped wrist across brow, leaving a white trail through coal-grime. Rupert continued watching and asking questions. Shelgrave leaned over the platform rail. "Well, Jennifer," he greeted, "how did it go in Bradford?"

"Most drearily," she replied. "I'm happy to be back."

He lifted a finger. "Then thou shouldst not at once be bent on pleasure," he chided, "but on thy knees in giving thanks to God, Whose victory is what's let thee return."

Rupert heard, scowled, and stepped to Shelgrave's side. Seeing the girl, however, he bowed. "Your Highness," the older man said, "pray let me present to you my niece and ward, hight Jennifer Alayne."

As she curtsied, a blush went over her like a tide. Shelgrave addressed her: "Have due appreciation of the honor of meeting his most gracious Highness Rupert, a nephew of our King, a Rhineland prince, made Duke of Cumberland—"

Jennifer had gasped. One hand flew to her mouth. She stared through eyes gone enormous.

"God help us, Rupert!" shrieked Prudence, and collapsed.

Jennifer knelt down beside her. "She's swooned, the poor old soul," she said, took the gray head in her lap and fanned it with a corner of her cloak. "There, there, fear not," she murmured. Prudence's lids fluttered. She moaned. Several men guffawed. Jennifer glared at them. "Nor laugh, you dolts!" she snapped. "She's ample cause for fear."

Rupert leaped to earth, strode to the pair, squatted, and chafed the woman's hands. "Alas, no cause," he said. His lips bent sardonically. "I know your pamphlets call me Prince Robber, Duke of Plunderland, and such; and doubtless it was fret about your safety which packed you off within those borough walls when word came I was riding north to York." He turned earnest. "A single time have I made war on women—"

Jennifer gave him an astonished regard.

"I did not know it," he explained. "Early in this strife, mine own band small, I sought to seize a house of rebels, who fought very stoutly back and held us off till powder was exhausted. I then found out that they were only few and that the manor's lady was their captain. I asked her husband to enlist with me, but he refused. I left them in their peace with their possessions. She had earned that right." He sighed. "Elsewhere—yes, I have often requisitioned, as is the practice on the Continent, and necessary in the Royal cause. When that has won, the cost shall be repaid." His smile grew lean. "Meanwhile, I am a prisoner and harmless."

"You speak so nobly, lord," the girl whispered. Red and white fled across her features.

Prudence struggled to a sitting position and spat with renewed courage: "No harm in him? He's mortal danger, although bound like Satan!"

Rupert chuckled. "Well, let this devil help thee to thy feet." She had scant choice. Once erect, she tottered backward.

"She needs support," Jennifer decided. "I beg your

pardon, sir." She went to give the maid her arm and shoulder, if not much attention.

"Take her within, and likewise take thyself," Shelgrave directed from the platform. "Your Highness, shall we be upon our way?"

"Until this evening, Jennifer Alayne," said Rupert. He took her hand and kissed it. Where he was reared, that was common courtesy; but her knees buckled. Since a horrified Prudence clung the more tightly to her, both women went down.

Rupert assisted them to rise, while keeping a blank expression and uttering meaningless murmurs. Finished, he bounded from their confusion. Ignoring a fixed ladder, he seized the handrail and swung himself aboard. The train came alive and thumped off across the bridge and southward.

"We should go in, dear Mistress Jennifer," said Prudence weakly.

The girl stayed looking after the smoke-plume.

Prudence stiffened. "Jennifer!" she said aloud.

The girl blinked. "Oh." She turned her face from that horizon. "Aye. Indeed. I come."

At the other end of the drawbridge, she paused to pet the watchdogs. Their tails dithered, they thrust muzzles into her skirt and laved her hands with interminable tongues.

"You're too familiar with those nasty hounds," Prudence scolded. "They're loud and dangerous."

"Well, not to me." Liveliness rose afresh in Jennifer. "Who else e'er gives them love?" She pulled ears and scratched necks. "There, Skull; good Bones."

"You are too foolish fond of animals." Prudence's glance went away, along the railroad to the last sight of the train. "And he," she mumbled, "the very Beast of Revelation—"

Jennifer went on into the house. Her servant followed. The butler closed the door.

iii

THE OBSERVATORY TOWER. NIGHT.

RUPERT took eye from telescope. "So I have seen the moons of Jupiter, and mountains on our own," he murmured. "It feels right strange."

"Did you not know erenow?" Shelgrave asked.

"I'd heard, of course," Rupert said, "but seldom had the time to think on it, except three years at Linz when I was captive; and other things then occupied my mind. Nor have I known an optic tube this good. I can forgive you much, Sir Malachi, for that you've opened heavens up to me."

He waved around sky and earth. A moon approaching the full enfeebled most stars but not the tawny planet. Light lay hoar on lawns, distant fields and hillcrests, black bulks of treetops; it ran down the river like spilled mercury. Against it, the lantern was dull which stood outside a rooftop storage shack. The various instruments had been removed from this and erected at the parapet, where they resembled tongues thrust out above snag teeth of merlons. Nearby, shadowy save for the glimmer on casques, breastplates, and halberd heads, those four soldiers who had the nighttime warding of the prisoner stood rigid. Doubtless they disapproved of what was going on.

The air was quiet, mild, full of green odors. Crickets creaked.

Rupert rested hands on bedewed stone, looked upward, and went on in the same low voice: "Now can I truly feel how we are crew aboard a ship that plies around the sun."

Beneath his high-crowned hat, Shelgrave's frown was barely visible. "Beware," he clipped. "Though God is merciful to us and lets us sweeten careworn sleeplessness —how well I know—with His astronomy, yet Satan can make this another lure. A moving earth is clean 'gainst Holy Writ."

Rupert raised brows. "I am no theologian, but I've known right godly men who've told me otherwise." His vision strayed across the guards. It made him hunch his back. Curtly: "No doubt you will deny the world is round."

"Oh, nay, I don't. That is acceptable. It has indeed been known since ancient times. Why, even in a dim and pagan Britain, before the Romans came, the fact stood forth."

Rupert's resentment drowned in interest. "How so?"

"Did not the anguished Lear cry out, *'Strike flat the thick rotundity o' the world!'*? I dare not claim the great Historian divinely was inspired; but with most scholars, I do believe he rendered truth exactly."

"I've often wondered," said Rupert in some excitement. "On the Continent so many records flamed away with Rome that he's well-nigh the only source we have . . . for an existence back in Grecian times of a first Kingdom of Bohemia, which had a seacoast, or a prior Russia. But did he draw on fact or on mere legend? How can tradition keep inviolate the virgin truth down tempting centuries?"

"When it is borne by God's own chosen people," Shelgrave answered solemnly. "They are the English, he their chronicler."

The ghost of a grin flickered on Rupert's mouth. "Well, I am half an Englishman. Say on."

Shelgrave paced back and forth, hands gripped beneath his coattails, talking rapidly. "How else will you account for English folk—and such they are, in character and speech, both elevated nobles and low commons—before the walls of Troy, in Theseus's Athens, in Rome and later Italy, in Denmark—save that the English race has spread out north from some old southern land which they must leave? And when we study well our English Bible, 'tis plain to see who our ancestors were: none but the ten lost tribes of Israel! Descendants who did settle by the way have melted into those localities and thus have mostly lost their pristine nature. But in far Britain they have stayed themselves, no matter Roman, Saxon,

Dane, or Norman—who're after all related in the blood.
And though they were beguiled by many lies, like Israelites since days of Abraham, they always kept a seed of
truth alive, which flowered in the great Historian."

Rupert tugged his chin. "It may be so. . . . I slept
once in his house."

Shelgrave halted. "You did?"

"A year ago upon this month. The Queen had lately
made return to England with troops and money. I es-
corted her to Oxford where her royal husband was. It
happened that we spent a night in Stratford. His own
granddaughter and her man inhabit the selfsame dwell-
ing, and they made us welcome. Next day I said a prayer at his grave."

Rupert leaned again on the battlements. Before his
eyes lay the gracious remnants of the abbey. He half
pointed. "If you are deep into antiquity," he asked,
"why do you seek to blot its glories out?"

Shelgrave joined him. The Puritan's voice harshened.
"We will restore the true antiquity—Jehovah of the
Thunders—and His Son who scourged the money chang-
ers from the temple—alone in heaven and in the soul
of man. My lord, I thought you were a Protestant."

"I am a Christian first," Rupert replied, still soft-spo-
ken. "In spite of errors, yon walls have been a fortress
of the truth."

"When once this man-consuming war is past, I'll have
them razed, plow up their very dead, and house mine iron
engine on the site."

"Barbaric! Why?"

"To keep away the spooks that still are seen ofttimes
by trusty men to haunt those ruins and the wildwood
there." Shelgrave gestured across his land. " 'Tis true
the Roman Church at first was pure, when good Augus-
tine preached unto the Saxons. But in the Serpent crept
with heresies and paganisms—worst in Western realms,
where Celtic so-called Christians held their rites in Ireland, Wales, and Glastonbury itself—"

"They say that Glastonbury was Avalon."

"If so, it grew corrupted after Arthur. And likewise
hereabouts, the Catholics soon made their peace with
diehard heathen ways. A saint and not a god went forth

in spring to bless the fields—what was the difference? The May and Morris dances were obscene, and Christmas nothing but a solstice feast. The folk continued to make offering of corn and milk and rites unto the elves, the while their priests did wink at it—aye, claimed that Puck himself became a Christian sprite!"

Shelgrave plucked Rupert's sleeve. "Make no mistake," he hissed, "they do exist, those things, as witches do, and fiends, and Lucifer, to mock the Lord and spring the traps of hell. I have a German book that you should read, *Malleus Maleficarum*, which explains it, and tells what tortures will call forth the truth, that fire and water then may cleanse out evil or rope and bolster smother it."

Rupert considered him for a while, under moon and stars, before he said: "And yet you are a student of astronomy! I think I'd best go downstairs to my cell."

iv

A ROOM IN THE TOWER.

BEYOND its walls hung gray weather, sun hidden behind overcast and occasional drizzle. Cattle, grazing in a nearby paddock, were a fantastic red upon deep green. Through an open window rawness invaded, against which popped the musketry of a hearthfire.

Rupert had been figurative in describing his quarters. The chamber was broad, comfortably furnished, its brick padded by rugs and tapestries. But he had shoved most things aside to make space for a worktable. There he stood driving a burin across the wax on a copper plate. From time to time he took a bite of bread and meat or a swig from an ale cup.

A rap resounded on the door, barely to be heard through oak and iron massiveness. Rupert grunted annoyance. It evaporated when Jennifer appeared. One of the sentries on the staircase posted himself in the entrance.

"Why, welcome, lady. What a fine surprise." The prince bowed. Though he wore stained smock, breeches, and slippers, while her garb was costly if plain and dark, his was the courtliness. She flushed, twisted fingers together and dropped her gaze.

Rupert stretched cramped muscles. "What should I thank for this?" he asked. With a grin: "And where's your keeper?"

"I . . . slipped from her," the girl whispered. "She never would have come."

"Aye, rustle in her starch and sanctity into my den of brimstone? Hardly Prudence!" Rupert laughed aloud. "But why've you come to visit this first time in these four sennights I've been counting here?" His merriment faded. Advancing to loom over her, he said carefully, "Your uncle doesn't like it very well, in spite of saying naught—I know the signs—he doesn't like that we are much together in walking, talking, playing chess or draughts, you singing to the pipe of my recorder . . . and that's in public view—" He remembered the Roundhead in the doorway and gave him a wry look, repaid in acid. "Ah, well, you have a chaperone of sorts."

"There is no need." She spoke toward her clasped hands. "Your Highness is an honorable man. I came . . . because you've long been shut away. . . . I feared you might be sick." The green eyes lifted in search. "But you look hale."

"I am."

"Thank God." It was no command—a prayer.

" 'Twas sweet of you to fret. Since we've been having such a rainy spell that naught's to do outdoors, my restlessness has turned itself to art, as erst in Linz, and soon I was too captured by the work to wish to leave it, and sent out for food." Rupert studied the girl. "Now instantly I know how I have missed you."

"Oh—" She swallowed. "May I see what you are doing, Highness?"

"An etching of St. George against the dragon, not yet triumphant but still locked in strife." She accompanied him to the table. Untrained, her look was mainly to the drawing from which he worked.

"How marvelously real," she breathed.

"And suitable to this our age," he said, turning grim. "Well, thank you, Jennifer." He tried to shake the mood off. "Will you not seat yourself awhile and chat?"

He placed chairs opposite each other before the hearth. She waited to take hers until he had settled down, shank across knee, fingertips bridged, glance quizzical. A smile eased the severity which most often possessed his countenance.

"In many ways, this place is just like Linz," he remarked, "including, yea, another damosel."

Jennifer stiffened. Firelight flickered across her face, its crackle went beneath her voice. "Who was she?" After a moment, in confusion: "Pardon my forwardness, lord."

"Naught calls for pardon, lady. Though, 'tis odd— have I not told you of Count Kuffstein's daughter?

You've asked so eagerly about my past—which no man's loth to tell a pretty maid—I thought you had my whole biography."

"No, you've passed lightly over those three years when you were prisoner in Austria." She leaned toward him. "I understand. The likenesses give pain." Her tone was troubled. "Then do not speak of them to me, Prince Rupert."

"I think I'd like to, if you will not mind," he said slowly.

"Then do."

Her gaze never left him. His went to the hues which wove in the fire. "This seems to cast a thawing warmth," he mused, "across a child born to the Winter King."

"The Winter King?"

"His nickname's new to you?" Rupert said, bending a startled attention back onto her. "Why, thus they called my father, for he reigned that single season in Bohemia. I know you know how England has been roiled by politics of the Palatinate."

"I am not learned, your Highness," Jennifer replied humbly. "As you've heard, I'm from a wild and lonely Cornwall coast. I got no schooling till I was fourteen, and in the years since then have been kept cloistered." Impishness broke through; she wrinkled her nose and giggled. "Please quote that not to Uncle Malachi."

Rupert laughed too, with a malicious glance for the sentry and his fellows. They were out of earshot if voices stayed low.

"You've told me almost nothing of yourself," he realized.

Her bosom rose and fell. "There's nought worth telling, Highness."

Gravity came back upon him. "Jennifer," he said, "with charm and merriment and . . . simply caring, you've kindled stars in this eclipse of mine. Today I see I've taken them for granted. I don't think I'll be here much longer—" At her strickenness, he nodded. "Aye. Reports come daily in how Cavaliers are everywhere in rout before the Roundheads. The London roads will soon be clear of them, and I'll be taken thither. . . .Well, my lady, if ever you have thought of me as knight, although upon the side opposed to yours, give me your token as in olden time—but let it be a memory of you. Tell me your life, beginning at its dawn. No matter if I've heard some parts before." He grimaced. "Remind me that you are by blood no Shelgrave."

Did she flush, or was it only red fire-glow? She stared into the flames awhile before abruptly turning to him and saying: "If you'll do likewise, Prince."

"A handselled bargain." Trying to laugh afresh, he reached over and laid his fingers about hers. She gasped, then clung; tears trembled on her lashes. The peering Puritan in the doorway bent neck around and muttered to a comrade.

Rupert released Jennifer and leaned against his chair-back. "Not quite a fair exchange," he observed: "because, you see, I'll hear what's mostly new—d'you understand I have not heard who your own father was?—while you'll be getting yarns I fear are shopworn."

"How can a tale of bravery wear out?"

Rupert squirmed a little. "Speak. Ladies first."

She responded hesitantly: "As you may know, my mother and aunt were daughters of Horatio Binstock, a Yorkshire merchant—Congregational, though easygoing, not a strict reformer. Mine aunt wed Malachi but had no issue. My mother, younger, wilder, then eloped with Frank Alayne, half French, half Cornishman, the captain of a ship . . . and Catholic. Her father having died, Sir Malachi avenged the slight by causing Dad's discharge. Thereon my parents had to seek his homeland, a hamlet on a rugged, wooded shore where he could be part owner of a boat that fished, bore freight, or smuggled as might be." She raised eyes from lap; finding his fixed upon her, she lowered them again. "There I grew up, the oldest child of four. Mine only education was some French from Dad and friends of his from 'cross the Channel. When Mother died, I must at ten be mistress, take care of those my siblings, and of Dad, who soon was drinking headlong as he'd lived. He drowned one autumn four years afterward. I fear we'd seldom been inside a church; but still the minister was good enough to write to London, to mine aunt and uncle. They, being childless, took us for their wards."

"How fared you with them?"

"Oh, they're not unkind—at least to us; the servants go in terror. We'd never been thus fed or clothed or housed. And we learned letters and . . . the true religion." Jennifer brightened. "And London is a fable come to life—those glimpses of it which I chanced to get—"

"Where are the other children?"

"Left behind, with Mistress Shelgrave, when Sir Malachi came north last year to see to his interests. He feared, like many, you, the dread Prince Rupert . . . would enter London soon . . . and might well sack it. . . . In both was he mistaken, I've discovered. . . . My sister's small, the other two are boys; but I, he said, had best come here for . . . caution."

"It seems he thought his wife could safely bide," Rupert said dryly.

The Roundheads, who had been huddled in a ring, dispatched one of their number downstairs. The two by the fire did not notice.

"And that is all my little life, your Highness," Jennifer said.

"No, no, the barest bones."

She raised her head. The light played ruddy in her braids. "Your turn, my lord," she challenged. "Thereafter comes the flesh for both of us—" She stopped, gasped, and buried blood-hot face in hands.

Rupert hastened to cover her dismay with speech: "Let's cast my bones and study how they fall. You've often heard them rattle, but you've asked it. My mother was a daughter of King James and Anne of Denmark. She wed Frederick, Elector of the Rhine Palatinate. They were a loving couple—thirteen children despite misfortune, I the fourth of them. Well, when the Protestants in Prague had cast the Emperor's envoys out a palace window, they asked my father if he would be king of free Bohemia, and he accepted. There I was born, but had not seen a year before the Imperial armies overthrew him. Their crown discarded for a crown now lost, my parents wandered fugitive about till they found refuge in the Netherlands. 'Twas granted for the blood of Silent William that flowed within my father's veins. His

widow and offspring still know straitened circumstances.
Together with my brother, Prince Maurice, I early went
to war, first in the aid of Frederick Henry, Prince of Orange, then, with Swedish help, in trying to regain the
Electorate our oldest brother claims. But what was gotten turned out to be me, for three years in the care of
Graf von Kuffstein at Linz while people dickered my release." Seeing her more calm: "You've heard all this."

She summoned courage to answer, "No, not about
that maid."

"Oh, she was Kuffstein's daughter, hight Susanne. He
was a good old man who liked me well and hoped that I
would join the Church of Rome. So far as he could rule,
my bonds were light—except for being bonds—not unlike here, including the most welcome company of a delightful damsel whom I'll ever remember with affection
and respect."

"I dare not hope to be . . . a new Susanne."

"You will be while this head is on its neck."

Jennifer jerked erect in her chair. "What mean you?"

"Nothing," said Rupert, discomfited. " 'Twas a sleazy
jest."

"A jest—or, nay—you're such a sober man—" She
surged to her feet. "You fear that Parliament—You
must be wrong!"

He rose likewise. "I do not fear those curs, whate'er
they do," he told her starkly. "Yet being curs, they're
reckless how they bite, and I have earned their hatred."

Her tone wavered. "But you're *royal*."

He fleered. "A gang who sent Lord Strafford to the
block on hardly a pretext, and hold in gaol their London's own Archbishop—nay, my lady, I'd not put regicide itself beyond them."

She half shrieked. The tears broke loose. She cast
herself against him. "They cannot—thou—they must not
—God won't let them—"

He held her with unaccustomed awkwardness. "Now,
now," he soothed. "Be not distressed, my pretty bird. It
may well be I judge too gloomily." His hand stroked her
hair. She clung the tighter.

A soldier stamped halberd butt on floor. Sir Malachi
Shelgrave hastened into the room. "What's going on?"

he sputtered. "What shamelessness is this?" He seized the girl's shoulder. "Thou Babylonian harlot!"

Rupert plucked his arm away, though cloth ripped between the fingers. "Sir, have done," the prince said through stiff lips. "If any fault is here, it lies with me. I spoke a thing which made the maid grow faint."

Jennifer sank to the floor and wept into her hands. For a while Rupert and Shelgrave traded glares. At last the Puritan declared: "I have to take your word for that, my lord, but must insist that she no longer see you, and hope that you will soon depart."

"I too," growled Rupert.

Jennifer raised her head, shook it, climbed back to her feet and stood fist-clenched, choking off sobs and hiccoughs. "Come," ordered Shelgrave. He beckoned and marched out.

She looked at Rupert like a blind woman. "Farewell," she got forth.

Few had heard a like gentleness from him: "And fare thee well, bright lady."

Alone behind a shut door, he sought a window and stood staring out into the thin rain. There went within him:

A dear, high-hearted lass—but oh, how young, and shieldless as the youthful ever are! My birth was barely seven years before; but I have ranged and roved and reaved so much that on this day of heaven's tears I feel it is an old man who's to be beheaded. I hope she'll find a better, safer love, and bear him many children like herself, yet keep my memory aglow the while, and sometimes smiling warm her soul at it.

Will Mary Villiers do the same in Oxford?

O Richmond's Duchess, I have been thy servant—thy servant only, gorgeous butterfly—the most thou wanted —and thy husband is my staunch supporter—I'd not shame a friend, no matter what a hollowness I have where thou shouldst be and art not. He straightened. *Well-a-day,* he told himself, *let's cut a few more lines in wax, my lad, not imitate the sky, which doesn't mourn as first we thought, but merely sits and snivels. For Fortunes's wheel has many turns to go, and where 'tis bound for, none but God may know.*

V

KIRKSTALL ABBEY. MORNING.

Many of the spare old walls remained. Ivy up their
sides, grass in floors and flagstones, rooks and bats
which were the sole congregation of the church, had not
had time to finish what Puritans would hasten. The clustered buildings blocked off view of the manor, and view
from it.

Jennifer passed between guesthouse and common
room, into the cloister. Leaves that climbed everywhere
about her glittered with water, and puddles shone like
metal. This dawn had finally seen sun. A few bits of
white fluff drifted across blue dazzlement. Birds jubilat-
ed. The breeze making stray dandelions nod was cool
and damp, however. The girl shivered a little and sought
what warmth might be stored in the corner of nave and
transept.

Her face was pale, save for darknesses around the
eyes. Fingers strained against each other. Her glance
drifted from unbelled belfry to crumbled punishment
cell. She said into vacancy: "I hear the linnet and the
lark declare that we have seen all murkiness depart. The
flowers flaunt their hues through brilliant air, and it is
only raining in my heart. When yesterday I heard how
great thy woe, a lightning bolt struck lurid hellfire white;
I heard the thunder toll, the stormwind blow, and
nothing else through centuries of night." She sighed.
"But day must break, and gales lie down to rest, and
sunshine hunt the clouds across the sea. Alone in nature
is the human breast, where grief, like love, may dwell
eternally." She bent her bared head. "Unless there come
an ending of thy pain, I must forever stand and wait in
rain."

After a moment: *But not in death that ending, my beloved! Thou didst dissemble far too skillfully. I never*

knew how deep thy shackles gall or that beneath thine easy pleasantries the block and ax are lurking—

A noise brought her around. "Oh! Who's this?"

The man who had slipped into the close halted at a reassuring distance. His frame, long and gaunt as a famine, buckled in an attempt at a bow. "Will Fairweather's tha name, good my mis'ess." The voice bobbed up by his Adam's apple made rusty an otherwise soft Southland tone. "An' today, at last, I can stand on the style of it. Be not afeared; you may fiand me a Tom o' Bedlam, but 'a war harmless long's they left his rhinoceros in peace, an' I don't 'spect you'll twingle miane."

He tapped the nose which dwarfed the rest of his head. As if cowed by that overhang, his brow and chin sloped backward, though some stubble fought a rearguard action. His smile showed crooked teeth, and little pale eyes twinkled beneath sandy hair. His smock was too short for him. Beneath breeches of better stuff spraddled shoes worn-out and holeful, evidently the best he could beg into which his feet might squeeze.

"Art thou a vagabond?" the girl asked slowly.

"Not quiate, mis'ess. A man o' parts—theeazam parts for tha time bein'. Uh, you be Jennifer Alayne o' tha Shelgrave house, ben't you?"

"Aye. But in the months I've dwelt here, I've come to know the neighborhood—"

"An' not me, eh? I pray you, listen. I hope in due coua'se to make everything as clear, an' to your gain, as a verse o' Scripture; call it a mica profit. But first I make boald to ask"—abruptly he was stretched tense—"how cloase a friend you be to Prince Rupert."

Jennifer sagged against the wall, whose ivy rustled and dripped. She closed her eyes, opened them again, and breathed.

"Ah." Will Fairweather nodded. "I thought as much. Well, me tha zame, mis'ess. If you knew how I've waited for this chance—! Thic mighty snuffle you hear comes from a month o' skulkin' in wet brush. Always you'd be with him, which meant four zurly Roundheads to boot —and how I wished to boot 'em!—or you war along o' zomeone else, oftenest a walkin' rail topped by a prune."

"Prudence!" Jennifer could not help herself, she must laugh.

"I'd plenty o' that—"

"I escaped from mine today, to be alone."

"Well, now we must boath leave prudence behind, mis'ess, for time's breathin' up our arse. Word goes, no Cavaliers be left under arms in East England, an' the rest be driven too far west an' zouth to have any way o' raidin' 'twixt here an' London. I think tha word be true. Countryfolk mark zuch things better an' pass 'em on faster than tha gentry might think, tha' havin' to fret 'bout crops what might be trampled an' women what might be zampled. Zavin' your reverence, mis'ess. Anyhow, tha way lies clear for hustlin' Prince Rupert off to tha Tower, an' I doan't zuppose Parly-ment'll be laggard about an invitation."

"No—"

Jennifer shook herself, straightened, and sped across the yard. Catching his hands, she cried: "Canst thou help him?"

Will stopped grinning. "*We* can, lady."

"Who art thou? What art thou? Dear God—"

"Nay, a different Person has thic post. I be but a tenant farmer from Somersetshire, 'listed in tha dragoons when tha King raised his standard, got near Prince Rupert on account o' bein' good at caerin' for animals. 'A kept no few—white dog, monkey, an' moare—tha Puritans yammered 'a must be a wizard an' theeazam his familiars, but 'twar zimply that 'a liaked pets . . . an' outzoldiered his foes . . . an' I chatter a lot, doan't I?"

Jennifer glanced around, "Well, I may be missed and tracked any minute. B-besides—keep me not hooked!"

Will hunkered down to scrub sleeve across a low fragment of wall. "Than zit, mis'ess, an' bear with me for tha love we boath bear him an' tha King."

The King? thought Jennifer dazedly. *No, not the King, that heavy Scot on England and on English faith and freedom—or thus I lately have been told— But Rupert—* She let herself down, clasped her knees, and stared. The ungainly figure shambled back and forth, talking:

"I'm only half desperate in trustin' you, good lady.

I've no choice—nor you 'bout me, if you truly wish him well—but I've heard everywhere as how you be kindly, mirthful, tolerant, a very zouth pole to thic northward-frozen stick your guardian. Moareover, I've dwatched you from afar as you walked alongzide my general, an' —There's tha one field where Rupert lacks shrewdness an' courage." Will shook head and clicked tongue. "Not that 'a's never planted palms on its hills, or with rod an' staff comforted what's in tha valley; zuch doan't stand to reason, though it do to attention. But either virtue in a woman maekes him shy, or 'a's always too occupied with war to scout a sweeter terrain an' wage a merrier campaign. Anyhow, I zaw moare in your gait an' stance than I think 'a did, or you yourzelf, maybe—" He jerked to a stop. "Hoy, I could light a fiere with your cheeks!"

"Go on or go away," snapped Jennifer.

"Forgive me; I be a barnyard fowl. Knowin' tha eagle Rupert—Well, to speak honest, I 'listed as much to have holiday from wife, ten kids, an' plow—not that I doan't cherish 'em, understand; 'tis only that they get to be, well, many—as much for a chance o' sport, an' maybe loot, as for my king an' tha Oald Way. But than I came to know Rupert. . . . On Marston Moor, befoare his eyes, I deserted him."

The wound in the voice made Jennifer sit erect. "He bespoke a once trusty man," she said indistinctly, "who let his dog go free to die, and fled."

Will cocked a fist. " 'Twarn't my fault," he rasped. "A blockhead groom— Well, I found scant space for 'splainin' mongst tha blades. An' when I zaw him trapped, it sim me best I slip free an' trail after him. What help might another prisoner be?"

"How didst thou follow him?" Jennifer wondered.

Will shrugged. "Mis'ess, I've poached my whole life, from Mendip Hills to Channel, from Avon River to Exmoor—an' moast 'round mine own hoame, in zight o' Glastonbury Tor but a countryzide damnably low, flat, oapen— If I couldn't track a Roundhead, five miles behind an' given no moare zign than his farts, why, dangle me aloft for tha crows on charges o' havin' cut off in their prime his Majesty's hares.

"At first I mingled with tha enemy, passin' for one o' them in tha turmoil." His manner bleakened. "An' turmoil 'twar whilst tha' butchered tha women."

Jennifer started. "What women?"

"Camp followers mainly, though zome war honest wives. An' when did bein' a whoare, or bein' Irish, merit death? Yet tha Roundheads put 'em every one to tha zword on thoase charges, not troublin' 'bout a trial." Will spat. "I think milord Jesus might have zomewhat to zay on thic, come tha Last Day. Meanwhile, let's hoape our Rupert wins free to smite 'em hypocrite an' sly."

The girl stared before her. "I'd give a world to disbelieve thee." She hauled her regard back to him. "Well, what then?"

"I kept near tha leaders' tents, zaw him taken into one an', next morn, stuffed in a cloase-guarded coach. I loped along on the verge o' sight; miane, tic be, not theirs, tha' not lookin' for an escoart."

"You *could*?"

"A man afoot can run down a hoa'se or deer, if 'a be in condition for it an' patient. An' I'd no carriage to pull, indeed no weight on me zave cloathes, armor, two zwords, an' a few pennies which, h'm, a zartin Roundhead had no further use for. I zaw tha prince delivered to his manor an' reckoned they'd keep him hereawa for a bit. Zo it behooved me to zettle down likewise, watch what happened, an' twitch a quiet tail before luck's mousehoale."

"Where might you bide?"

"Around about. 'Twould be wrong to name names, but this land grows Stuart loyalists like thistles. A haymow heare, a backdoor dish o' beans an' bacon theare, a plump an' lusty goodwife whose husband's long absent in tha war—There be plenty wanderers, not just tinkers but tha uprooted. Takin' due care, I've drawn no moare notice than was needful in reconnoiterin' tha local gossip."

"And for Rupert!" Jennifer leaped to her feet. "Hast thou a plan? What can we do to, to save him?"

Will took a stance and peered long at her. "Thic depends on you, Mis'ess Alayne."

She confronted him. "How?"

"Let's first zee if I grasp tha nettle right," he said with a new hesitancy. "'A's locked into his rooms, too high in that as-tro-logic tower for a jump out a window, an' zentries beyond his door . . . each night. Ben't thic zo?" (She gave a stiff nod.) "By day 'a may walk abroad, in limits, but never beyond zight o' his warders unless tha're content just to zurround tha jakes. No help in thoase hours, the moare zuch when our allies be o' night."

"Allies? Who, in his aloneness?"

"I've followed tha Oald Way, an' zometimes on it met others unliake me," said Will ambiguously. "Let's first break him loose, shall we? Around my waist, underneath this farmer garb I've begged sine 'twould be unwise for a full-clad dragoon to go clumpin' about—I've coiled a roape. It could as well go inzide your skirt. If you can slip it to Rupert, he can snake out thic window we bespoake, this very eventide."

"Christ have mercy! I've been forbidden to see him."

"Surely you can brass yourzelf off as havin' a special message or zome zuch need, get by tha men at his door, zay unzuspicious words whilst you let tha roape an' a noate of explanation fall behind zomethin' what bars their eyes but not his. Can't you? Tha . . . others . . . tell me you've stomach for great deeds; an' heare's a mere schoolgirl prank."

"Well—but 'tis not that easy, Will. The watchdogs would clamor—"

"Not if you quiet them. Zo I be toald."

Now she peered at him for a time. Drops clinked from leaves onto stone. A cloudlet crossed the sun and made a moment's chill.

"Who told thee?" she asked.

His look grew steady as hers. "I could zay 'twar a peasant who'd watched you befriend two four-foot slaves; but I daere not lie. Zee you, mis'ess, 'tain't enough that you slip him the means to slide down, nor stand below an' accompany him over tha bridge for to keep them hounds mute. 'A doan't know tha country, an' I dast not come nearer tha house than this. You must needs guide him to a zartin place in tha wildwood. There I'll wait with what weapons I took from Marston

Moor, an' a couple o' requisitioned hoa'ses. An'
. . . our friends, miane, Rupert's, yours if you'll
let 'em be . . . you'll meet them too. Further than thic
I mayn't speak heare, zave to swear that inzofar as lies
in their power an' miane, you'll steal home to your bed
unharmed in any way."

She wrenched her glance from side to side and answered wretchedly. "Save in mine honor."

"Not one of us will touch you other than as a brother."
Will made a chuckle. "We'll be too chased."

"I mean the duty that I owe my guardian . . . and
my religion—"

"Rupert has his own."

"And I have Rupert, if he does not me. . . ." Jennifer flung back shoulders and head. Light flashed along
her hair. "So be it, Will Fairweather, blessed man!" Her
words clanged. "Quick, tell me how I may fulfill thy
plan."

"Let's go inzide tha church to talk o' this, that none
may zee us an' think aught amiss," he suggested. "At
best, tha road we tread be dangerous to England an' to
Rupert an' to us."

She nodded and led him through the arched doorway.

vi

OUTSIDE THE MANOR. NIGHT.

A full moon frosted darkness of house, town, and ruins. More brightly it covered river, trees, grass that had begun to sheen and glimmer with dew, cropped fields, forest crowning the northern hills. The sky arched less black than gray-blue; the stars therein were shy. Air beneath was cool, barely astir, hushed save for the purling water.

Jennifer, stooped to keep a hold on the neck of either hound, saw a thing like a thin serpent writhe from under the battlements of the left tower, forth across Andromeda before it fell and was lost in murk. She drew an uneven breath. The dogs sensed her dread. One whined, one rattled his chain. "Hush, ye," she whispered frantically. "Repay what ruth I've shown with silence."

A new blackness thrust out. Rupert slid from his window to earth. Crouched, he hauled on one of the twin strands down which he had come until the entire rope —which he had passed around some piece of furniture —lay at his feet. He moved toward Jennifer cautiously, not to alarm the hounds. Meanwhile he coiled the line around his shoulder like a bandoleer. Once more he was clad in the rough garments and high boots of war.

Moonlight made the girl and him silver and shadow. She cast herself into his arms. He hugged her hastily. A dog growled. She broke free, though her fingers stroked his hair as she did, and spent a minute bent, soothing the animals. Rupert stood above, his whole body aquiver. Eyes and teeth gleamed in the face he turned heavenward, horizonward. "Free, free," he breathed in glory. "The padlock taken off the world. God's death, I'll suffer mine ere caged again."

Jennifer rose, took his hand, led him over the drawbridge. None troubled to raise it at night or post human sentries, after the Cavaliers were driven off. The weed-darkened moat lay like a pit beneath.

They had gone a few hundred yards when Rupert deemed it safe to speak. "Thus far I've heeded every word . . . thou . . . wrote," he said slowly. "But 'tis not right to further hazard thee. Go back within. I'll fare on overland and think no prayer that does not hold thy name."

Under the hood of her cloak, he could barely see her head shake. "Thou canst not go alone, afoot, unarmed. I am to take thee to a place I know from household pleasure trips, off in the wood. There we will find the helpers that await thee."

"What helpers?"

"Save for him I scrawled about, I do not know—am more than half afraid to guess their nature—Oh, but 'tis thy life!" Beseechingly: "And Rupert, if thou owest me any thanks, grant me these few more hours to be by thee."

The colorless luminance could not show whether he flushed; but he stared at the ground. "Thou'rt being very reckless, Jennifer," he warned, "in more than one way."

Her answer was firm. "Nay, my dearest dear. Since I have taken this resolve to risk not only life but maybe hell for thee, my recklessness would lie in hanging back from word as deed." She drew breath. "We've miles to go. Let's stride."

THE FOREST.

Moonlight splashed silently on leaves, streamed down white flanks of birch trees, flowed undergroundishly in the gloom of oaks but fell at last from it to dapple the earth. There mushrooms and anemones peeped through those blankets the years had drawn over themselves when they grew old. A fallen trunk glowed blue. The air was warm, heavy with odors of soil and growth.

Oberon trod forth. A spider-woven cloak swirled

from his shoulders; crystals flashed across his tunic, or were they dewdrops? He raised a horn to his lips and winded it. The call went searching down the corridors.

Again he blew, and again. Firefly twinkles came bobbing among bough and boles. They shone every tint in the rainbow, and as soft. When they were near, it could be seen how each was a gleam in the upraised palm of one who bore the shape of a tiny human—though too beautiful to be truly human—flying on moth-wings.

Oberon lowered the horn. "Ho, Faerie folk!" he cried. "Where's Queen Titania?"

The swarm flickered and weaved about him. After a while the breeze-voice of a female answered: "I lately flitted past, Lord Oberon, and heard her say to Puck she'd fain begone, if he would be her company and guide and saddle two swift night-winds for to ride southward and south, in flight from poisoned town, blowing through goodfolks' dreams like thistledown, to seek our loved, abandoned home in Greece and scout if we might there at last find peace from Turkish curses—not be driven forth again to this now likewise wretched North—"

"My Petal," Oberon sighed, "if I let thee have thy way, till dawn thou wouldst rehearse what we well know." His tone grew urgent. "I've instant need of Queen Titania. Go, everyone, disperse in search of her, till she's been overtaken and fetched back to meet me at the ancient standing stone." Grimly: "There is no hope in Greece, or anywhere, if we forsake this sorely stricken isle, for the disease will gnaw behind our heels, all ways around the globe, and meet itself. Nay, we must make a stand while it is small. Our chance of victory seems smaller yet—but I have taken omens and cast spells, and sensed a destiny within two men whom I've contrived to bring here. . . . Be you off!"

He shouted the last words, and waved his staff on high. The starfire at its tip flashed briefly brilliant. On a sudden wind, which moaned among the branches, his elven subjects scattered from sight.

THE OBSERVATORY TOWER.

A trapdoor swung back and Sir Malachi Shelgrave climbed out onto the roof. Beneath the moon, he scarcely needed his lantern. Perhaps its yellowness tempered for his vision the icy lucency around.

Shelving it on a wall of his instrument shack, he opened the door to that and piece by piece brought forth telescope, quadrant, astrolabe, bronze-and-crystal celestial sphere, worktable, calipers, books, charts, notepaper, inkhorn, quills. . . . Last was a pendulum clock, always kept going. Before he wound up the weights, he put spectacles on his nose in order to compare the time shown on a watch he took from the wallet at his belt.

Nigh midnight. Witching hour, he thought, and shuddered. *I almost envy the superstitious Papist with his cross. But nay. A sign or idol is no shield. 'Tis grace of God, conferred on righteousness, holds off the prowling demons of the dark.*

He dropped to his knees, raised face and folded hands, and spoke in a voice made shrill by pain: "God of my fathers, I, a stumbling sinner, implore Thy mercy. Thou, omniscient Only, seest hell's corruption roiling in my breast. Such filthy things as snigger in my sleep, to bring me gasping wakeful and . . . still haunted—" His neck bent downward, his fists punished the stone roof. "Why can I not forget those youthful years I spent astray in hell's dank, stinking wilds, drank, gambled, swore, poked into hairy caves, until that night my dying father's curse blasted away the scales upon mine eyes? Did not the Lamb's pure blood then drown old Adam? Why has that corpse so often left its tomb, these past few years, to smirch with rotten fingers my thoughts— aye, even when my niece sways by—"

After a while he could look aloft once more and say with a degree of steadiness: "Thou foreordainest everything which is, and everything that Thou decreest is good. Thou plungest me into this lake of fire to burn the dross out and make hard my steel, until my soul's a swordblade for Thy war"—his words quickened—"that holy war Thou call'st on us to wage, to humble haughty kings before Thy might, cast idols and idolaters in dust, then take possession of the whole wide world—the promised land of Thy new chosen people: redemption-blazing English Israelites."

He sprang to his feet. "I hear Thy voice, Jehovah Thunderer! I've strength to smite, remaining in mine arms." He lifted them, fingers crooked as if to grasp something. "Or if it be Thy will that I not fight, but forge instead the iron thews of power . . . why, I am doing that already, Lord. But this I pledge, to work with doubled force, and make vile lust the fuel of my zeal."

After standing for a few minutes he added calmly, "Tonight I'll quench my fire and balm my burns in the cool chastities of measurement amidst Thy stars, till sleep returns, or dawn."

He unfolded the tripod of his telescope.

vii

A GLADE IN THE FOREST.

TREES were a darkling wall around, with frosted parapets. Moonlight whitened grass, daisies, cowslips, primroses; dew, which chilled and soaked feet, made shards of brilliance. Near the middle reared a monolith, twice a man's height. Though the weathers and lichens of none knew how many years had softened its edges, it remained a stern thing to see.

Two horses stood at the border of the opening. Common farm beasts, they bore nothing save tethers. A steady *crunch-crunch* and sweet smell of broken herbs rose from their jaws.

Will Fairweather lounged against the stone and used an eating knife to pare his nails. He had put back on his dragoon's outfit, sans Royalist tokens, in spite of its woeful condition. A cavalry sword hung at either hip. He sang to himself, low enough that one might have called it a mumble were it less off-key:

> *"Oh, whan I war in love with thee,*
> *'Twar hey, derry, down, derry, down tha*
> *livelong day,*
> *For thou didst love to wrassle me,*
> *Down amidst tha bushes an' down upon tha*
> *hay;*
> *An' whan tha stars winked bawdy eyes,*
> *'Twar hey, derry, down, derry, down tha*
> *livelong night,*
> *For moare than moon did than arise,*
> *Down upon tha mattress until tha down*
> *took flight.*
> *But whan—"*

He broke off. Rupert and Jennifer crashed through undergrowth, out beneath the sky. Their clothes, snagged, soaked, stained, were worse for hard travel than they themselves. Nonetheless she sank gratefully among the flowers.

Rupert bounded through them. "Will!" he roared. "Thou old rascal!" He seized the man and hugged him till ribs creaked.

The other staggered. "Whoof! Your Highness overbears me. A month's baitin' by Roundhead dogs ha' lost you no foa'çe. Pray take caere, lest you make my breastplate into a buckler." He recovered his balance, to stand in front of the prince's height and bulk for a span of silence before he asked: "Did Jen—Mis'ess Jennifer 'splain how 'tis, in tha note she smuggled you?"

"Aye." Rupert's glance went admiringly to her. "I wish most of my officers could write such a dispatch, clear, complete, and terse. Our cause would be in better case. She even revealed thou'st no blame in what happened to Boye. Not but what I couldn't forgive thee that, or anything else this side treason, which word I do believe thou canst not tell the meaning of—after what thou'st done."

"Not done; begun. We've starvelin' little to go on, my loard. Zee, I plucked an extra weapon for you off tha battlefield. I marked where yon two hoa'ses war kept outdoors, an' this night liberated 'em; but they ben't any Pegasuses, no zaddles came in the bargain for them mighty sharp-lookin' backs, an' we'll have to cut bridles from this roape you carry. Nor could I hoist moare'n a chunk o' bread an' stale cheese from tha dame who gave me barn-room; she war eager to visit me there after dark, aye, but her own zausages she keeps under lock an' key. How much money has my lady got together for us?"

"Why, I never thought—" Rupert turned back toward her.

She touched a purse at her waist. "No better than a few florins," she told him sadly. "I'm never allowed more at a time."

"Well, we'll forage as we fare," Rupert assured them.

"Across half or moare of England, acrawl with ill-wishers?" Will protested. "Tha word o' your escape'll splatter as fast as relays can gallop—or faster, unthanks to them damned zemaphoare things along o' tha railways. No doubt there'll be a whoppin' price on you. An' a man o' your Highness' zize an' bearin' ben't just easy to disguise."

"We must try—travel by night—"

"An' if we do zimply rejoin tha Cavalier cavalary, what'll we find? All tha news can't lie, 'bout how Cromwell an' tha rest be smashin' our zide like with sledgehammers. You'd rally 'em zome, no doubt, my loard; but I fear 'tis too late to do moare than stave off tha endin' awhile."

Rupert scowled. "What else does honor allow, save a return to serve the King?"

"There be ways an' ways o'zarvin' him, loard." Will plucked Rupert's sleeve. "Come, let's rest our feet by Mis'ess Jennifer. She needs to hear this too, I be toald."

"Told?" Rupert asked sharply. "By who?"

"Thic's what I aim to tell you, my loard an' lady, if you'll listen."

Rupert peered about before he shrugged and followed. When he settled into the grass next the girl, she took his arm. He kept stiffly motionless. Will Fairweather buckled at waist and joints, like a folding rack, as he joined them.

The moonlight streamed, the horses cropped, a sighing went through unseen leaves.

Leaning forward, his big hands flung now right, now left in awkward gestures, Will said, unwontedly earnest: "My loard an' lady, I be a Christian man. You must believe 'tis zo; else we be done. Oh, aye, I've zinned tha zeven zins, an' moare; ha' broaken Zabbath, stolen, poached, caroused, an' zee scant hoape I'll ever mend my ways—yet still tha Faith's in this ramshackle zoul, an' I repent me that I can't repent a longer time than from tha mornin's headache to tha first bowl o' yale what drives it out. I do believe Christ Jesus is our Zaviour, whose blood got shed for even zuch as me."

He filled his narrow chest before going on: "But shouldn't than God's oaverflowin' grace wash oaver everything what 'A has maede? If human flesh be grass, tha grass itzelf should liakewise be an object o' His love, tha fish, tha fowl, tha beasts—all what 'A maede. I wonder if maybe tha fiends in hell be just too proud to take tha love 'A offers." (Rupert stirred and frowned.) "Aye, aye, my loard, thic's heresy, I know. It ben't for me talk o' zuch-like things. Zave this one pw'int"—he lifted a finger—"that there be alzo creatures what reason, talk, yet be not whoally men. I speak not o' tha angels, understand, but bein's in an' of our common yearth, though ageless an' with powers we doan't have. Well, we got powers tha' doan't, an' zome zay we got immortal zouls an' tha' do not. A simpleton liake me knows naught o' thic. I only know that many, if not all, mean well, however flighty oftentimes. They be unchristened; zo be animals; an' neither kind war ever in revolt against tha will o' heaven, war it, now? If 'tis no zin to care for hoa'se or hound, why should it be a zin to have for friends tha oalden elven spirits o' tha land?"

Jennifer shrank from him, closer against Rupert. The prince had gone impassive. "That's heathendom!" she said, aghast. "They'd lure thy soul to hell."

"Zome would, no doubt; but than, zome humans would. What harm can be in common usages what maybe zailed with Noah in tha Ark, when men an' beasts an' weather war as one? If 'tis allowed to zet a bowl o' milk for your graymalkin sine 'a catches mice, what's wrong with showin' kindness to a harmless hobgoblin what will work or ward a bit? As for those ones what dwell apart from men—"

Rupert stirred. "Thou'st met them thine own self?"

"Well, zeldom, loard. But zome few times I have, beneath tha stars, when I war . . . questin'; for my family has ever shown their kind its due respect. We never cut a tree nor kill a beast without first barin' head an' drawin' cross—"

Jennifer was doubly shocked. Will gave her an apologetic smile. "—thic zort o' thing, to them what share tha land," he finished. To Rupert: "I'd maybe chat awhile, or swap a cup—their wild an' spicy mead for plain brown yale—or watch 'em dancin' lovely in a ring to music zeemed like played upon my heart. I never zinned with 'em . . . own I'd liaked it, but I'm too hoamely for a Faerie lass. . . . Have I done ill in this, my loard?"

"Say on," Rupert told him quietly.

"Well, skulkin' hereawa in meager hoape o' doin' aught to help you or tha King, an' yet not willin' just to quit, go hoame, be shut for aye inzide tha dismal stall o' Roundhead ways—an' Christ, be preached at, too!—I came to theeazam woods in zearch o' hares. There zome-one found me, an' we spoake an' spoake until tha daybreak flogged tha stars away; an' afterward again by night— Your Highness, that's how I got tha courage to strive on; that's how I learned our Mis'ess Jennifer might have a mind to help in your escape." (She covered her face.) "An', short to zay, we hammered out a plan."

Will rose. "Well, loard, I gave my handshake in return, to promise you would come an' hear them out. Tha' will not foa'ce you—nay, tha' couldn't that—but honestly, I zee no other way than takin' what small help tha've got to give. Pray, will you hark to them who'd fain be friends?"

Rupert stood too. Jennifer scrambled up, clinging to his arm. The prince's countenance was impassive, his tone steady: "I will."

"Oh, nay!" the girl pleaded in tears. " 'Tis peril of our souls."

Rupert took both her shoulders, looked into her eyes, and said gently: "Not so. The Puritans have lied to thee. I've read, if thou'st not, the Historian. Not only dwellers in antiquity had good, and little ill, at Faerie hands, but wise and Christian men in modern times. Aye, even magic arts of certain kinds are lawful if they're used with right intent. Recall the neighbors that thou knew'st in Cornwall. Like Will's, did they not follow olden ways?" (She nodded dumbly.) "And dost thou think them damned on that account?" (Slowly, she shook her head.) "Then do not now." (She fought forth a smile for him.) "Good lass! What heart thou hast!"

He released her and turned to the other man. It exploded from him: "Go summon, as thou wilt, thy miracle."

"Thy free consent has served to call us here."

That singing tone made Rupert whirl about. Two stood before the stone. Tall they were, uncannily beautiful of form and ivory features. Their eyes shone as if by inner moonlight. The outer radiance sparkled on high crowns of curious shape, on the glitter of the male tunic, the sheen of the female gown. Above them, behind them, flickering around their pale hair, danced and glowed small winged shapes.

At their feet squatted one more solid, broad and thick-muscled—though standing upright he would scarcely have reached Rupert's belt buckle. His head was round, snub-nosed, pointy-eared, shaggy; eyes glinted over a raffish grin. He wore leather and leaves.

Will louted low and stepped back. Jennifer joined him within the shadows. Her hands were folded, her lips moved silently. Rupert trod forward. He bent his neck the least bit, for the least moment, then met the unhuman gazes and said into the hush: "I think I do address King Oberon."

"Thou dost," the male answered.

The man bowed to the female. "Then likewise Queen Titania," he said.

"Be welcome to our Half-World kingdom, Prince," went the melody of her voice.

"I thank your Majesties." Rupert hesitated. "The rightful title? You know that presently I serve King Charles, and save that he unbind me from mine oath, I'll hold me free of others—under God."

The royal pair neither fled nor flinched at the Name. Jennifer began to ease. Will saw, and smiled at her. They looked back to the glade, where only Rupert and the horses seemed quite real.

"Thou seest we pass the test," boomed the dwarfish one. "Wouldst try us more? Why, then I'll list for thee the saints and angels. Their catalogue rolls trippingly— Walburga, Knut, Swithin, Cuthbert, Cunegonde, Matilda, Hieronymus, Methodius, Claude, Gall—"

"Be silent, Puck," Oberon commanded. "Show more solemnity." To Rupert: "Forgive him, Prince. Unaging Faerie folk too oft blow rootless on the winds of time, and ripen not to wisdom like you mortals."

"You flatter men too much, your Majesty," Rupert said.

Titania's hands fluttered white. "Enough!" she begged. "The cruel dawn comes on apace, when we'll be powerless and thou pursued. Make haste!"

Oberon nodded; the plumes swayed and shimmered on his crown. "Indeed. But first I'd best explain to thee, Prince Rupert, why we lend our aid in this thy mortal quarrel. It is ours. We elves are spirits of the living world, the haunters of its virgin loneliness, the guardians, helpers, healers of all things in nature, whence we draw our nourishment."

"You're sometimes tricksy, sometimes terrible," the man said.

"Why, so are earth and sea and sky and fire. Were there no wolves and foxes in the woods, the deer and conies soon would gnaw them bare." Oberon paused before adding bleakly: "Unless man use his poisons, guns, and snares. That can bring order of a graveyard sort, until unpastured rankness chokes and burns. Best he show reverence for Mother Earth. The Old Ways help to keep him true in it, wherefore they win the blessing of the elves."

"As long as this leads not to heathendom—"

"It need not. We've seen peoples and their faiths past counting come and come and go and go. From reindeer hunters in an age of stone to warriors in brazen chariots, we were familiars of the seed of Adam. When iron came, it was more difficult, for that's a greedy fang against the wilds, and bears a cold and sullen force within which sears our kind if we do merely touch. But after restless years came balancing. The yeomen wanted luck upon their fields, and love and sons and grandsons in their homes, and warding off of demon, ghost, or witch —and in exchange for this gave us our due."

Titania observed softly: "If fewer forests, we know richer fields; and in a maiden's love or baby's laugh, the wonder wells as from a secret spring."

"The Christian faith, whatever else it changed, made small discord within that harmony," Oberon went on. "As long as no one worshipped us as gods—a star-cold honor we have never sought—the priests did not deny our right to be, and let the people dwell at peace with us and with the land. Meanwhile, their bells rang sweet."

"They did but change the names—" Puck muttered, "the names—the names."

Both Rupert and Oberon frowned at him, and the king continued hastily: "When Henry Eighth cast off the rule of Rome, to us 'twas naught but mortal politics. The Church of England did not persecute us, nor care to end the Old Ways in the folk. But then—"

"The Puritans arose," said Rupert, for Oberon faltered at the uttering.

"They did." The king lifted a fist. No matter his height and handsomeness, it looked strangely frail, almost translucent to moonbeams and encroaching shadows. "That wintry creed where only hell knows warmth; where rites which interceded once for man with Mystery, and comforted, are quelled; where he is set against the living world, for he is now forbidden to revere it in custom, feast, or staying of his hand; where open merriment's condemned as vice and harmless foolery as foolishness; where love of man and woman is obscene—there's Faerie's and Old England's foe and woe!"

Jennifer gulped, clenched fists, stiffened herself, and piped timidly, "Oh, nay, sir, that's not altogether true—" None seemed to hear her. Rupert stood stone-massive and moveless; Oberon and Titania kept their eldritch eyes on him; the elven lights danced blue, gold, purple, green, ruby, giving glimpses of tiny frightened faces.

Will Fairweather squeezed her elbow. Puck sidled to the fringe of the glade and around it, until he hunkered near her feet.

Meanwhile Rupert said, to those twain who were like swirls and currents in the moonlight that poured around him: "Your Majesties are not of human blood. What have theologies to do with you?"

Oberon drew his cloak tight, as if a wind had arisen —in the white wet stillness of the night—from which its gauze could shield. He spoke nearly too low to be heard: "A creed which bears no love for Mother Earth, but rather sees her as an enemy which it is righteous to make booty of, to rape, to wound, to gouge, to gut, to flay, then bury under pavement, slag, and trash, and call machines to howl around the grave . . . that creed will bring that doom."

His head drooped. "But long ere then, with wonder, woods, and waters, we'll be dead. Already soot and iron shrink our range. When every churchly minister abhors us and hunts us out . . . no longer are we strong. We cannot stand before anathemas. First England, then the world—"

Elven swift, his resolve returned. He straightened and declared aloud: "The Royal cause defends the Old Ways, knowing it or not. Whatever be the faults—the arrogance of King and bishops, squalid greeds of nobles, lump-stodginess of yeomanry and burghers, and gross or petty tyrannies these breed—still, such are found in every human clime; and you'd at least preserve what keeps your kind from turning to a pox upon the globe, and would not scour the Faerie realm from off it."

He raised an arm. "My spells, my wands, my secret silent wells descry for me a faint ambiguous hope, though not its form, borne by the three of you. Therefore we aided thine escape, Prince Rupert. Now we would give some further help and counsel, if thou'lt accept it. Then we've shot our bolt, and can but wait to see where it may strike."

Though hardly moving, the man seemed to crouch. "By the eternal," he whispered, "it shakes the teeth and bones when such a gauntlet's cast before the feet. Yet Arthur took it. Dare I be afraid?"

"I am, I am," Jennifer almost wept. "What dream has fallen on me? O Mother, come and help me to awaken!"

Will laid an arm around her shoulders. "Thou'st tumbled into eeriness, poor lass," he murmured hoarsely; "but one grows used to anything erelong."

"Why must they be this oratorical," grumbled Puck, "and how, when chins are dragging on the ground? Be done, be off; and if the Roundhead shaves so ye can't beard him, give his nose a tweak. Howe'er," he added after a moment, "be sure to wear that gauntlet, Rupert, for 'tis a sharp and thrusting nose indeed." He cocked his head to look at Jennifer. "I feel an inkling thou wilt also ride on this adventure." He delivered a gunshot slap to her bottom. "Well, thou'rt nicely cushioned!"

She jumped, gasped, and smacked his face in return. He leered. Indignation burning out terror, she stared back toward Rupert. The prince had not noticed the by-play. Standing as if at attention, he said, "Within the bounds of faith and morals, sir—and common sense— I'll fare by your advice."

A smile drifted across Oberon's lips. "No doubt we need a careful qualifier," he said; then, grave again: "I fear I can but send thee on a search, and where and what to seek know only darkly. Thy King, thy cause, thyself cannot prevail unless the Earth herself may fight for thee. So spake the prophesying spells I cast. But how shall Earth, mere soil and rock and water, mere air and life, resist an iron Death?

"There once were words and tokens full of might. It may be these can raise their elements in threatened children of old Mother Earth. But the North's great magicians long are dust, and naught remains save feeble country witches and such poor powers as we keep in Fa-erie." Oberon shook his head, a slow back-and-forth weaving. "And yet," he breathed, "what oracles that I could seek gave half-heard whisperings about an isle far to the south, in realms I do not ken—for they lie west of Greece where once we dwelt—an isle where was a mighty mortal wizard not many years agone—"

"High Prospero?" barked Rupert.

"Then thou hast read the chronicle thyself." Oberon trembled, like moonglow on a lake when the breeze passes over. "I think 'twas he. I could not learn for sure. Nor could my spells and sendings search it out. Belike he left the place invisible, that none might find and use his tools for ill, without foreseeing good would someday need them. Its friendly sprite knows nothing of our woe. If thou couldst fetch those things—"

"Where you have failed," Rupert asked, "how shall unmagic I discover them?"

Queen Titania flowed forward. Rupert dropped to one knee. "I bow to beauty," he exclaimed.

She smiled and touched his head. "Nay, to weakness,

Prince," she answered softly. "Thou must have read
how I was made a fool." Casting a mischievous glance
at Oberon: "Though if, instead of Bottom, it'd been
thee—" (Puck snickered.) She gestured the man to rise.
Quickly as had the king, she grew solemn.

"Ye mortals do have powers, do know things, which
are for aye denied the Faerie race," she said. "Among
them is the strength of mortal love." Wistfulness tinged
her speech: "Mine ageless, flighty kind knows love
. . . of sorts . . . but simply pleasantly, like songs
or sweets. True human love is not a comedy; time
makes it tragic. In those heights and deeps rise dawns
and storms beyond our understanding, the awe and the
abidingness of death."

She raised her hands. Abruptly in the fingers of each
was a ring. One was larger than its mate, but otherwise
they were alike: circlets of silver in the form of an asp
which bit its own tail, its head the bezel crowned by a
many-faceted jewel.

"These rings which I uphold before thy gaze were
forged in Egypt centuries away, by the last sorcerer of
that old land, to aid a lordly pair who were in love. So
long as each stayed true to plighted troth, the glowing of
the stones would guide them on tow'rd where the means
of fortune for them lay: the closer aim, the brighter was
the light." Titania sighed. "He proved too weak, too
politic for it. The flames went out for both, who failed
and died.

"By twists and turns, the treasure came to us, who
lack that strength and purity of love which kindles it."
Like a stooping hawk: "But thou art mortal, Prince!
With this for compass, thou canst seek the isle, and on
the way know where is help or refuge. Thy right hand
wilt thou need for reins and sword. Wear this upon the
left."

Jennifer clutched her breast. Rupert was as shaken.
He took a backward step and stammered, "I have no
one—"

She leaned near. Her hair floated cloud-wan, bearing
odors of thyme and roses. "Not Mary Villiers?" she
whispered.

He made as if to fend her off. "She was never mine."

Jennifer broke from her companions, sped through the dew-bright grass. "Leave off thy gramaries on him, thou witch!" she yelled.

Titania smiled as she withdrew to Oberon's side. "Here's one to make exchange of vows with thee," she said.

Rupert caught the maiden's wrist. "Be calm, they mean us well," he began. She halted, but faced the queen and challenged:

"What dost thou mean?"

"Thou heardst us speak, my child," Titania responded gently. "Take each a ring and give it to the other, pledging faith, that he may have a torch to show his way, and thou thyself what safety thine bestows."

Jennifer stood awhile, staring first at her, then at Rupert, there in whiteness and shadow. The moon was lowering and a thin cold ripple went through the air. At last the girl said, "I cannot give him what he owns already."

Beneath the oak, Puck remarked to Will, "If he'll not take the maiden's ring she proffers, he is a fool, unless his softness lies elsewhere than in the brain."

"A liavely wench," the man agreed. "How spendthrift be't, to risk thic slender waist."

Rupert looked long at Jennifer in his turn before he joined his clasp to hers and said, as carefully as if his tone might shatter something of crystal: "My dear, I am not worthy of thy troth. And 'tis a pledge unsanctioned by the law or holy Church—"

Her words stumbled. "It only is forever."

"I know not, nor dost thou. Let me remind that thou and I are worlds and wars apart. Nor do I like this pagan ceremony."

"But . . . thou'lt go through with it . . . to get the help?"

He nodded. "I am a soldier; and it is my way to charge ahead into the teeth of chance. If thou wilt stand me true till I return, or till I fall, I'll do the same for thee. Then afterward, if such be fate, we'll talk."

She told him through tears, "I'll live in hope of what thou then may'st say."

"Kneel, children, here before the sacred stone," Oberon commanded. They did, hand in hand. As he stepped in front of them, his elves made a whirlpool of dim fire above his crown. He laid palms upon their heads. "By oak and ash and springtime-whitened thorn, through ages gone and ages to be born, by earth below, by air arising higher, by ringing waters, and by living fire, by life and death, I charge that ye say true if ye do now give faith for faith."

They answered together, like speakers in sleep: "We do."

Titania came to her lord. "Place each a ring upon the other's hand," she told them (they obeyed), "and may the sign of binding prove a band that joins the youth to maiden, man to wife, and lights the way upon your search through life."

Oberon and Titania together: "Farewell! And if the roads ye find be rough, keep love alive, and so have luck enough."

They and their followers were gone. Darkness overwhelmed the glade.

"Where art thou, darling?" Jennifer cried. "Suddenly I'm blind!"

"The moon has slipped below the treetops, dear," he answered. "Bide unafraid till thou canst see by stars."

Puck nudged Will Fairweather. "I likewise have to hurry on my way," he said. "Methinks this night has not yet done with pranks."

"We too must travel off, tha prince an' me," the man replied. "When once his landlord finds 'a's left tha inn without a stop for payin' o' tha scoare, we'd better have zome distance in between." His voice was troubled. "I caered not for his magickin' myzelf. Her heart war in it, but not whoally his. Half done, it could recoil if 'a ben't caereful. . . . An' we doan't even know which way to head!"

"To west, I'd say, where ye can find a ship." Puck advised. After a pause: "And, h'm, to speak of inns and such— My friend, if sorely pressed for shelter, think of this. There is a tavern known as the old Phoenix, which none may see nor enter who're not touched by magic in some way. If flits about, but maybe ye can use his ring to find it, or even draw a door toward yourselves. . . . I must be off. My master calls. Away!" He was gone.

Eyes grown used to the lessened light, Will made out Rupert and Jennifer at the rock.

"I hate to send thee back, alone and weary." The pain was real in the prince's voice.

"But we can do naught else," she said. "I will abide, and pray for thee and love thee always, Rupert."

They kissed. She felt her way off into the forest murk. Awhile he stared after her, until he shook himself and spoke flatly: "Well, camarado, let's prepare to sail, while tide is ebb and wind not yet a gale."

viii

THE SCULLERY OF THE MANOR.

It was unadorned red brick, floor sloping to a gutter which drained into the moat. Above an open hearth with a flue reached a swivel-mounted hook for the great kettle wherein water was heated. Firewood lay stacked beside. Nearby stood a raised counter and sink. Elsewhere buckets, tubs, tools, utensils crowded shelves or hung on walls. The gleam of copper, the deep tints of crockery made this the cheeriest room in the house.

Late at night it had grown cold, though. Sir Malachi Shelgrave's breath puffed white. The clatter of his shoe-soles stopped when he did, but got answered by the creak of the door to outside. Shadows swung monstrous as he raised his lantern.

Jennifer came through. Seeing him, she caught one tattered breath and swayed backward.

"Hold, slut!" he belled. "Stand where thou art or be run down."

She could not completely obey. She crumpled. Legs sprawled across the floor showed slim through rents in a stained and dripping skirt. Stiff-elbowed on hands, head fallen between hunched shoulders, locks tumbled around cheeks, she let dry sobs quake through her.

Shelgrave loomed above. "I see why God kept me awake this night," he said deep in his throat, "that from my towertop I might espy thee come slinking o'er the bridge tow'rd this back entrance thou must have left unlatched—how many hours?" Violently: "Speak, harlot!"

Still she fought for strength and air. He set lantern on counter. Stooping through the glooms, he seized a fistful of hair and yanked her head back upward. His other palm cracked her cheeks, right, left, right, left. Her neck rocked beneath the blows.

"What foul swineherd hast thou sought," he panted, "to wallow with him in what mucky sty? Ungrateful Jezebel, thou'lt get no peace till I have squeezed the pus of truth from thee."

"I did no wrong," she got out, gasp by gasp through the punishment. "I . . . swear to God—"

He released her and straightened, spraddle-legged, knuckles on hips. The tall hat cast a mask across his face, through which glistened eyeballs. "What, then?"

"I too tossed sleepless," coughed from her, "thought a walk might help . . . unthinking wandered far, and . . . lost my way—"

"A maid alone, out after dark? Go to!"

She lifted her arms. "I pray thee, uncle, by the bonds between us—"

Light flashed off the third finger of her left hand. Shelgrave pounced on that wrist. He gripped it abundantly hard to draw a wail of pain. For a minute he stared, before he snatched it off. She nursed the hurt against her mouth. The finger was red where he had skinned it in his haste. Her eyes upon him were those of a trapped doe.

"Who gave thee this?" he whispered at last. Over and over he turned it. The stone sparkled like any costly gem. A yell: "I'll have no further lies!"

She huddled mute. He raised a foot as if to stamp her teeth. She braced herself against the wall, arms and knees drawn up for shield, and waited.

He lowered the foot. "A royal thing," he mumbled. "Is't from the Prince of Lies—?" Shock made him lurch. "The prince. Prince Rupert—" He whirled and roared: "Nafferton, awake! What butler art thou, snoring in thy bed while hell walks loose? Ho, Nafferton, to me!" Echoes flew hollow around. Faintly came the barking of the aroused watchdogs.

Nightshirted, his butler fumbled from unlit corridor and kitchen into the scullery. "Go to the guards outside Prince Rupert's room," Shelgrave ordered. "Find out if he is there. Be quick, thou whelp!"

"Aye, sir." The man's jaws clattered. "Let me but light a candle at your lantern. 'Tis deathly dark."

"Make haste, or learn of death." Shelgrave snatched a carving knife off a rack.

Gaze averted from Jennifer, Nafferton got a taper kindled and fled.

Shelgrave stared at the girl. She watched him test the knife edge on a thumb, over and over. A smile of sorts stretched his mouth. "What else might send thee forth at midnight, eh?" he said. " 'Twas plain as filth that thou'd grown overfond of him, that royal devil. This day past, against mine own command, thou sought'st him out."

"There was no secret in it, uncle, none." Her tongue tried to moisten lips but her voice remained parched and uneven, scarcely to be heard. "How could there be? I knew that thou wouldst learn. I frankly told the guards how I had lost a keepsake from my mother I had shown him and thought might lie forgotten in his room. They let me in. We spoke in their full view, he helped me search around a little while, we found it not . . . whereon I said farewell."

"And at the farther side of that apartment, when curtains of his bed or his broad back screened off the soldiers' glance for just a heartbeat—did he then slip this ring between thy paps?" Shelgrave tapped it with the knife. A clear little chime went under the hysteria of dogs, the thick hush everywhere else in these shadows.

Jennifer climbed stiffly to her feet. She must lean on a wall to stay upright, and the breath whined in and out of her. But she lifted her head and answered with more steadiness than before. "Thou'st guessed aright. A token of . . . his love. I meant to keep it hidden till the peace . . . but this night I could not forbear—"

"Well, traitress," he interrupted savoringly, "befouler of the house that sheltered thee, what say we cut the nipples from those dugs lest thou shouldst nurse a devil-brat of his, or make thee noseless like so many whores?"

"No, no, God help me!" She choked off the scream, filled her lungs, squared shoulders; and the eyes which met his were now lynx-green. "I have rights in law," she snapped. "Hale me before a jury if thou wilt. What else thou pratest of would outlaw thee."

He cast the knife down so it rattled across the bricks. "I have a guardian's right, at least, thou wanton, to strip thee bare and flog thy back and butt till such foresmack of hell has chastened thee."

An approaching uproar swung their attention to the kitchen entrance. Out of it burst a halberdier. The cresset he had snatched from a bracket in the tower streamed red gleams across helmet, cuirass, and a face whose strictness had well-nigh dissolved in terror. Behind him came Nafferton, and other servants wakened by the noise. They dared not venture into the scullery; they crowded the archway instead.

"Sir Malachi, your prisoner is gone!" the soldier bawled.

Coldness descended upon Shelgrave. "Thou'rt sure?" he asked.

"We ransacked every inch at once when your word came to look inside for him." The man groaned aloud. "The rest still search—there is no trace to see— How might he have escaped? We heard no sound. It must be true he is a black magician. What bat-wings bore him off?"

"Cease whimpering," Shelgrave said. "No fiend has power over godliness."

"But I . . . I am a sinner."

"Thou'rt a man. Go bid thy squad make ready to pursue, likewise the day watch and my kennelmaster. We'll ride within the hour."

"Into the dark?"

"The dawn's not far. And every moment's priceless for picking up a scent ere it grow cold." Shelgrave leaned toward Jennifer and whispered, "Thy stench at first . . . or Rupert's if they're mingled. We've articles aplenty ye've both used." Louder: "Get busy, there! Light up the house, pack food, prepare as for the chasing of a wolf. Thou, Nafferton, send Prudence Whitcomb hither"—he paused briefly for thought—"and Sim the under-groom." A babble and surging had started. He raised arms to quiet it, glowered, and said, each word a hammerblow: "Have care, ye folk. Ye've kept the secret well that he was here, the Devil's dragon pet. I charge you now, on pains more dire, keep still that he is gone. It would encourage the iniquitous. Nay, wait till he is safely off in chains to London. *Then* make known what trust was ours."

He chopped a hand in signal. They dispersed. Though the sound of their runnings and callings grew greater, and light seeped in ever more bright as flames were brought to life, Shelgrave and Jennifer had a while alone.

He said to her almost sadly: "Do not insult the wounds thou'st given me by claiming thou hadst naught to do with this."

She answered in the same quiet tone. "Nay, it is true. I'd planned a ruse of war. By hiding of my ring and new-made rags, I hoped discovery would be belated and nowise linked to me. Did not Our Lord command that man and wife forsake all others?"

He started. "What went between you?"

"Less than I would wish," she sighed.

"How did'st thou aid him? Unforgivably?"

"A rope let fall from underneath my skirt, a note which said that I would soothe the dogs and guide him to the hiding woods. Naught else."

"This ring gives thee the lie, I think. There's more. But if thou wilt deny on Bible oath—"

She shook her head.

"Nay? Then I must presume a deeper thing than fancies of a brach in heat: like witchcraft. This serpent ring could be the sign of Satan, and Rupert freed by wizardry, not wiles." He brought fingers near her throat. "If thou hast strayed that far tow'rd hell, recall what Scripture plainly bids: *'Thou shalt not suffer a witch to live.'*"

She closed eyes and fists, opened both, and said, "I swear to thee by Christ I am not such. Now I will speak no further."

"Thou'lt change thy mind." Shelgrave looked about. A man, ugly, unkempt, and smelling of manure, slouched in the outer doorway.

"You wanted me?" he said.

"Aye, Sim," Shelgrave replied. "I've seen thee curbing stubbornness in beasts. 'Tis work that thou enjoyest. Bide a bit."

The wait was short until Prudence arrived. It might have been shorter had her proprieties not demanded a hasty gowning. She had overlooked her hair, which flew in gray fizzles. "What is't, Sir Malachi?" she asked from the arch: then, spying Jennifer, hurried toward her, arms outstretched. "Oh, poor dear lamb! Where hast thou been? And bruises on thy cheeks—"

"Have done." Shelgrave's tone checked her. "She is no lamb, this swart she-goat that slipped the wolf we kept loose from his cage."

Prudence clapped hands to mouth, pop-eyed. Sim tittered. Jennifer confronted them.

"I'm on my way for his recapturing," Shelgrave said. "Meanwhile, ye two take her into your charge. Abuse her not, but keep her close confined in her own chamber, seeing no one else. She may have food but never, never sleep."

"I can't do that, though she be sold to hell," Prudence protested.

"I can," Sim declared avidly.

"I tell ye, harm her not . . . as yet," Shelgrave instructed. "However, when she starts to drowse, then shake, or shout, or pinch, pour water on her head—" To the girl: "It is the mildest ordeal that I know. I wonder if thou'lt dare to thank the God Whom thou'st betrayed, that I am merciful." Curtly to the others: "Be off with her. I'm off upon my hunt."

THE FOREST GLADE.

Above solid blacknesses of trees, stars wheeled silently toward dawn. Though soaked with dew, the grass showed dim gray, the standing stone mottled leaden. Mists drifted ghost-pale.

Racket ripped their quiet. Dogs bayed, men shouted, horns clamored. In trampling of hoofs and crashing of brush, the pursuers broke through.

"Holla, halt!" Shelgrave shouted. He had lost his hat in the woods; the dome of his head gleamed tombstone white. "The hounds're going wild!"

They were in truth ramping and roaring about the

open ground. The kennelmaster sprang from his saddle, flailed his whip among them. "Heel, heel!" he called into their chaos. Shelgrave's steed, skittish as the rest of the half score, drew close. The keeper raised glance from pack to leader and cried, "They've caught some scent 'round here that maddens them."

"A fiend," wavered a voice from the stormy shadow-mass of the troop. "May heaven pity us this night."

"Hell gulp that fiend!" Shelgrave rapped. " 'Tis Rupert's slot we want." His horse screamed and reared. He leaned into stirrups and reins, slugged the animal to a halt.

Likewise did the kennelmaster beat order back into his charges. They were a dozen, mostly bloodhounds, three tall staghounds among them, disciplined and not long to be daunted. Akin in that much, the Roundhead riders brought their mounts under control. The one which had no man upon it still stamped and whinnied, but a gauntleted hand clamped firm on its bridle.

Armor sheened fitfully; otherwise the band were murky blurs. "Sir Malachi," a man ventured, "this was exhausting work, to grope through lightlessness—"

"We had a path," Shelgrave retorted.

"Most of the way. But nonetheless, we're worn. Were it not wiser to await the sun?"

"Our quarry hasn't." Shelgrave stiffened. "What's that sound I hear?"

A wicked snickering raced around the glade. The mists swirled thicker, into nasty shapes. Hounds growled and huddled close together. Horses grew restless anew. The rank smell of their sweat blent with the sourness of man's.

"We've fumbled to forbidden ground, I fear," the kennelmaster whispered. "Look yonder." He pointed. Everywhere among the trees, whose twigs bent over the Milky Way like claws, wavered dull-blue lights. "Corposants, those lures of death." The stillness seemed to deepen beneath stridencies. "Owls hoot and ravens croak too hungrily."

"Sir Malachi, let's home," implored a soldier, "if yet we may."

Shelgrave drew his sword. "Who does forbid this

place?" he said. "At worst, some spooks. What do you fear the more, their puny spite or wrath of God for scuttling from your duty? Whip on those curs! A trail must lead from here."

A horn sounded, far off but rapidly nearing. Though no breath of the dank air moved, there went a noise of great winds and of hoofbeats in the sky.

With spurs and crop, Shelgrave made his horse carry him around the rim of the glade. He slashed at brush and branches. "Take that in your uncleanness, that, and that!" he yelled above the chopping. "If ye have power, here I am for target."

The dogs plucked boldness from his example. The kennelmaster held two by their collars and let them cast about. Meanwhile he, like his companions, kept peering uneasily aloft.

The din overhead became a storm. Skulls rang to that unseen gale, thunder of gallop and howl of wolves. Huge over the treetops passed a rider. They could just see the antlers on his head, raking across stars gone alien. His horn-blast tore through their guts.

"Herne the Wild Hunter!" shrieked a man. He hauled on reins, wheeled his plunging horse, and made for home.

Shelgrave was near. He spurred his own beast, came alongside, gripped shoulder, and heaved. The Roundhead fell from the saddle, struck ground, rolled over, and sat dazedly up.

Meanwhile the heaven-rider had vanished. They heard his noise dwindle until Shelgrave's scorn clanged more loud:

"Aye, maybe 'twas him—that old wives' yatter, bogle fit for babies, whom fat Jack Falstaff wore the aspect of. It brought him the mistreatment he deserved . . . at human hands. D'ye hear me? Human, human! No doubt 'tis true that Rupert is in league with hell, whose minions now would seek to thwart us. But since we broke his cause on Marston Moor and sent his shattered bandits scattering—behold how impotent hell really is! These heathen spirits of the wilderness are sapless, if they only can send visions. Ignore them, or else curse them if ye think they're worth the trouble; never stop to fear them." He reared his horse. His blade flared on high. "The hounds are baying, Ironsides, away! We'll have the sun erelong to see our prey."

They lifted a cheer, ragged at first, swelling as the sounds around them ceased. The dogs found scent and settled into a lope along a deer path. The kennelmaster and the toppled guardsman resumed their saddles and fell in. Shelgrave commenced a hymn of war. Soon the deep voices behind him had joined.

ix

A RIDGE ABOVE A VALLEY.

RIDING along its crest, Rupert and Will had sunrise and the descent on their left. Brilliance, shadows, and morning fog blurred the bottomland; a thin iron gleam could just be glimpsed. Elsewhere stretched intensely green pasture, speckled by white lady-smocks and golden cuckoo-buds under a sky the hue of harebell. Two cottages were in sight, miles off amidst clumps of trees; closer, a shepherd boy leaned on his crook and gaped at these strangers.

Behind them, to north, the horizon-hidden mills of the new age were beginning to smear heaven.

Rupert thumped heels into the ribs of his horse. "Get on, thou ambling crowbait," he said to no noticeable effect.

"I'd not condoane mutiny," Will remarked, "but while my head an' heart wring their hands at this floutin' o' your Highness, my backzide rejoices. My kingdom for a zaddle!"

Rupert eased. "Well," he laughed, "if thy rear guard wants to preach sedition, let it be downwind of me. What's this kingdom thou offerest?"

"Why, tha one I'd ride forth for to conquer, as might be in America, did I have a zaddle. Meanwhile, my loard, let's be content to rock along slow, hearin' tha larks an' dumbledores, snuffin' cool sweetness—though for thic I be better gunned than you, zir, by no few calibers—an' drawin' as little heed as we can till we've zafely lost ourzelves in countryzide. Than'll be time for to think o' luncheon. For now, would tha general caere to break his fast?" Will opened a greasy leather pouch at his belt and fumbled after the bread and cheese within.

Rupert nodded absently, his mind already gone in calculation. "Let me conjure up a map before me," he muttered. "Straight overland to Chester, perhaps a hundred miles or somewhat less. We may hope it remains in friendly possession. If not, 'tis at the gateway of North Wales, where the folk are stoutly loyal—"

"My loard!" Will exclaimed. " 'Ware!"

Rupert twisted about, clapping fingers to sword. "What?"

Will pushed scraggly straw-colored hair aside to cup an ear. "Rearward. Hounds. D'you hear tham?"

Faintly beneath the rustle of grass around fetlocks, heavy clump of hoofs, carol high overhead, sounded that living music. "Some squire might be after fox," Rupert said. There was no lilt in his voice. It roughened: "Or deer, today when any clown may rob the King."

"Maybe," Will answered skeptically. "Tha' be nearin' quick-like." He slapped his mount's neck with the rude reins he had fashioned. "Best we pick a hidin' place. Yonder spinney?"

"That won't screen us from dogs," Rupert reminded. "At most, it may help us make a stand. Hoy!" He and his companion beat their animals into a trot.

Presently the huntsmen came up onto the ridge, entering distant view. Sparks glinted eye-hurtingly among them. "That's sun off armor," Rupert said.

Will smote palms together. His stubbly features twisted. "Oh, God, General! Tha' warn't zuppoased to miss you at tha house for hours yet."

"It seems they have, though. I can guess how." Rupert's own lips bent in anguish. "Poor Jennifer."

After a moment he shook himself and said to the wind, "Nay. I think I dare hope better. I've seen how fondly her uncle's gaze follows her about—one touch in him not sanctimonious or mechanic, that may make some angel smile— If he punishes her, he'll not be too severe, surely."

"Tha'll be with us,"Will declared. "What's your counsel, zir?"

The warrior filled Rupert. "Keep moving," he said. "Find a strong point where we can't be taken alive, and can make them pay for us—"

"Through my noase."

"—unless, by happy chance—" Rupert leaned over,

shaded eyes from sun and strained them at the valley floor. The mists were breaking, to show more clearly the railway line and semaphores. "I chose this course 'gainst your advice, Will, because of what's there, thinking perhaps— Let's seek downward. More cover, if naught else." He sent his nag on a slant along the slope.

This concealed the followers for a while. When they again became visible, they were close enough for sharp sight to make out details: eight men in helm and cuirass, one in Puritan civil black, one in a red coat who shouted thinly-heard orders to the pack of hounds. Seeing the two ahead, he winded a bugle.

"Aye, Shelgrave in truth," Rupert snarled. "He'll overtake in minutes. Gee-up! *'Raus mit dich!'*" Drawing sword, he pricked a bony haunch till its owner lumbered into a gallop. It took horseman's skill to stay on, bareback. Will lay behind, gripping mane, flailing with flat of blade. The hillside leveled out, the rails drew near. Likewise did the Roundheads, their halloos, and the savage song of their hounds.

A hoot responded. Around a shoulder of the ridge, some two miles north but headed south, came a train.

Rupert's ring flared in glory. He didn't notice.

The locomotive puffed, boomed, spouted smoke and sparks, a black monstrosity in that serene landscape; he had rarely seen a sight more beautiful. After it, clacked its tender and half a dozen open, empty cars. It must be bound for a colliery, that the mills be kept fed.

Rupert's horse snorted and shied. "So-so, my bully," he soothed. Through knees and hands he let confidence flow. "Ah, good, brave fellow, stout fellow, *echter Knecht*—" Glancing over a shoulder, he saw the mettlesome animals of his pursuers buck, rear, and bolt. Gleefully he cried to Will, "Thanks, man, for choosing stolidness like this!"

Onward. He gauged speeds and distances, made himself into a centaur, reached the rails a few yards and seconds ahead of the engine. Roadbed stones grated beneath hoofs. The driver shouted something indignant, unheard through grunting and clangor. He hauled on a cord; his whistle blasted forth shrillness. Then Rupert's horse stampeded. But then the prince had come alongside. Heat, vapor, greasy fumes torrented over him. He grabbed a handrail and swung himself onto the platform.

The driver's grime-black face opened in terror; his tongue was incredibly pink. The stoker, more bold, whacked with his shovel. Rupert caught the handle in his left hand. He overtopped either of them by nearly a foot. His sword gleamed free. He poked air, gestured a command. The crewmen scrambled onto the fuel heap in their tender. Crouched, gibbering, they saw him work the levers which vented pressure and put on brakes.

The train rocked to a slowdown. Will Fairweather had lost his seat, tumbled stern over bow in the grass. As he crawled up, the staghounds rushed him. He drew saber—*snick, snick, snick,* blood fountained scarlet under the sun, the dogs flopped right and left, the rest of the pack milled in yelping confusion. Meanwhile the Roundheads struggled to keep their saddles.

"Hurry, Will!" Rupert called.

The dragoon pumped his legs. Astoundingly fast for such awkwardness, he reached the locomotive. Rupert jerked a thumb at driver and stoker. They caught his intent and leaped off. Rupert snatched Will's hand and hauled him aboard. "There's the firebox," the prince said. "Shovel those coals like a devil assigned to a Covenanter, if ever thou'dst shovel manure again."

He made whistle shriek and bell clang to frighten the horses further. Beneath his grip, wheels gathered speed afresh. Will took an instant to bite his thumb at the riders before he started work.

The train was gone when Shelgrave's party had restored order. They sat for a while staring at each other in a silence broken by the gasps of their mounts. Foam dripped from bits, sweat-smell boiled off lathered flanks. The dogs lay nearly as worn.

"Well, Sir Malachi," said the kennelmaster at last, "what's to be done?"

Shelgrave straightened. For all his pallor and blinking eyes, he seemed in that moment more Ironside than any of them. "We signal ahead, of course," he snapped. "If that fails . . . I'll consider what next." He spurred his animal. It was only capable of a stumbling walk.

A SEMAPHORE STATION.

At the second message tower he reached, Rupert halted. It was a tall wooden frame, upbearing two arms painted in bright stripes and tipped with polished brass. Blocks led tackle to a bench, where were fastened a pair of ratcheted winches by which the apparatus could be moved. It stood in front of a plank hovel, from whose interior the aged operator tottered. Boys and oldsters were cheapest to hire for this work. They did not need especially keen eyes, though the companion constructions right and left poked barely into view. Telescopes were part of their equipment.

"What's amiss?" he quavered. (Rupert vaulted down gigantic, in a thud and a puff of dust.) Squinting closer: "Nay, thou'rt no crewman . . . no uniform . . . hair to thy shoulders—God help, a Cavalier!"

"Intending thee no harm, gaffer, if thou'lt stand peaceful by," Rupert said. He stalked to the winches, drew sword, slashed the ropes across, and reeled them in. "We've need to disable communication awhile. To that end, I must chop these lines like herbs for dinner —and, h'm, I'll take that pretty optic tube as well."

"An' tha coade book," Will added from the engine platform, where he had been curiously examining the controls. "'Twill feed our fierebox. I wager zuch be harder to replaece than coards or even spyglasses. An' for what pittance a purse-lipped Puritan doles out, who's spent free time a-learnin' o' their litany?"

Rupert slapped his thigh. "'Fore heaven, thou'st a head on thy shoulders!"

"Tha aim o' tha gaeme's to keep yours on yours, my loard. Me tha'll hang, if this Adam's apple o' miane doan't upbear tha weight."

"We'll not burn the book, however," Rupert decided. "Further on, after we've broken a few more links in the chain, we may wish to launch a message of our own. I'll think on that."

His blade had meanwhile been whacking. Satisfied that no repair was possible without replacements, he entered the cabin, took the volume, smiled bleakly when a glance at the title page showed that the printer had registered this a few years ago with his Majesty's stationer. Stepping forth again, "The telescope, if thou wilt, gaffer," he said. "Fear no wrath of thine employers. Thou'rt helpless against us."

"So Ay am. Thank God for that, sir." The old man pressed the instrument into the young man's clasp.

Rupert lifted brows and looked down upon the small stooped figure in the shoddy smock. "Thou'rt loyal to the King?"

"Ay beg you, breathe no word," the operator answered. "Not only me 'ud be kicked out to starve—that's no great matter, not since my Sarah coughed out her lungs in bloody bits—ay pled for a little coal to warm the one hencoop room we had, but after rent an' beans, what was left to buy with? . . . Not me, sir. My son, Sarah's an' my one son left alive, an' his wife, an' our grandchildren, let 'em lose their places on the looms an' lines in Bradford, an' what's to become of 'em? 'Tis hollow enough they already are." He tried to stand erect and meet the prince's eyes, but had spent too long a lifetime bent.

" 'Twas otherwise in my boyhood, sir," he said. "Ay saw a last bit o' the gone ways, an' often Ay've cursed luck that Sarah an' me wasn't born somewhere else this here progress ha'n't reached. Not that Squire was any angel, oh no, sir. Nor was't pleasure hunching over a sickle, sunup to sundown, till knees shook too sorely to uphold a lad. But we belonged, sir, we had our right's well as duties, going back to Earl Siward. Eigh, Squire 'ud make us grind our meal on his stones at his price; he'd make us drop what we had in hand to beat game for his hunting, though did his keeper catch us takin' a hare out o' the hundreds nibbling our cabbages, 'twas a whupping or a day in the stocks. . . . But 'fore God, sir, Squire never fenced off no common, an' he never cast nobody from house an' home, nor'd his lady leave nobody alone an' unhelped when sick or old . . . an' sir, God save the King."

Will shifted from foot to foot. "We be none too far from where we left yestre'en, Highness," he warned.

"Aye. Fire up our oliphaunt." Rupert clapped the hunched shoulder before him, turned, and soared onto the platform. Gauges told their tale, the shovel clattered and grated before brawling flames, arms rocked on eccentrics, the locomotive jerked into motion.

The operator stood tiny beneath the semaphore, waving till his visitors were out of sight.

FURTHER SOUTH.

The countryside remained hilly but had changed from pasture to cropland. Cornfields ripened beneath the sun, hayfields reached smaragdine. The latter were being harvested, mostly by lines of scythemen followed by women rakers—for hereabouts independent farms survived among estates, half-timbered homes and outbuildings, wind-gnarled apple orchards—though sometimes the whirling blades and teeth of a modern horse-drawn mower might be seen, worked by three or four hirelings. The fragrance was so overwhelming that it blessed every reek of tar or oil. Clouds were piling in the west, enormous white and blue.

The train banged on its way. Rupert clutched wheels, hauled levers, peered at meters and at the shining road before him. It was joy to brace legs against the pulse and shake of speed. Heat and smoke were an honest breath of freedom. They did not really bar off sky or land. He laughed, a flash amidst soot, and broke into a riding song of the Continental wars. From time to time he pulled the whistle lanyard.

> *"Morgenrot,*
> *Morgenrot,*
> *Leuchtest mir zun frühen Tod?*
> *Bald wird die Trompete blasen.*
> *Dann muss ich mein Leben lassen,*
> *Ich und mancher Kamerad!"* (*Toot, toot!*)

Will Fairweather saw the firebox gorged for a while, gusted a sigh, and racked his shovel. He tapped Rupert's arm. "B'r leave, my loard." When the prince glanced around: "I ben't ungraeteful, zir, for your foarezight what guess God might zend this heare roallin' kettle along for us," he said through the din. "But ben't we, well, zort o' bound to faere where it wants to? An' I doan't reckon one nest o' rebels smells any sweeter'n another."

"Nay. However, I know these roads."

Will gaped. "You do? I never put credentials in them stoaries 'bout your Highness's pets bein' his familiars; but now—" He scratched his gritty head. "A little tin mouse?"

Rupert set wheels and levers, lowered himself to a bolted-in bench, and explained: "See thou, I was ever taken with mechanic arts as well as alchemy and the like. Herein Sir Malachi and I are of the same breed, beneath raised hackles. He was delighted to show me what he had and what he planned. No doubt he thought it might help convert me, too—he was often after me to receive the *soi-disant* minister whose church he attends in Leeds, and would give me no chaplain for myself—" His scowl grew dark as the dust upon it.

"Sine tha Bread an' Wine wouldn't be forthcomin' anyhow," Will observed, "your Highness might's well tighten his belt an' go thirsty for tha Spirit."

Rupert nodded. "Not the first time. At Linz they were Jesuits I refused to see." Memory of that liberation brightened his mood in this. "Well," he continued, "among other things, Shelgrave took me for a good many rides on his private train, letting me drive when I wished: pistols cocked and primed at my back, of course. We talked much of what he and fellow magnates have done, and what they hope to do in future. No denying, they dream grandly. I looked at maps, timetables, bills of lading; and I'd naturally studied similar things earlier, when planning my campaigns; and there aren't but a few long stretches of railroad in England; and a military chief needs an exact memory. The upshot is, I know the web as well as anyone. Indeed, since I can recall what we Cavaliers tore up, belike I know it better than Shelgrave."

"Than tha general has a plan?" Will tugged his exiguous chin. "Stupid question. Tha general always has a plan. Or a scheame or a ruse or a wile or a plot or zomethin'."

"May God speed it. And I trust He will, for He's already let the builders lay tracks—barely before the war erupted—bypassing such dangerous-to-us big towns as Manchester or Sheffield. We'll need fresh coal and water at Buxton, not far ahead now. None come to take its waters in these uneasy times. Hence I expect few people at the station and assume we can overawe them. We'll need to, for a message would not be believed that did not originate at a regular depot."

"Message, zir?"

"Aye, by semaphore to Stoke-on-Trent, where again we must feed and slake this brute. It'll tell how we're on special business and are to be helped in every way, despite our appearance. We'll slash the cords behind us, of course, to block countermands. At Stoke we switch onto a line running due west. The one thence to Chester was cut, and if 'tis been repaired, that was by unfriendly hands. But the one I've in mind ends at Llangollen. The plan was to build south from there, to connect Welsh coalfields with Midlands manufactures. The war's halted that, Llangollen's a mere terminal of no interest to anybody, and . . . Wales is for the King."

"Moast zaggishly reckoned, your Highness," Will beamed. "Worthy indeed o' tha victor at Powick Bridge, Edgehill, Brentford, Cirencester, Birmingham, Chalgrove, Whitebridge where you routed 'em ere breakfast an' went back to finish shaevin', Bristol, Newark—" Abruptly the knot bobbled in his scrawny throat. "Uh, my loard, beggin' your pardon, not to carp, you deem —however—"

"What is't?" Rupert surged to his feet. Will pointed into wind and cinders. Far over the hills, but growing, lifted a plume of smoke.

Rupert snatched the telescope. "Aye, another train on this track," he growled. Muscles bunched in his tattered, blackened sleeves. "I feared that might happen. . . . Nay, better said, I knew the odds were it would. We're not on any schedule, or even the route we're supposed to plod."

Will spat on his shovel. "At least I needn't wield thee no longer." To Rupert: "M-m, Highness, if an oald . . . ranger . . . might zuggest, yonder's a clump o'

woods, an' beyond's a ryefield just right for comin'
through, meetin' nobody."

"Thou'd not abandon this faithful mount of ours,
wouldst thou? Why, I'm shocked as they oncoming will
be." Rupert laughed aloud, though it was more war cry
than merriment. "Lay on the coal!" He stood to the controls.

Will looked dismayed but resumed his labor. "Well,"
he mumbled, "if we be goin' to play Robin Hood on tha
bridge, you've tha zize to be Little John."

The other driver screeched whistle and slammed on
brakes. In rumble and whoosh, he came to rest. Rupert
stopped more leisurely. The last few yards he advanced
at an easy rate, till cowcatchers nearly touched.

The unknown crewman leaned across his overlook
and bawled furiously: "Who art thou, whoreson runa-
gate and knave? What thimblewit of a dispatcher sent
thee? Back, back!"

Rupert's answer came as loud, more deep, very mild:
"We're nighest Buxton and its sidings. 'Twill expedite us
both if thou giv'st way."

His opposition, a burly redhaired fellow accompanied
by a still more bearlike stoker, waved fists aloft. "Dolt!
Read the crest emblazoned on this boiler: Westminister,
Birmingham, & Manchester! And thou, a wretched local of some kind, hast gall to ask that I unschedule me?"

"The war's left only stumps of thy proud line. Now
do be reasonable and back up. I've business more toward than draper's goods or even beer, if that be in thy
wagons."

The driver seized a wrench. "I'll business thee!"

"Oh, wilt thou, good my friend?" Rupert's blade
snaked free. He went himself like a tiger, in half a dozen
bounds onto the top of his own engine and down the
lengths of both, till he stood above the other steering
board and lazily swung bright menace through the
smoke.

"Methinks it would be Christian to oblige me," he
purred. Wrench and shovel clattered to deck. The crewmen stared slack-jawed at his bulk and his weapon.
"But since ye are this loth to do a favor, why, I will do
it, and give you a ride in one of your own freightcars,

safely locked. Climb down to earth, now; do not seek to flee. I've longer legs than you, 'tis plain to see."

Will unbarred and slid back the door of a carrier, secured it after Rupert had prodded the prisoners in. "I reckon here's where we change trains, my loard," he said. (Rupert nodded.) "A moment, pray. I'll further look inboard." At the next wagon which he examined, he uttered a yip of glee. "Here's brew indeed, whole casks o' nut-brown yale! We'll not go thirsty, though we may go stale."

"Our prize's tank and tender are quite full," Rupert said. "To Stoke or further, 'twere a steady pull, save that for speed, we first must turn around, and send that message." He stroked scabbard and hilt. "So, we'll seize the ground."

In a few minutes the North country locomotive stood deserted, watching its Southland sister progress steadily backward.

X

BUXTON.

As Rupert had guessed, the little town was not frequented for its mineral springs in these unhappy times. It seemed to dream almost empty between its high surrounding hills, beneath a heaven half open and half mountainous snowy clouds: one wide street lined with gracious old buildings, a marketplace with a fine old cross. A few homes stood further out along meandering lanes, dominant among them at the west end a mansion raised in the days of Elizabeth.

The railway station was down by the River Wye, in order that a steam pump might keep the water tank loaded without need to sink a well. Otherwise there were coal bins, switchyard, semaphore, shedlike house, everything gaunt and dust-gray. Chuffing in, Rupert grimaced. "Such ugliness—here—comes nigh blasphemy," he said. "If naught else, they could plant a garden, as I've seen done in other places."

" 'Twar formerly, my loard." Will pointed to a weedbed. "No doubt tha new warder be a true Puritan, his miand on higher things liake cabbages." He glanced at the barrel lashed onto the platform bench. "Think you 'a's got a cup to spaere? After thic sweat that general an' me lost, hoistin' this monstrous weight o' beer to a handy plaece, what shaeme we let tha bigger part splash free whilst standin' on our heads to drink from tha bunghoale."

"We might better seek food," Rupert reproved him. "Or to carry out our mission."

His gaze traced the course he must follow to point the train properly south. His experience was not sufficient that the maneuvering would be easy, given six cars for tail. Carefully, he inched toward position.

The stationmaster came forth. He was a big, rawboned person in somber garb. A scar seamed his brow, running into close-cropped gray hair. His limp did not make him less fierce-looking. "A Roundhead veteran, pensioned off with this post," Rupert muttered to Will. "Handle him like a hot petard, if we're to capture the station."

"Halt!" the man cried. "What means this?"

Rupert obeyed in a hiss of vented steam, leaned over the rail and answered, "Emergency most dire. Bandits."

"Aye—you in your Popish mane!"

"No, hold, sir. I own I fought for the King, but being taken prisoner and finding 'twas not truly his cause, I've become Sir Malachi Shelgrave's man—you've heard the name? My comrade and I were riding secretly in a van, as guards, lest robbers strike, which they've been doing further north. We looked not for them hereabouts, but found our way barricaded only a few miles hence. Ere we could act, driver and fireman were slain. Then did we come forth and chase the rogues, doing some execution; but since we could not go on, we must needs return."

The Puritan had stood rigid beneath Rupert's smooth word-flow. "Indeed?" he responded. "Evil news forsooth. Let me fetch my codebook, that I may broadcast it at once." He hobbled into the stationhouse.

"Keep lookout from here," Rupert whispered to Will. "I'll secure him." He jumped down to the flagstones beside the track and strode toward the house.

The stationmaster emerged. In his belt was a pistol. At his shoulder gaped a blunderbuss. "Let go thy sword!" he screeched. "Arms aloft ere I blow out thy treacherous brains!"

Rupert stiffened. He saw finger go tense on trigger. "I'd love to do it, Cavalier," the stationmaster said.

Rupert's hands went up. "You're much mistaken, sir," he began. Inwardly: *Yon bell-mouth tolls the knell of all my hopes.*

"We'll see about that," was the reply. "If proper authority certify thee honest, thou'lt go free and, if thou'st a grain of sense, thank Ebenezer Smail that he's cautious. Too hellish many masterless men—worse, fugitive Cavaliers—a-prowl these days. I think ye're two of 'em;

but better hang tomorrow than be shot today, ha?" A shout: "Thou on the cab! Sound thy whistle, summon me help!"

Will stooped forward, brought palm to ear. "Eh?" he said. "What?"

"Pull the whistle cord, thou sicksoul! Else I've a bolus for thee, after thy fellow sufferer has swallowed his pellets."

"Zir, I be very deaf," Will said in the flat tone of those who are. "I zee you oaverwrought 'bout zomethin' or 'tother. Maybe zuspicious of us, hey? Can't blaeme you, no, can't blaeme you. We've no fear o' tha sheriff. I'll be happy to do your little wish, if you'll come nigh that I may hear."

Smail glared. "Stand fast," he told Rupert. Crabwise, to keep the giant covered, he approached the locomotive.

Will simpered at him. "Look, I unbuckle my zaber in earnest o' faith," he called. The weapon dropped on the stones. He leaned far over the side. "Pray, zir, cloase an' loud."

He has a thought, Rupert knew. *When the Roundhead's gone as near as he will, I'll make distraction. . . .* "Ha, beware!" he roared from full lungs.

In the instant when eyes flickered, Will Fairweather whirled over the rail. His boots spurned it, he soared through a meteor's arc, he struck Smail and they went down together. The blunderbuss crashed.

Rupert sprang across the paving. Dragoon and stationmaster rolled about at each other's throats. Rupert got hold of an ear, dragged Smail's head around, drove fist to chin. The man went boneless.

Will crawled from beneath. "What a snock!" he gasped. "It shivered me too. Did you kill tha lout?"

"Nay, he'll but sleep awhile. Thou—" Rupert seized the narrow shoulders. "Oh, Will, thou couldst'a been slain!"

"Tha blast did tickle my whiskers, zir." A shrug. "'A be a fool, him. Never zaw that for me 'twould'a been better indeed, gettin' blown oapen right off, than waitin' to dangle." A grin. "Think o' tha mess I'd've left for him to scrub."

Rupert remained grave; nor did he let go his clasp. He spoke slowly; "My valiant friend, say no more 'lord' to me. From this day forth, I would be 'thou' to thee."

"What? H'm? I doan't follow your Highness nohow."

"Is't not English usage? When two of German kind would be dear comrades, they agree they'll henceforward call each other *du*—'thou,' not 'you' on either side. I'd fain make it thus between us twain."

The dragoon blushed and shuffled his feet. "Oh, really, zir, thic ben't riaght. I'd never bend this tongue 'round zuch a way o' speakin' to your Highness."

Rupert frowned. "I want it so."

Will snapped to attention. "Aye, zir. If you . . . thou zay'st zo. I zuppoase tha order doan't hoald whan we be with other great loards like, like thy Highness?" He pulled loose. "Zir, we've no time to spill on speeches. Tha bang o' thic gun be bound to draw onlookers."

Rupert nodded. "Right thou art. Don thy saber again. Reload the blunderbuss—there must be powder and shot in the stationhouse—bind mine host here inside—shoo off whoever comes, telling them our bisiness is secret, urgent, and official. I doubt any'll be armed. Nevertheless, we need haste as we need air. I'll uncouple the wagons, turn the engine, signal ahead that we're on a special mission—clear tracks for us, have refills for man and machine alike ready in Stoke—then disable the semaphore. God willing, I can get it done in an hour."

"I hoape I fiand a cup," Will said. "After thic zort of hour, my gullet'll be too parched for practicin' these thous o' thine till 'tis had a princely rinse. Be that why tha Germans drink on it?"

THE BOUNDARY OF CHESHIRE AND SHROPSHIRE.

Rain-brooding weather had slowly been driving eastward, and now the locomotive was headed straight into it. The afternoon was blue-gray, sunbeams which slipped past ponderous cloud masses a brazen color which, despite its hardness, pervaded the green of meadows and leaves until they seemed to glow by their own light. Farmsteads huddled widely strewn across ever steeper hills, hamlets were rare along the serpentine railbed. Wind shrilled chilly through chug and clatter. Sometimes it bore a few drops; they stung.

Will hunched to warm his hands at the filled firebox. "Brrrr!" he said, "Why've we not walls an' a roof around us?"

"Has a helmsman shelter at sea?" Rupert answered from where he stood.

"On zome ships 'a do."

"A wooden cab would too likely catch fire from stray sparks."

"An' an ieron one'd cost. 'Tis cheaper to replaece men as tha' get cough an' fever. Though o' coua'se your Puritan measter will tell you 'a leaves 'em out in tha oapen for to strengthen their moaral fiber."

Rupert adjusted a valve. "Have cheer. We ought to be in Llangollen about nightfall."

"Couldn't we wait till tomorrow, an' meanwhile fiand dry quarters? It ben't zeemly tha Prince Palatine arrive like what might be called a drowned rat, zave that rats got better zense."

Rupert shook his head. "We met a surprise in Buxton, well-nigh lethal. Recall how suspicious they were in Stoke—"

"Tha' stoaked us, though. What a ham!"

"—no matter that they'd received our message. Were't not that Cromwell's conquered so widely around, making it hard to imagine anyone defying him still, they might well have tried to hold us for investigation. Sithence . . . thou'st seen the burnt-out shells of houses. I know not how far the Roundhead sway extends. Too chancy, stopping to inquire anywhere short of Wales."

Will clanged the furnace door shut and rose to stand beside his leader. "Canst thou not ask o' thy ring?"

Rupert turned a whetted glance upon him. "What mean'st thou?"

The dragoon gestured at the asp circlet. Its jewel glinted wan. "Thic, what Queen Titania gaeve. Aim it at a buildin' along our way. If help's within for us, tha

stone'll light up." He hugged himself and sneezed.
"True, maybe 'twoan't reckon just keepin' us dry
o'ernight, with a posset or a cup o'mulled wine inzide,
be worthy of its tellin' us about. Howsomever, no harm
tryin', hey?" He yawned prodigiously. "We've had no
rest zince yesterday morn. Thy Highness be young, an'
made o' well-oiled steel; but take pity on an oaldster
who'd dearly love a nap if 'a didn't keep gettin' roused
by tha clunkin' o' his eyelids."

Rupert scowled at the facets and rubbed a bristly
cheek. "Um-m-m . . . the further in hours and miles
from yonder moon-dream, the less real it seems. What
did truly happen? And why?"

" 'Twar real enough to maeke thy ring a beacon this
mornin', when thou drew'st near tha train what delivered us."

"Indeed? I saw not."

"I did, my loard. But than, beliake I be in tha habit o'
heedin' zuch winks, an' thou not."

"No doubt. Which one of us does right? How far dare
I obey this thing around my finger? A single inch?"

"Hoy, theare! You'd not cast the treasure away,
dwould you?"

Rupert's shoulders slumped beneath their own weariness. His voice dropped likewise. "I'm duly grateful to
thee, trusty Will, and . . . Jennifer . . . and, well,
perhaps those others. Yet what can we be safe in thinking of them? They could be gaudy lures, mere will-o'-
the-wisps above a thin-decked pit—the Pit itself. Or
tricksters, stirring us to rush about as boys may stir an
anthill; they're not human. Or, if well-meaning, fools
who toy with flame. Or fools more shallow still, too
worldly-wise to bear in mind the next world."

His companion stared aghast. "Highness Rupert!
You'll not now let tha Calvinist in you o'erriede tha
Cavalier?"

"I do not know." Torment filled the words. "I do not
know, forgive me." Then suddenly the prince drew himself erect. "Aye, I do! Take it howe'er thou wilt, this
much is certain: we cannot go astray if we but follow
the Word of God and duty of a soldier."

"Too strait a road, if straight-aimed at defeat."

"But free of snares and mire. God's will be done, for laurels here on earth or crowns in heaven. Meanwhile, I swore an oath to serve my King, not chase a moonbeam when he needs me most. We'll seek his court."

"Moare liake, his beggared camp," Will grumbled. Rupert didn't hear. Will shivered and squatted down to tap a stoup of ale.

Clack-clack went the wheels. They were on a level stretch, no need for guidance. Rupert twisted his ring about and about. *Should I then cast this off me, overside, like something glowing blue-white from the fire?* he wondered unhappily. Decision: *Nay, that would be a craven deed itself when I have no more knowledge than I do. Unworthy of a knight, that I should spurn a love-sign humbly given by the hand of one who dared ask nothing in return save that I let her dare the world for me.*

A smile tugged faintly at one corner of his mouth. *She's a mere maiden—merry, though not Mary; a commoner, albeit comely—yet oh, so very England! I recall how I, a youth first visiting this isle, when steeplechasing, wished that I might fall and break my neck, to leave these bones in England. Yon English wheatfield, stalks as slim as she, sun-ripened, goes in ripples like her walk; its hue and heaviness bespeak her hair; the soul above it is no butterfly to flit and preen on jewel-broidered wings, but rather is, I think, a youthful hawk already riding lonely on the wind.*

He shook himself. *Ha' done! Belike I'll never see her more. Or if I do, in peaceful after years, 'twill be with puffed politeness to her spouse and presents for their eight or nine plump children. I hope he doesn't seek to curry favor. . . . That's if the King wins. If the King wins. If.*

A sharp curve appeared in the tracks ahead. Rupert took back the steering.

LLANGOLLEN.

Between lowering sky and shouldering shaggy mountains glowed a last brimstone bar of light. Against it hulked the ruins of a fortress, upon a conical hill a mile

or so beyond settlement. The town was roofs and steeples rising out of dusk along the River Dee. From its
railway station, downstream, one glimpsed the graceful-
ness of an ancient arched bridge. Bells chimed through a
cold, muttering breeze.

A pair of great pole-mounted lanterns cast glow upon
the terminal, though this walled off any clear view elsewhere. Approaching, Will asked, "Why yonder lamps
whan tha western liane ben't in use?"

"Perhaps it is," Rupert replied. "If a loyal force is
posted hereabouts, they may well send a train on short
runs after supplies. Let's trust the cargo can feed us ere
we tumble into bed."

"Could be a pallet in gaol, thic." Will stooped to peer
through dimness. "I zee no kindlin' o' thy ring."

"Should there be? I thought it was to shine at extraordinary help or opportunity, not simple friendliness." Rupert stood quiet for a clock-tick. "Aye, conceivably the
enemy's won this far. Keep that blunderbuss ready;
here's the pistol in my belt. We'll not debark till we're
sure. At need, I'll back us out again, and we'll be gone
to earth well before they can organize their chase."

As he slowed to a halt, his eyes scouted. A few wagons stood on a siding, lumps of black. On the station
pavement were the usual boxes and barrels, a pair of the
usual horsecarts for carrying off freight. Otherwise was
emptiness. No candlelight showed in the stationhouse
windows. "Holla!" Rupert hailed through a final gush
of steam. "Who's here?"

A dozen buff-coated musketeers leaped from the
door and pelted to disperse themselves. Their captain
poised boldly in place. His helmet and sword gleamed
beneath the lanterns. "Hold!" he shouted. "Declare
yourselves!"

"Tha' spied us from afar an' maede ready— Let's
go," Will chattered.

"Who are ye?" Rupert demanded.

"General Cromwell's Independents," the captain
snapped. "Speak."

"Tha' *war* ahead of us, Fiend thunder 'em," Will
hissed.

"Get between him and me," Rupert whispered back.

"Let him not see my hands readying us for escape. I'll talk meanwhile—

"Ah, good," he responded aloud.

"You say that, from under hair like yours?" the captain scoffed.

Rupert thickened his accent. "Dis iss no var uff ours, good sir. Ve're artificers from de Dutch statholder, come to study your British trains for him. Ve vere trying dis vun, by leaff uff de master in Stoke-on-Trent, ven ve saw such a vild-looking gang uff men ve t'ought best ve make speed. Good to see ve haff come in de same hands ass ve left in Stoke."

The captain's tone grew more amiable. "They'd not have known, there. 'Twas but this day we entered. Semaphores've stood idle and trains been frightened off whilst fighting was in these parts." His alertness never slackened. "Well, come on down. I'll need to bring you in for questioning. Have no fears if ye're honest. Why, no doubt General Cromwell himself'll wish to talk with you."

"Vun moment, pleasse, vile ve make de enchine ready — Ah!"

Pressure was back at the full. Rupert threw in reverse drive. The locomotive clanked into motion.

The captain yelled. Muskets barked, not only from around the paving wherever cover was to be had, but from the sidetracked vans. Bullets clanged off the boiler and whined away.

Two soldiers darted out of shelter of a crate. They hurled themselves against a horsecart. Will saw their intention. His blunderbuss belched orange flame, inky smoke, leaden hail. The wagonbed shielded the men. They shoved the vehicle across the tracks and shook triumphant fists. "Do your worst, heretics!" one taunted.

"I've naught to do it with," Will keened, clutching his discharged weapon.

The tender struck the wagon. Wooden frame crunched beneath iron wheels, to block and jam them.

"Out, out, men!" the captain cried. "Ring them in! If they surrender not, slay them!"

Fearless in their faith—or shrewdly gauging that they

would meet no more serious gunshot—the Roundheads swarmed from both sides. Rupert drew saber and slashed at the ropes securing the ale barrel. A welter of soldiers hurried to form a line on the pavement beside the track.

Rupert dropped his blade and seized the cask. Muscles swelled to rip his shirt down back and front. In one swing he raised the great object over his head and hurled it among those Puritans.

He was a very light drinker. Will alone had not much diminished thirty-six beer gallons. Counting the oak itself, some four hundred pounds struck ground.

Staves splintered and flew on an outward volcano of brew and foam. The sundering crash was followed by screams, gurgles, and strangled ungodly curses.

Rupert retrieved his saber and was in the air before the barrel smote. Landing on shattered flagstones, blade aloft, "*En avant!*" he roared, and led Will through a chaos of drenched, overbowled, lurching, beer-blinded or half-drowned Ironsides.

More darted from behind locomotive and tender. Three of them, fast runners, sped at a slant to intercept the fugitives near the stationhouse. One, who had not used his musket in the volley, brought it up. Rupert shot him. It was no mortal wound; to hit with a pistol at that distance was rare. But the man sank to his knees, hugging a broken shoulder. His companions had their swords out. "Thou to the right, Will, me to the left," Rupert called. He attacked. A spark-showering blow knocked the Roundhead weapon loose. On the return, Rupert laid the man's thigh open. Meanwhile Will hurled an otherwise useless blunderbuss at the nose of his opponent, which made it easy to disable him too when they closed.

On past the station, into the dusk. "They'll rally and be after us," Rupert said in rhythm with his feet. "Reinforcements; dogs if they can get 'em; surely guides, willing or not, who know this country. Those're wildwood hills before us. Be thou our leader."

"We'll need moare than woodcraft, my loard," the other answered.

A MOUNTAINSIDE. FULL NIGHT.

Somewhere in the thick wet tangle of forest, a stream clucked. Louder came snap and crash as Rupert fought his unskillful way through brush which his companion parted easily. Faint but clear tolled the voices of hounds.

"*Dood ok ondergang!*" Rupert panted. "I'd liefer meet a line o' Switzer pikemen than these damned claw-twigged withes. How canst thou find thy path? 'Tis black as an Ethiop's bowels."

"Fiand it we boath must," replied grimness from the murk. Thunder boomed. "E'en if yon rain comes zoon to wash out our slot, 'tis too laete. Tha' be on our track itzelf, broaken limbs an' trampled shrubs."

"My doing," Rupert admitted. Pride flashed back into him. "I'm a hunter, not a poacher."

"Aye," Will snorted. "Thou ben't woant to slip on a deer unbeknowanst an' fell him by one quick shot. Nay, thou'lt chaese him a-hoa'seback till 'a can drag his weight no further. There be a Frenchy naeme for each staege o' his terror an' weariness, not zo? Well, Prince, naeme them in thyzelf tonight!"

That anger brought Rupert up short. "Forgive me," he said. "I meant no offense to thee—was only trying to excuse mine own clumsiness."

"Aaahhh. . . ." Will's resentment faded. "How can I rail at a man big enough to talk thus? I was a-feared for, well, not just my carcass, loard, but ten kids in Somerset . . . aye, their mother too."

"Thou canst evade the chase."

"An' thou canst not. Come along. What we got to do be fiand yonder beck I hear, wade down it a ways for to break our trail, take squirrel hospitality o'ernight, an' hoape—can this be done in time— Hoy! Almighty God! Look!"

Light burst on Rupert's left hand. Ruby, bronze, gold, emerald, turquoise, sapphire, amethyst, it streamed from the jewel facets, forth to bring gaunt unshaven faces, matted hair, sweat-tunnels through coal-dust, vivid against the middle of the night, and to blaze back out of eyes.

"Tha elven ring," rattled in Will's throat. "Help's nigh."

"Or damnation is," Rupert mumbled. "Thy plan might well save us. This'd go . . . a different way."

Thunder bawled anew. Wind soughed ever louder in leaves, boughs creaked. "Hark'ee," Will said, "cavalry-men liake thee an' me, moare callouses on zoul than even arse, our kiand miaght well fiand they've 'listed un-der Nick's banner. But Mis'ess Jennifer, dost thou really zuppoase 'a could maeke *her* his recruitin' zergeant?"

Rupert stared for a heartbeat into soft incandescence before he responded most quietly, "Thou'rt right. We'll follow where the ring aims."

That proved to be almost a backtracking, diagonally down the mountain. In any other direction, the jewel be-gan to dull. In this, its brilliance made travel easy. Nonetheless, hounds and horns pealed closer amidst the noises of approaching storm.

And so I rest my faith on Jennifer, Rupert thought. Aloud: "I think not the ring's simply discovered whatev-er 'tis we're seeking. Else we'd've known on the way hither. Nay, what power it has must've drawn something toward us—"

"Which war not too far away, as't chanced," Will added; "but than, tha West's where moast magic lingers. Robin Goodfellow toald me things miaght happen thus. . . .Hoo, heare comes our rain!"

Some lightning glare had blinked through foliage. Ab-ruptly it seared past leaves etched white over black, while thunder cannonaded and wind bore forward the first mighty rush of water. Drops flung past branches were so swift and cold that they burned.

Woods gave on a patch of grass and blossoms. There stood a building, single-roofed, of no unusual size or form though sufficient for two stories and—it could just be seen—with beam-ends carved in fanciful shapes.

Rupert jarred to a halt. "Who's raised a house like that in wilderness?" he exclaimed.

"Nobody, loard. Nor will it stay heare long." His fol-lower urged him ahead. Rain cataracted across them.

At the massive, bronze-studded front door they stopped. Above it was fastened a bush; above that, a signboard rocked under its bracket. "A tavern, zarvin' wine," Will observed through the uproar. "Nay, wait. What's this? A flowerin' thornbush, in tha midst o' zummer?"

Rupert's eyes were for the sign. What light there was revealed how a bird of rare beauty, plumage long and like gold tinged with flame, carried a branch of cloves to a nest it was weaving. "A phoenix near its death and resurrection," he said. "I've never met that namepost—"

"Tha Oald Phoenix," Will breathed. "Tha inn whereof Puck toald me . . . yesternight? No liafetimes moare agone nor thic?"

"Ho-ah!" The call was nearly lost in wind, rain, thunder. Out beneath flaring heaven trotted a band of men and dogs.

"The Roundheads!" Rupert snatched at sword, moved quickly to cover the luminance on his left hand.

Will tugged his tattered sleeve. "Bide, my loard," the dragoon said in awe.

"Come on, come on!" The Puritan leader waved his own blade. "On after them, or e'er this gale they've raised by wicked wizardry sponge out their track!"

The pursuers toiled across the glade and vanished among darknesses beyond.

"They sensed us not," Rupert stammered, "nor spied the very house—"

"Tha' got no ring off Mis'ess Jennifer," Will answered. "Let's us two try what drink be found inzide."

He took hold of a handle molded in form of an elephant's head and trunk. The door swung smoothly open. Rupert led the way through. As he crossed the threshold, his jewel fell to an ordinary luster. For this while, its work was done.

XI

THE TAPROOM OF THE OLD PHOENIX.

WILL closed the door behind himself, barring every hint of storm. Windows likewise were tightly shuttered. The men kept right hands at hover near sword hilts and glared about.

But the chamber was altogether peaceful. Indeed, the strangest thing was its homelikeness. It might be somewhat wider than was common for a country inn, but if so, that was not by much. Massive ceiling beams, subtle-grain oak in floor and wainscots, long central board and benches, a few small tables with straight-backed seats, were familiar. In a handsome stone fireplace a blaze danced to its own merry boom and crackle, casting forth pinewood fragrance as well as warmth, flanked by several armchairs which were intricately carved and ivory-inlaid but whose cushions had plainly comforted many a body over the years.

The contents of the room were perhaps more unusual, as if sailor patrons had brought gifts from a whole world. Upon the mantel rested a giant hourglass and two seven-branched candlesticks of twining brass. The light from these were joined by that from tapers sconced around the walls. Their gleam picked out a number of pictures whose kinds, styles, and subjects made a somehow harmonious turmoil. On the right side stretched a mahogany bar with a brass footrail and surprisingly up-to-date beer pumps, guarding racks of bottles and drinking vessels. A nearby door must lead to the kitchen, since lingering savorinesses drifted thence. In the adjacent wall, opposite the entrance, another opening gave on a corridor and staircase. Beside this lifted a high, crammed set of bookshelves. Next to it, a desk held writing materials and two globes.

Rupert's glance gulped the setting as it hunted the

persons. They were not many: a barmaid, a man and woman seated at the fire, another couple at one of the little tables. Their conversations chopped off when the Cavaliers appeared. Yet the regard they gave was neither hostile nor wary; it was frankly curious.

The man by the hearth sprang erect and hurried toward the latest arrivals. "Good eventide, good sirs. Be very welcome," he greeted. His voice was deep and rich, bearing a trace of West country accent.

Rupert looked hard at him. "You're the . . . proprietor . . . of this Old Phoenix?" he asked.

The man nodded. "What may your wishes be?" He raised a palm, smiling. "Nay, let me guess. Ye've fared through rain, in striving and distress. A bath, dry garb, hot food, a cup of cheer, a bed, then breakfast, ere you go from here."

Still Rupert considered him. While more quick on his feet than most, he was stocky beneath an overlay of plumpness. His face was round, rosy, snub-nosed, brown eyes a-twinkle, chin clean-shaven; only his complete baldness made it memorable. His garb was equally nondescript, though of superior material. Yet something about him breathed an air at least of Puck.

"Our purse is lean," Rupert warned.

The landlord made a dismissing wave. "We take no money here." At their astonishment he laughed. "If Faerie gold turns into autumn leaves in mortal wallets, what's your gold to us?"

Rupert stiffened. "This is a kittle place we've blundered into," he told Will under his breath.

"But friendly," replied the dragoon, now standing almost at ease.

"Aye, to those who seek us out," the landlord said. "Fear never paying such unholy price as might be taken in the Venusberg. My sole reward for hospitality is meeting folk like you, within whom burn the stars of many worlds and destinies. I love to watch them meet and hear them yarn." Seriously: "Indeed, I may not really touch their lives. Methinks, for instance, ye've escaped some peril. Well, ye could not have come upon this house had there not been another refuge for you."

"A brook an' treetop," Will nodded. "Me, I'll choose

your bed." To Rupert: "Fear not. It war *her* toaken led us heare."

The prince shook himself. "Aye." With a stiff grin: "Maybe I'll grow used to trollery." To the landlord: "I thank you much, and offer you our names. I am Prince Rupert, exile from the Rhine, and this my comrade is Will Fairweather."

The other bowed. "I've many names," he answered. "Let you say Taverner. Now follow me upstairs. Hot water waits, soap, towels, grooming gear, and change of clothes. Ye must return them when ye leave tomorrow; yours will be ready, clean and dry and mended. We've eaten here, but you'll be brought roast beef and what pertains to it, to dine at ease while settling private-ly what your desires are. A room is fitted for each one of you. I hope your wish will not be 'Straight to bed.' "

"Nay, we'll return"—Rupert gave a salute of courtesy to the rest who were present—"and make acquaint-ances."

As Taverner led them out, past the bar, Will half choked and Rupert himself broke stride. That was not due to the woman behind the counter; chubby, cheerful, gray hair in a bun, she was like a female version of the landlord, and might well be his wife since she wore a wedding band. But from here, one got a direct view of the hearth.

"Thic wench in yonder armchair," Will whispered. "Hoo, hoo, hoo!"

"Whoe'er she is, she's not for likes of thee," Rupert cautioned.

Taverner might have heard, since he remarked over his shoulder: "Ye'll find your fellow guests tonight forthcoming. We get some surly ones; but mostly not. Here all alike are far beyond their worlds, and none may leave by any other door than that wherethrough he entered, nor bear off much more than rest and cheer and memories. Thus, in a way, whatever happens here has not quite fully happened. That's a freedom whereof no few avail themselves. Pray, come."

The three departed from the chamber.

The man at the table, who had sat clutching a tankard

while he observed, brought it to his lips for a mighty draught. "Aah!" he said. *"Det gaar godt."* He addressed the young woman opposite him with a slight lilt. "Who might those fellows be?"

"I don't know." Like him, she spoke an English never native to England, though with a different accent. "They look kind of Renaissance? Except I didn't think people grew that big in those days. The dark one's just about your size and build."

Her companion was in truth huge. His face was good-looking if not extraordinary, save for a slightly dented nose; his yellow hair was cut short and he went beardless. He wore trousers and open-necked shirt of stout brown cloth, boots cobbled for rough use. "Well," he said, "things may not be the same in their world. Thou, uh, actually, in my own time-line—I mean the one I started out from, this trip—giants did exist now and then, 'way back in the Middle Ages. Like King Harald Haardraade of Norway, who died in 1066 trying to conquer England one jump ahead of the Normans. He stood seven feet high."

"Then no doubt the same was true in my history," she answered. "They're so similar, yours and mine, maybe identical till, m-m, didn't we decide about 1900?"

"I tell you, I don't belong where I came from."

She patted his hand. "I know. Take it easy, Holger. I am trying to help you." She was a winsome lass, tall, slender, features pert, eyes blue as the man's. Ruddy-brown locks fell past her ears. Her garb was a feminine, green version of his. On the left breast shone a silver pin in the form of an owl.

"If we had more time!" he said. "What can I learn in a night?"

"Well, we don't. I'll simply have to cram what I can into that square head of yours, before Mister Boniface politely but firmly sends us on our separate ways."

"Why can one only spend a night per visit?"

"Isn't it obvious? Anything more, and there might be too decisive an interaction. This is neutral ground." The girl drew breath. "Suppose, oh, suppose I happened to meet Abe Lincoln here—I'm sure he's eligible, whether or not he ever actually did find his way to a door—well, given a lot of time together, I probably couldn't resist warning him against Ford's Theater. Lord knows what that might do to his world. Make a new continuum? I'm not sure if that's possible. However, I am sure that nobody less than God has the wisdom for it. I suspect we're bending the rules already, you and I."

"You're very kind," he said.

"Nuts! I'm having fun." She sipped from her glass of wine. "But look, when those two guys come back, I'll want to talk with them. After all, I am on an exploratory project. So let's get as much done as we can until then." She stood up. He made to do the same. She gestured him off. "Stay put. I'm going to see if anything helpful is on the bookshelf over there."

She crossed the room with a limber stride. Holger settled down to his beer. The woman in the armchair leaned forward. His glance crossed hers, and locked.

With sheer material, trim, jewelry and other accessories, she had turned what was supposed to be a decorous stola into something spectacular. The sumptuousness beneath her clothing made this irrelevant to any normal male. She ran fingers through midnight tresses and gave him a smoldering smile.

"Damn," he lamented, "I wish I could talk to you."

She crooned, to be heard only by him: *"Da mi basia mille."*

"Det var som Fanden! I've forgotten practically all the Latin I ever had, except for church." Slowly: "However, is language required?"

He half rose. His erstwhile partner saw, and called: "Hey, take it easy, lover boy. Sex and mathematics don't mix. Or hadn't you heard?"

"Oh, well, look here, Valeria, I'm simply trying to be polite—"

"Yah, I know that kind of politeness. And you told me you're seeking your own true sweetheart. Do you or don't you want some how-to instruction?"

"Sure." Holger slumped. His sheepish glance at the other woman got a return both sullen and sultry. He fumbled for pipe and tobacco pouch.

Valeria ran her eyes over the books. They were as

various in titles as in size and binding. Her fingers
stroked the celestial globe on the desk beside. The ter-
restrial sphere was equally detailed, marking in special
colors places like Atlantis and Huy Braseal.

The landlord re-entered. Approaching Holger, he
asked, *"Vil Herren ikke gerne ha' et Krus til?"*

"Jo, Tak," the big man said; then: "Why talk Danish? Yes, thanks, I would like more beer, Herr Kro-
mand. I've never had better."

"Quite a compliment from your nationality," beamed
the landlord. His English changed accent again as he
raised his voice. "I say, pet, the gentleman 'ere needs
another pint of the dark."

"Coming right along, duck," the barmaid answered.
She pattered to fetch Holger's tankard and fill it afresh.

"Would you care for a drink yourselves?" the Dane
asked them both.

"Aow, thanks, sir, but I got me place to tend," said
the barmaid. "Might draw meself a mild-and-bitter,
though."

"And I've me own 'ostly duties," the landlord added.
"The poor lady over there ain't got anybody else 'ere tonight what can talk with her. Besides, I think you're
busy. You come join us when you can, what?"

He sought the woman by the hearth, resumed his
chair, lifted his goblet to hers, and proceeded in their
conversation.

"Hey!" Valeria warbled. "Yippee! Here we are—So-
kolnikoff, *Introduction to Paratemporal Mathematics.*"
She took a closer look. "And, yeah, right beside it, the
Handbook of Alchemy and Metaphysics, so I don't even
have to go upstairs for my copy." She grabbed the two
volumes, plus paper and pencils off the desk.

Back by Holger, she drew her chair close to his and
sat down. "Now, look," she told him, "I can't teach you
everything they've learned in my world. Anyhow, I
don't claim to understand more than the elements myself. And even our experts still have some pretty large
areas of ignorance. But the theorems I do know let me
cross from continuum to continuum, with a fair proba-
bility of landing in whichever one I want, or a reasona-

ble facsimile of it. I even deduced there had to be an interuniversal nexus. That's how I found the Old Phoenix. You did it by accident, didn't you?"

"Well," he said defensively, "at least I have been traveling too."

"Yah!" she gibed. "Using the spells from that superstition-riddled medieval grimoire you located—an unguided missal if ever I saw one. You could hunt through the time-lines till you died of old age, in its random style. Or no, not that long: till you met something too tough and smart and mean. Had several narrow squeaks already, haven't you?" She tapped a book. "Okay. You did once take an engineering degree. You should appreciate a systematic treatment. You may get a glimmering of how to cast a transportation spell that has a better-than-chance likelihood of taking you where you want to go." She sighed. "I hope, for openers, you've got the wit to grasp the fundamental ideas of the transcendental calculus, because that's how we prove the theorems you'll need, and without understanding, you can't get any good out of them."

Holger reached for the volume. "Please explain," he said meekly. "You shouldn't take all this trouble for a stranger.".

"Aw, hell, I like you, man." Valeria started to talk and draw diagrams. The other woman chatted with Taverner-Boniface-Kromand, though her attention kept straying. The barmaid waited in amiable patience.

XII

LATER.

RUPERT and Will came into the taproom, cleansed, remarkably refreshed, the former regal, the latter gawky in robes of timeless cut but many colors. They paused at the entrance. Rupert's glance was caught by a picture unlike most of the portraits, landscapes, and action scenes around: a colored print of a glossy kind new to him, eerily beautiful in its vista of a starry night wherein floated a branded silvery globe encompassed by shimmering rings.

The landlord beckoned. "Ah, welcome, guests," he hailed. "Come take your ease and drink. What is your pleasure?"

"Beer!" said the two like a single mouth.

The landlord chuckled. "I thought 'twould be."

Rupert led the way to the hearth. "You're far too kind, good Master Taverner," he said.

"Nay, Highness, I'm a fat and cunning spider, albeit male, which weaves a subtle web bedewed with ale and wine and stronger waters, and thus ensnares a singing swarm of lives, to batten on the fables that they bear." The landlord waved at armchairs. "Do join us. Oh, but first I must present you." He spoke to the woman, with an appropriate gesture: *"Rupertus, filius comitis palatini Rheni, et Guillermus, miles et famulus suus."* To the men: "And this is Clodia Pulcher, come from Rome."

Will leered at her. Rupert was dumfounded. "That Clodia—Catullus's Lesbia?" he faltered. (His host nodded.) "But she is dead these sixteen hundred years!"

"Not in the world that is her own, my lord. And here may come, from every time and clime, aye, every cranny of reality, whoever finds a way to find the door and brings uncommon tales wherewith to pay." Taverner winked. "She is an often guest, our Clodia: tonight

97

in disappointment growing sulky till your arrival. Sit ye, sirs, I pray."

Rupert curbed himself, bowed over the woman's hand, kissed it, and greeted her: *"Salve, domina; ad servitium tuum."*

She beamed and purred in reply, *"Oh! Loqueris latine?"*

Rupert shrugged. *"Aliquantulum, domina."* Too bemused to struggle further with the language, especially when his pronunciation and, no doubt, grammar were so unlike hers, he settled his great frame beside the landlord's.

The barmaid arrived with two brimful tankards. She curtsied as she handed one to Rupert, saying, "Here's for your Highness." Giving Will the other, she added more casually, "And the same for thee. I hope 'twill smack you well."

"I thank thee, goodwife," said Rupert absently.

Will picked a chair next to Clodia's, though her attention remained on his master. Goggle-eyed, he little marked what a noble brew he drank.

Valeria nudged Holger. "Let's join the party for a while," she suggested.

"I could use a break," he agreed. "You know, I damn near flunked differential equations in college, and now you spring this stuff on me."

She threw him a sharp glance. "Look, friend," she said, "given your background, you ought to know already that God never felt obliged to make the universes easy for us to understand."

"Or easy in any way," he sighed. *"Naa, da,* let's go." He put pipe in mouth, tankard in fist, and sauntered along.

Clodia, who had been getting no response from Rupert, ignored Valeria but turned the full battery on Holger. He gulped. "Twenty lashes with a wet eyeball," Valeria muttered. To Rupert and Will: "Good evening, gentlemen."

The prince rose and bowed; his follower was too rapt. "If you'll allow self-introduction . . . lady—" His voice trailed off.

She smiled. "Not used to women in slacks, are you?

Sorry. I'm Valeria Matuchek, from the United States of America, if that means anything to you." She extended her hand. He hung fire a moment, decided there could be no harm in showing her a courtesy to which she might not be entitled, and kissed it as he had Clodia's. "Hey!" she said. "You know, you're the first man I've ever met who could do that with real authority?"

Rupert straightened, to tower above her and reply, "I do not comprehend, fair damosel."

"Our accents are sort of thick, mutually, aren't they? You sound a bit like Holger—here, Holger Carlsen, from Denmark, though he's spent a lot of time in my own country, on a different hyperplane."

The two big men clasped hands. "I'm Rupert, of the Rhine Palatinate," the Cavalier said, seeking to establish good relations. "My mother's mother was a Danish princess—Anne, queen to James of Scotland and of England, two countries which have been close friends with Denmark since days of Hamlet, if not further yet."

Holger raised brows. "Hamlet?"

Valeria shushed him, urged him into a seat, and took one herself opposite Rupert. "Suppose we swap information," she advised. "We haven't got such an awfully long time for that; better headlong then hesitant. You're from the Rhineland, did you say, Rupert?"

"By right of blood alone—a stuff more thick than water, goes the adage, but too thin to mortar soil in firmness 'neath my claim," the prince answered wryly. "At present, as the nephew of King Charles, I'm fighting on his side against revolt. Mine English friend and I were lorn in Wales, beset by Puritans and other dogs, when we got . . . guidance . . . to this happy place."

Valeria sat upright. "Wait a minute! King Charles—Puritans—you mean Roundheads?" (He nodded.) *"When* are you from? I mean, what date would you say it is?"

"Why-y . . . I've lost track of what it is exactly—but August, sixteen hundred forty-four—"

"Ahhh," she exulted. A slender fist clenched on the arm of her chair. "How much do you know about the situation—parallel universes and all that jazz— Nothing, h'm? Well, look, Rupert, I'm from America. You know America, don't you? Where I come from, it's independent countries. And . . . when I left home, the year was 1974. Holger, there, left in 1950—but not the same 1950 as I was busy being born in."

Rupert grew most quiet. "This well's too deep for Will," complained Fairweather. Turning to Clodia, who was obviously furious that neither Rupert nor Holger paid her any special heed, he added slyly, "And eke for thee?" Her glance crossed his and came to rest.

Taverner leaned back, ankles crossed, fingers bridged, altogether delighted. The fire was burning down. A gnomish figure bustled from the kitchen doorway to lay on more wood. The barmaid took empty vessels with an equal clatter, filled and returned them.

"You're from tomorrow, then," Rupert said low, "as Clodia is from the ancient past; and distant lands?"

"Not quite," Valeria denied. "I'm not sure how well I can get the idea across, but I'll try. Look, you were born into the world you know. It has such-and-such qualities—geography, astronomy, laws of nature, kinds of life; people, nations, societies; a past, a present, and a future growing out of these. Right?" (Rupert nodded.) "Well, imagine some important event had turned out differently in the past. A battle lost instead of won, that kind of thing. Give me an example."

Rupert's bewilderment was yielding to fascination. He cast a look at Holger while he tugged his chin. Finally: "Well, say Prince Hamlet had not died in vengeance, thus making Fortinbras the Danish king, but had, instead, become the king himself. The dynasty had many English ties. He might have come and helped his kinfolk here to overthrow Macbeth, the Scots usurper. Once planted on the isle, the Danes might next remember King Canute, not long agone, and turn on Norman William when he came. Since Denmark only, of the Northern lands, had cannon then, however primitive—"

"Hvad for Pokker?" burst from Holger.

"Take it easy," Valeria told him. "He's from a different time-line. . . . I wonder, I wonder—" Fairly aflame with enthusiasm, she leaned forward. "Let's get the theory of this out of the way first, shall we, Rupert?"

Will saw his leader struggle for insight, remarked to Clodia, "I thank the Loard I war not boarn to think," and clinked his tankard against her wineglass. She smiled straight at him. He choked, "I ne'er wot one could stagger in a chair."

Valeria was proceeding: "Well, if you can imagine history might have switched onto a different track, take the next step. That is, suppose both outcomes are real. One world where, uh, Hamlet died young; one where he went on to take the Danish crown and stop the Norman conquest. Both happened. Can you accept that?"

"I dare not say what limits God has laid on His creating," Rupert breathed. "But how can this be?"

"Two whole universes . . . two whole space-time universes, stars, galaxies, countless planets—differing in a single detail, and of course in the consequences afterward—Except it isn't like that, really. These universes have always been distinct, from the beginning. It's just that this is the first point where the differences between them get noticeable. Besides, we haven't got merely two universes. Nobody's proved, in my world, whether there's an infinity of them, or whether the number's finite but enormous—N factorial, to be exact, where N is the total number of matter and energy particles that exist. . . . You can picture the cosmoses as lying parallel to each other, like the leaves in a book. That isn't strictly true, either; they occupy the same space-time, being separated by a set of dimensions—"

"Hold on, Valeria," said Holger. "Have pity. You're close to losing me overboard, and poor Rupert looks as if he's going down for the third time."

The girl relaxed and laughed at herself. "Sorry. You're right. Uh, Rupert, think of it this way. A lot of different worlds. Some almost the same as yours, some totally alien to it. In some, for instance, there's a kingdom of England, A.D. 1644; in others the date is different; in still others, the kingdom never existed. Even the laws of nature may vary. What's possible in one world is not in another, and vice versa. You follow me?"

Rupert ventured a smile. "Through quicksands, marshes, brambles, rain, and night."

"And if a person knows how, he can cross between them," Valeria continued. "You savvy? After all, this is a pocket universe you're in."

Rupert drank deep. "At least its beer speaks comforting of home," he said to Taverner, "though sweeter, like a long-forgotten dream."

"I know what's sweeter, aye, a sugartit," Will whispered. He squeezed Clodia's hand. After a glance at oblivious Rupert and Holger, she gave a shrug, which quivered in numerous places, and fluttered her eyelids.

"You are from . . . elsewhere, Mistress . . . Matuchek?" Rupert asked. "That name is from Bohemia, like me."

"Elsewhere and elsewhen," she said, "though the words aren't especially meaningful in this context. That is, I don't belong to your future. I doubt if your world will look remotely like mine, by the time it reaches its own 1974. Certainly neither world of Holger's will."

Rupert stared at the Dane, who puffed his pipe before explaining in a diffident tone: "Well, you see, I'm a peculiar case. I belong—I was born in—a universe where the Carolingian myths are true. You know, Roland and Oliver and the rest."

"You're too modest," Valeria said.

"No, I just don't want this discussion to get worse complicated," he replied. To Rupert: "Never mind how, I got cast into an altogether different time-line—a time-line where magic doesn't work, except maybe in areas like ESP—or, again, never mind. I'm trying to find my way home. I have had nothing to go on except a spell which carries me through space-time barriers, all right, but doesn't have any direction to it. After a lot of mishaps—the last was with a clutch of Aztec gods, and I barely escaped in one piece—I'd picked up enough assorted hints and clues that I could fumble myself to this inn. By my good luck, Miss Matuchek was here."

"I don't believe that was pure coincidence," Valeria said. "However, let's skip that. The point is, Rupert—Holger's twentieth century and mine are quite alike, rationalistic, industrialized, the Western countries mostly democratic. Only they're quite unlike, also. For instance, in both of them, the USA and Germany were on opposite sides in the First World War. But his Second World War, that he fought in himself, was against Germany too —and Japan and Italy—while mine, that my parents fought in, was against the Saracen Caliphate. I suppose the differences were mainly due to paraphysical forces. Either they're as weak in that adopted cosmos of Holger's as he thinks, or else nobody there has discovered how to degauss the effects of cold iron, as they did in my world about 1900."

"Anyway," Holger said, "on her Earth they've made a science and technology of magic—"

"Paraphysics," she corrected. "Or the Art, if you prefer."

"Whatever. She's being very nice to me, giving me some valuable pointers. Maybe she can do the same for you, Mister—Herr—uh, Prince Rupert."

"Perhaps," Valeria said dubiously. "A lot would depend on your background. Is it science-oriented like mine? How much math do you know? That kind of thing." She braced herself with a drink before adding: "Also, to tell the honest truth, I'd want more information about you. No offense intended, but you could be serving some cause I'd think it was wrong to help."

"Or maybe I would not take help from you," Rupert snapped. "What are you doing here, in boy's disguise?"

Valeria smiled. "My, you really are from a different milieu! Well, I don't mind explaining, if the explanation will make any sense to you. In my home, this is perfectly ordinary female dress for a rugged outing. And as for my purpose, I'm on a field trip, collecting material for a master's thesis. It's not so long ago that people in my universe first managed to cross into others. We're still measuring the parameters—"

"How lawful are your thaumaturgic arts?" Rupert demanded.

She bridled. "Completely legal."

"Wait, I think I see what he's after," said Holger. "You remember, Valeria, I told you how in my world, the Carolingian one, that is, elves are mostly enemies to man. Maybe something like that is true for Rupert."

The girl spent a moment thinking, before she nodded at the prince. "Okay. Listen, please. Where I come from, there's nothing inherently good or bad about the Art. It involves a set of forces. We can use them morally or evilly, wisely or stupidly, same as anything else. Why, my father's a werewolf, my mother's a witch, and they're two of the dearest people you'll ever meet. Some of my best friends are halflings."

Rupert had likewise invested time in thought. "I pray your pardon, Mistress Matuchek," he responded. "I stand myself in dept to Oberon." (She started, and gave most intent attention to his speech.) "This ring I have of him and of his queen—and from one other—led me here tonight. Ere then, I'm told, its brilliance blossomed high, as we approached that steam train which we seized and drove this day from Yorkshire into Wales."

"Now, wait a little," Holger protested. "Oberon I know something about; *ja,* the English Civil War too— in fact, I seem to remember reading about a Prince Rupert who was in it—but steam trains?"

Valeria leaped up. She shivered in body and voice. "Hold it! I may be onto this paradox. Gimme a minute, will you?"

Her pacing shoes clacked beneath the crackle and rumble of fire. Its light wove through candle-gleam, soft over Rupert's tautness, Holger's puzzlement, Taverner's glittering-eyed observation.

Will nudged Clodia. "Mesim a taele'll shortly start to wag what I know well, an' would but brush thee off," he murmured. "We got a common language, thou an' I. 'Tis oanly partly spoaken with tha tongue. What zay we steal away an' practice it?"

Valeria whirled. Her finger stabbed at Rupert. "You talked about Hamlet and Macbeth—as if they were both real," she cried. "Contemporaries, even. You said you'd met Oberon and . . . Titania . . . yourself. Well, did Romeo and Juliet ever live? King Lear? Falstaff? Othello? You mentioned cannon in Hamlet's time. How about, by God, how about a University of Wittenberg already then? Did they have clocks that struck the hour in Julius Caesar's days? Was Richard the Third really a hunchbacked monster? Did Bohemia ever have a sea-coast? Does witchcraft work?"

To each flung question Rupert nodded, as if these were blows hurled upon him.

"Okay, then"—Valeria tensed—"do you know the name William Shakespeare?"

"Of course," Rupert said dazedly. "He was the great Historian."

"That's it!" Valeria turned to Holger. "If, if you could start in a world . . . where the Carolingian romances are the literal truth . . . why not the plays of Shakespeare?" she stammered. "It figures, it figures. They'd've been technologically a little ahead of my world since an early period—though just in certain areas—still, their Industrial Revolution commencing in the seventeenth century, and maybe getting tied in with Puritanism—" Swinging back: "Oh, Rupert, we've got so much to talk about!"

Holger shook his head. "I think I better go work those problems from the textbook you gave me," he said.

"Of course. Poor dear. I'll come help you later on." She stooped to brush her lips across his forehead. "But I've *got* to talk to Rupert as well. Don't you see? Besides Shakespeare being an idol of mine, I always had sympathy for the Cavaliers. Maybe that was schoolgirl romantics; and anyhow, the issues may not be identical in Rupert's home. I doubt very much he could absorb the kind of instruction you're getting. But at least, I must have a certain hindsight over his period. It's possible I can counsel him, influence events a tiny bit for the better. I feel obliged to try."

Will climbed to his feet, Clodia undulated to hers. "Beg pardon, loard," the dragoon said. "Thou wilt not need me moare?"

It took Rupert a second to pull his mind their way. Then he grinned a trifle, rose, and bowed. "I must not," he responded. "Ladies e'er go over princes."

"But . . . princes . . . they go over commoners," said Will reluctantly; for Clodia was thrusting curves at his master.

Rupert clapped the soldier's back. "And commoners o'er ladies, on this night. Myself, I'll be discoursing till the dawn. May weariness not soften hardihood."

"Nay, zir, I be quiate firm in my resolve." Will took
the woman around her waist. She sighed toward Rupert.
His look had returned to Valeria and Holger. Clodia
snuggled against the man she had. They slipped upstairs.

Holger voiced a harsh chuckle and sought his books.
Valeria and Rupert settled themselves for conversation.
The landlord listened.

XIII

THE FOREST. MORNING.

RAIN had washed the air glittering clean. Each leaf stood vivid against sun-spattered shadow. Birds rejoiced. It was mild and getting warmer.

Rupert and Will halted at a spring. Water gurgled through a sward which the latter traveler bent to feel. "Plenty dry to lie on an' catch no wheezles," he reported. "We should sleep snug like in yonder flyin' inn."

"Oh?" Rupert half smiled, half yawned. "Didst thou sleep? I'm nigh as disappointed as Mistress Pulcher."

"Marry, nay. Never a wink, believe me." Will spoke dreamily. "Again an' yet again, a gallop on the sweetest o' mares. What pity thou got to exercise no moare than thy tongue. Let me tell thee—"

In swift irritation, Rupert snapped: "Spare me an old swiver's tale. Be glad I spent my time learning what I did. It may prove all that'll keep thy weasand unhaltered for bragging."

"I be zorry, your Highness," Will apologized. "I should'a remembered how tha liakes o' thee must stay awake an' afoot for to ward zilly sheep like me. Uneasy hies tha head what caeres for clowns."

Rupert calmed. "No matter. I ought not to have bared teeth at thee in that wise. But we're both worn to the bone. Two days and nights without rest! Surely 'twas a magic in the hostel which let us keep strength. Since we left it—" Both men sat down. "A-a-ah-h-h. Corporal Gabriel himself couldn't blow reveille for me till afternoon at earliest."

"What do we do than?"

"We'll to the coast. A matter of fifty or sixty miles, albeit slow ones since we must fare warily. I think we'll get food, shelter, and help from common folk, for love

of the King. With luck and diplomacy, passage across
the Channel. In Holland I'll coax money from my
kindred for continuing on southward."

Will's drowsiness retreated. "Than thou'lt follow—
Oberon's rede—an' not zeek tha Royal camp right off?"

Rupert nodded. "Aye. Those twain from the morrow
did persuade me. The woman particularly spoke of hor-
rors that it clogs my throat to utter. True, her history of
this hundred-year is not precisely the same as what we
know—yet far too close. I'd be traitor indeed, did I act
as if unaided man may snatch a happier outcome from
the jaws flensing our poor land."

"What did they prophesy?"

Rupert shuddered. "Worse than a cavalier defeat.
The King himself beheaded."

Will's jaw struck his Adam's apple. "Can't be, my
loard!" he gasped. "Why, 'a . . .'a be tha King!"

"The Stuarts grow no armor on their necks. In truth,
the man and maiden told me, this regicide will . . . did
prove, in their worlds, to be but the first through centuries to come. And always the same thing follows, terror,
tyranny, those who claim to speak for the people standing on their backs to do it. In England, at last, a
restoration—" Rupert hesitated. "Mark, I say no ill of
the Prince of Wales; he's a bright, likely, and likeable
youth. But year upon year of exile would corrupt him.
His reign would be merry but ruinous. Why, there'd
even be war against the Dutch, who befriended me and
mine. And they'd smite us on the sea, aye, sail up the
Medway with a broom at their admiral's masthead for
scorn. And thus, after the second Charles, erelong his
whole dynasty is cast off a throne whose pillars are rot-
ted irredeemably weak. . . ." Rupert's fist smote the
turf, to thump in its softness. "By God's own lightnings,
it shall never be, if quest of mine may help!"

"An' miane, my loard," said Will quietly. "An' maybe
Jennifer's."

Rupert looked heavy-eyed at his ring. "How does she
fare?" he wondered. "Not ill, I trust. She may have been
chastised, but surely now has rest."

"As we do too." Will lay flat, throwing an arm across

his face. After a moment, during which he stroked the silver asp while gazing down woodland corridors, Rupert followed the example.

JENNIFER'S BEDCHAMBER.

It was sparsely outfitted. A few books, some half-done embroidery, a vase which had held flowers, an etching of the infants Jesus and John with their mothers, were touches of herself; a chest from olden times was riotously carved; the rest of the furnishings stood prim. Mid-August heat broiled and blazed through the windows.

She stumbled. Prudence Whitcomb caught her, quavering, "There, lamb, poor lamb, lean on me again."

Jennifer gripped the woman's arm till fingernails left welts. It did not seem she could have that much strength remaining. Her hair hung lank and tangled around a face which was mostly skull; the green of the sunken eyes was washed out and red-rimmed, in the dark caverns where they lay parched; her gown was stiff and reeking with the sweat of days.

"Move!" said the Roundhead soldier at their backs. He stamped the floor. "If she stops, she'll fall."

"And sleep." Prudence glowered over her shoulder. "Or swoon. Thou'lt haul her awake by shakings, shoutings, drenchings, as through all these past days and nights. And still thou callest thyself a man!" She spat at his feet.

"I'd not call thee woman, old harridan," he retorted. "Were't not for thy comfort, this witch would long since have yielded."

Jennifer moaned and reeled on, upheld by her attendant, around and around the walls.

"Witch?" Prudence screeched. "Thou'lt meet witches in truth, Righteous Gerson, when hell receives thee."

"I'll first see her hang in this world, I think; and belike these too, hag, who abetted her willfulness. Had Sir Malachi not commanded thy presence—"

"Knowing the goatishness of . . . him—" Prudence jerked a thumb in the direction of the bed, "and thine,

I'll wager, underneath that tin sanctimony—" Jennifer's feet tangled. Prudence barely caught her. "She *must* sit down."

"But may not sleep," the guardsman said. "When we've worn away thine own meddlesomeness, crone—"

"That'll come more from the crawling of my flesh, that I must take my rest in sheets which Sim's befouled, than from they milk-souring malice, Gerson."

There went a stirring beneath the blankets, and the under-groom thrust his hedgehog pate above them. "I hear my mistress longing for my mattress," he gibed.

Prudence sniffed, turned her back, and helped Jennifer to a seat. Sim emerged, yawning and scratching. A louse crept from his shirt. He caught it, cracked it between his teeth, and strolled to stand before Jennifer's empty stare.

"Is my lady ready to speak, pretty pray you?" he sniggered.

"Nay." The girl's answer could barely be heard.

"Ah, well, no haste for my sake. Here's an easy task, and a pleasureable when't comes to rousing you." His look glinted at the black-and-blue pinch marks which covered her arms and neck and what the disheveled gown showed of her bosom. "Drowse whene'er, you will." He stretched, belched, farted, and gaped. "Meanwhile, Righteous, thou may'st go off watch, soon's thou's brought us food and drink."

The soldier nodded. He was at the exit when Jennifer's body slumped back in the chair, her head lolled loose. Sim laughed and snatched a handful of hair. Prudence clawed at him. He grunted. A push sent her staggering. He slapped the prisoner's cheeks, one, two, one, two. "Awake, awake, behold the gladsome day," he caroled. "Tonight thy hornèd lover comes for thee, not so, witch? Say, who aided thee to stick those horns on him? Wake up, wake up!"

"Na-a-ay," Jennifer whimpered.

He released her. She crumpled to the floor. "I'll speak," jarred forth. "Let me sleep, dear God, I'll tell you anything if you'll let me alone."

Prudence knelt to cradle her. "Well, hurry!" the servant yelled. "Fetch your damned master." Gerson swallowed, flung open the door, and sped off down the hall-way.

"So she's broken at last, hey?" Sim lounged against a bedpost and picked his nose. "What shame."

"Aye, now thou goest back to the dungheap that begot thee," Prudence said. "Bowels of Christ, whate'er made a man I thought was just order this done to a helpless maid?"

"She'd plenty help from below," Sim declared.

Jennifer sobbed, though no tears were left in her.

Sir Malachi Shelgrave hastened in. "Has her contumacy indeed ended?" he exclaimed. Planting himself above the girl: "Art ready to confess they vileness?"

"Torture wrings forth words, sir," Prudence pleaded. "Mere words."

"Torture?" Shelgrave lifted his hands. "What art thou babbling of? This is my ward. Never would I spill a driblet of the blood she shares with my wedded wife. For her correction, the saving of her soul, I commanded she be kept awake, that she might meditate on her sin until she repented; no more than that, as thou thyself art witness." To Jennifer: "Now tell me what happened and what's toward."

She raised her sunken face. "If I may sleep," she mouthed.

"Indeed, indeed. Thou shalt have every peace that nature craves, and thy body will heal with thy spirit, when once this venom has drained out of thee. Hearken —sleep not yet; hearken, I say! I'll take thy Bible oath that the testimony thou givest is true and complete, free of any least evasion or falsehood. Dost understand? By thy hope of salvation must thou swear."

"I understand. . . . I think. . . . I know not what I think," she whispered harshly. "Oh, bring the Book, uncle, I'll swear on it a hundred times over, if I may but afterward make it my pillow."

SHELGRAVE'S STUDY.

It was a large and somber-paneled room, full of heavy furniture. Folios, quartos, excellent pictures, a bust of Cato the Elder, a hearth-fire did not much relieve

the austerity. Windows stood open to blue dusk and a
sound of crickets.

The owner sat at his desk, writing with one of the new
steel pens by the glow of one of the new glass-chim-
neyed lamps. A knock brought up his high, gleaming
head. "Come in," he called.

The butler entered to announce: "The Reverend Nobah Barker, sir, assistant pastor of our church in Leeds."

"I know him," Shelgrave said dryly. "We would fain
be closeted. Let no man interrupt ere suppertime,
though it were General Cromwell's very self."

He stood to shake his visitor's hand. "Welcome, my
friend. 'Twas good of thee to come."

"Thy note held intimation of a duty," was the nasal
reply. While Barker was a comparatively young man,
stooped shoulders, round paunch, and shuffling gait
would have fitted an older one. In a long, lantern-jawed
face, his eyes were twin hailstones beneath the flat
brown hair. Against his garb, which was otherwise
black, the clerical cravat showed more grubby than
white.

"Affection has its duties, has it not, as does that fel-
lowship we share in Christ?" the host said. "I could have
asked the help of many else; but thee I know and trust.
Sit down, sit down. Here's coffee newly shipped from
Genoa, within this pot above its spirit flame—a fresh invention of our wondrous age. Thou takest cream and
sugar, I recall."

"Let us not chat too much of worldly things," said
Barker, accepting the edge of a chair.

Shelgrave pinched lips together. "It helps me keep the
Devil off my mind. He's prowling near, and I must bat-
tle him whilst unwise rivals seek to shackle me. How few
I dare rely on! Mine own kin—"

"Who? Jennifer? I saw her not in church this Sunday
past. They told me she's been ill."

"A loathsome cancer I've no certainty that e'en the
sharpest razor may excise. And yet my duty is to essay
it. A duty still more powerful than this—to God and
country and our holy cause—drives me the selfsame
way. But meanwhile, Nobah, discretion's of the essence.
I'll explain."

Having filled the cups which waited on an end table, he sat down opposite his guest.

"Thou'st shown me favor and hast aided me, as elder of our humble congregation, since first thou heard'st me preach." Barker said. "I am right grateful that thou hast been the instrument whereby God's grace has helped unworthy me to rise."

"The merest step, from deacon to assistant. I'd see thee go much further if I can. But now I stand in direst need of help."

"Thou'lt have it, godly Malachi. Thou'lt have it."

Shelgrave's knuckles whitened over the frail cup handle. He stared past the other. "Let me speak blunt," he said. "A man in great pain or a man in great danger has no wit for honing words on; he can but drive them into the target by what might is left him; and I am both those men.

"Hark'ee. I told thee in confidence how Rupert, prince of bandits, was held captive here till they could fetch him to London." (Barker jerked a nod.) "That's a sigil of my faith in thee, Nobah. I knew thou couldst be an influence over my household folk should any of them show signs of blabbering; for we dared not risk somebody like his madcap brother learning where he was and mounting a raid of rescue. . . . Well, he's escaped."

"God's mercy smite that Assyrian—like this!" Barker shouted. The great gesture of his hand would have been more dramatic had it not held a cup. Coffee billowed across his face.

Shelgrave hardly noticed. "And worse," he groaned, " 'twas by seduction of my ward—aye, Jennifer Alayne. She aided him."

Barker, who had pulled a handkerchief from his sleeve, stopped mopping himself. "Indeed? Oh, horror! . . . Yet say on, poor man. Lay forth the shame in full, each word, each stroke, that I may know how Satan worked through him and counsel thee. How did his wiles prevail? In what wise did he deal with her? How often?"

"Would it had been simple fornication! But nay, she's a maiden still."

"Ah-ha! Italian ways? Go on, go on!"

"I tell thee, 'twas no common fleshly lust. She swears on the Book, by every oath I can compose, Rupert and she have never touched more than lip to lip."

"Oh." Barker resumed his scrubbing.

"And I'm assured, now those willful lips are finally unbarred, she speaks truth. I've come to know her. She's pious in her half-Popish fashion, would never perjure herself—might indeed have escaped suffering, had she sworn at once to some plausible demi-truth which I do believe she'd've had the wit to devise on the spot. Besides, what broke her will was prolonged sleeplessness enforced, a tool wherewith I've had experience. I wish the good men pursuing witches on the Continent knew more about this means. 'Tis better than rack or wheel, if used aright."

"And hale, she'll feel more fear at execution."

"Hold!" Shelgrave snapped. "They'll not . hang *her*. . . . Well." He hunched himself in self-possession. "Let me be brief; later thou canst hear the full account. It seems a man of Rupert's, slinking after him like a dog, lured Jennifer into setting him free; and this man had been put to it by those heathen sprites which haunt our wilds and ruins." At Barker's shock, he nodded. "Aye, she named none less than Oberon and Titania; and sure it is, chasing him, my men and I were pestered by phantoms. That was after I caught Jennifer trying to slip back into this house. . . . Though I've wrenched the story from her, Rupert remains at large. No word of him, either recaptured or rejoining the enemy. But 'twould be rash to postulate the crows have picked his bones."

"What then about him and his midnight legions?" Barker asked. His shivering congealed into resolution. "Nay; righteousness is fearlessness. More coffee?"

Shelgrave let him pour, while rising to unlock and open a drawer in his desk. "The demons counseled him to seek magical aid in Mediterranean lands or waters," he continued. "She can't recall details, being but poorly read. However, I think we'd best suppose he's off in that direction. The danger of his success is as worth fretting over as a possible outbreak of plague. To guide him, he got a ring, whose stone shines brighter as he comes close to what may help him: bottled hellfire, no doubt. She was given one too, which has the same property." He made a smile. "Behold how God can work also through the instruments of evil! This was the clue which led me to her guilt. Here."

He held it forth.

Barker dropped his cup into his lap. "Eeh!" he wailed. "Cast it away, that fearful thing, away!"

"I took thee for a man of courage, Nobah," Shelgrave said.

The divine flushed. "Forgive. It was a nasty, swift surprise, like clasping of a well-known hand to find that suddenly the fingers are all snakes." He stood—the cup smashed—pointed at the ring, and intoned, "Thou forging of Beelzebub, beware! Let heaven's levin blast thee in its wrath!"

Drip, drip said the coffee from his breeches.

"Prithee, peace." Shelgrave put the ring aside, gripped his guest's shoulders, eased him back into a chair, stood above him, and spoke rapidly, reassuringly: "See here. We're men of practicalities, thou and I, as well as pieties; we know what part of both our work and our reward lies in this world. If God Himself, as I say, did use that unholy object to reveal unto me the extent of sin and guile—as the golden calf showed Moses how our ancestors had fallen—why, is't not a sign of His? Does He not mean for us to use this maggot out of the Devil's flesh to gnaw the under-devil Rupert?"

Barker squinted a long while up at him before answering, "Thou hast a plan. I know thee, Malachi."

"That I do, and thou'rt at the core. Listen. When sad, misguided Jennifer wears the ring, 'twill always light and guide her whithersoever best serves the enemy's fell purpose—or *would*, were she traveling freely. I've studied magic, as one must study a disease to find the cure. It has a blind, mechanic quality; in itself, it no more distinguishes friend from foe than does a loaded cannon.

"Well, then. Does it not stand to reason, both rings will point at the same goal? Let her follow hers, and Rupert follow his—both ought to show plain signs, after their wearers have reached the Midworld Sea—why, inevitably as moths to a candle flame, those two will be brought to a meeting point. Now if she's under the guard of trustworthy fighting men—bearing in mind Rupert's a fugitive, who at most has one or two desperadoes at heel—"

"But Rupert is of royal blood as well," Barker objected. "He'll first to Holland, and fetch many friends."

"I've thought on that, and doubt it," Shelgrave said. "He may indeed go there for some funds, though that's an impoverished court of exiles which his mother maintains. However, the Dutch are mostly Calvinists, who'd recoil in horror, aye, arrest him, did he reveal what his mission really is. And he'd not spend time trying covertly to gather a troop who would go along. Remember, not only is he himself impetuous, his King Charles cannot hold out for many more weeks unaided. Therefore, he'll sacrifice recruitment for the sake of haste—and, as I say, come to his destination with no following worthy of mention. Oh I could be mistaken. Those who go after him should proceed with care. But I feel sure they'll find that a small, determined band can take him."

Barker gulped. "I have a feeling thou intendest me to lead this expedition, Malachi."

"That I do. I'm too well-known, have too many affairs, mine absence would too soon be marked. Moreover, none save I can keep a hatch on the news of Rupert's escape; I know what persons in this household I can use to frighten silence into the rest; if London sends after him too early, I can write back that he's ill and must not travel. The word that he's loose would shake our armies."

"And do thee little good in Parliament," said Barker shrewdly.

"Well, I own there are spiteful backbiters who'd dearly love to drag me down. They must not; for most of the work remains undone to which the Lord has appointed me. Besides, Jennifer . . . herewith I give her a chance to win redemption, whereas if her misdeeds became public knowledge whilst Rupert is free, I fear nothing could save her from being hanged for a witch. And, finally but fondly, Nobah, I think of thee. Thine opportunity."

Shelgrave intensified his gaze on the seated man and continued with slow-voiced earnestness:

"Thou hast a godly soul which hell can't swerve, and understandest witchcraft's darkling ways, so 'twould be hard to hoodwink thee by spells. Moreover, thou art like a son to me, the son wherewith the Lord has not seen fit that I be blessed; unless, like Abraham— Set that aside. A triumph such as this will open every road to thine advancement. In time, thy preaching could make Europe quake."

Barker moistened his lips. "But traveling 'cross country, just with her," he husked, "to meet at last . . . not merely devils . . . *him?*"

"Thou wilt have company, his eight stout guards," Shelgrave promised. "Thou know'st them well for strict and valiant men. There's Righteous Gerson and his younger brother, Sword-of-the-Lord; Jashubilehem Brown; Goforward Meeker; Increase Waterman; Uriah Prickett; Nehemiah Scudder; Zerubbabel Throckmorton —all good men. They'll lay Prince Rupert low and bring him home, or else his wicked head for London gate." His words were kindling the dull eyes below his. He shouted forth: "And Nobah, think what glory will be thine!"

XIV

A FISHING SMACK.

SKY and water reached in the same iron hue. Beneath the overcast went blue-black clouds swollen with rain. Chill, misty, shrill in movement, the air soon blurred out eyesight; there was no horizon. The boat rolled and pitched to the chop of whitecaps. It smelled of tar and old catches. A man stood at the tiller, another at the rail beside Will and near Rupert, who sat on a bench at the cabin entrance. Each one wore a shabby woolen pullover, the prince's badly strained across chest and shoulders; but the cavalrymen kept their own hose and boots instead of the sailors' patched wadmal and bare feet thrust into wooden shoes.

Tacking, the boat came about in a creak and thump of boom, a rattle of faded-red canvas. Will lurched, nearly fell, caught a stay, and swore. "God founder thee, thou spavined, knock-kneed jaede! Dwouldst cast me off?"

"Speak not thus," Rupert reproved. "Or dost thou not know 'founder' has a different meaning at sea?"

"Tha less I know o' tha zea, tha happier I. Dwould 'twarn't zo eager for to make *my* 'quaintance. It comes leapin' o'er tha zide to licke me like a lollopin' zalty dog."

The hard-bitten, gingery-haired little man with them grinned. "Pe glad you're not seasick, Sergeant. Not that anybody e'er died o't; no, none ha' peen that lucky."

"Oh, but I be zick o' tha zea indeed, Captain Price."

"Ap Rhys, if you please. Owen ap Rhys."

"Beg pardon. I forgot zometimes how Welsh you Welshmen be. Pray keep your leeks out o' this hull whilst I be aboard. How long'll that last, think ye?"

"Hwell, since we've lately passed the Scilly Isles—"

"Silly for sure, waterlogged's tha' must be."

118

"—and the hwind is foul, hwithout sign of pettering soon, and we've the Channel to run and then the narrow sea till we reach Holland, it could pe days."

Rupert frowned. "Meanwhile a Navy vessel might come on us," he said, "and the Navy's Roundhead."

"Have no fears o' that, your Highness," ap Rhys assured him. "My folk have peen smuccling since Noah came to harpor. Can we not slip free, the hwell has a false pottom, room peneath for you and your man if maype a touch crowded."

"To lie liake herrin's in a crock," Will grumbled, "an' smell liake 'em a foartnight after."

Rupert ignored him. "I'd fain tell thee once more, skipper," he said, "how thankful I am that thou and thy son do hazard this—despite my warning thee that exiled royalty is longer in pedigree than purse."

" 'Tis for the King, sir; though to pe sure, when he's pack on the throne, if your Highness might say him a hword on pehalf of honest fishermen who must needs eke out their meaccer living py foreign trade—"

"Indeed I shall. Thou'd wish the duties lowered or abolished, eh?"

Ap Rhys stood appalled before answering: "St. David preserve us, nay, sir, nay! What hwould that *do* to the trade? Nay, higher tariffs if ye hwill, heaven-high, put . . . fewer cutters—?"

"Ship ho!" cried the helmsman.

The three others scrambled to peer ahead. The shadowy shape grew swiftly solid before their eyes. It was a smallish three-master carrying two courses of square sails, including on the bowsprit though not on the mizzen, where the lower one was lateen. The hull was sleek, inward-sloping, ornamented with gilt figures upon red and black timbers. At the flat-countered and rather low stern fluttered a gaudy banner.

"Not Navy," said ap Rhys. "A double-decked pinnace. Foreign."

Rupert nodded. "Argent, a lion rampant azure between four crosses potent or," he said. " 'Tis the flag of Tunis."

Will gasped. His arm snapped from the stay, to point at his lord's left hand. The boat pitched and he tumbled.

Sprawling, he still pointed and yelled, through wind and Welsh exclamations: "Thy ring, Rupert! Ab-b-b-blaeze!"

"*Lieve hemel,*" the prince whispered into that surging rainbow. "Yon must be . . . well-wishers to our cause . . . straight-bound for the waters we seek— Turn!" he bellowed. "Intercept them!"

"Arcue not hwith the Flying Dutchman," ap Rhys called in terror. "Opey!"

His son swung the tiller. The boat came about once more in a sharp heeling. Will clattered across its beam, into the scuppers opposite. A wave came through and over him. "Be thic our luck?" he wailed. "To fare tha whoale damned way by zea?"

ABOARD THE TUNISIAN SHIP.

Rupert swung himself up a Jacob's ladder and leaped the rail. Will clambered slowly behind, burdened by his rusty armor, declaiming oaths. The smack fell away, caught wind, started off north-westward. Rupert paused to wave and shout: "Farewell, dear loyal friends! Good voyage home! When I return, I'll bring you back your King!"

Thereafter he drew his attention inboard. Sailors stared from their work and muttered in their native tongue. They were swarthy, full-bearded men whose loose-flowing gowns were girded to the knees, caught by sashes which also held curved knives. The officers were European, clad accordingly, though in Southern wise, their hair long, their own beards and mustachios trimmed to points, crucifixes hung around the necks of most; and a black-robed Roman priest was among them.

Rupert bowed to the couple who stood immediately before him, braced against the roll of the deck. "Your Graces greet me graciously indeed," he said, "in granting me this passage to your land."

"We could not well do less than that, nor would, since the first joyful startlement we felt on recognition of your Highness's self," replied the woman, low in her throat and smiling. Though she was young, the cloak wrapped around her did not hide fullness of figure or gay elegance of garb. Jeweled pins secured a mantilla on high-piled ebony hair. Her eyes were nearly as black and more lustrous, in a curve-nosed, heavy-mouthed, olive-skinned face. The girl who stood behind her was pretty, but scarcely noticeable in her nearness.

The man on her left also suffered by contrast, despite the rich dark fabrics which draped him: being short, grizzled, spindle-shanked, beak-featured, and green from seasickness. "Eet was a large surprise," he quavered in English more accented than hers.

Rupert glanced down at himself and remarked ruefully, "In truth, your Grace, I was less well transported and accoutered than when we knew each other erst in Oxford."

"You'll soon have garments fitting to your size and dignity," the woman promised. She indicated the girl. "My serving-maiden Niña plies a deft needle— *Santa María! ?Que?*"

Rupert saw his companion crawl over the rail. He laughed. "Will Fairweather, a centaur but no merman." Seriously: "He was the foremost 'mong my rescuers and never flinched through our adversities."

"Until we struck this craedle o' tha deep what bears zo wet a baebe," growled the dragoon. Seeing that he confronted people of quality, he removed helmet and tugged forelock. "Forgive your zarvint."

"Know we are fortunate—" Rupert stole a look at his ring, but it had reverted to a normal luster. "This ship bears home the ambassador of his Majesty of Tunis: the noble Duke of Carthage, Don Hernán Ferdinando Juan Sebastian del Monte de Gavilanes y Palomas."

"Whoof!" said Will.

"Therewith his gracious lady, Doña Belinda," Rupert finished.

"Our captain, Highness, Don Alonso Mena," said the duchess, indicating a burly man who gave Rupert a nautical salute.

The duke, who had been swallowing ever harder and more frequently, brought a hand to his mouth. "Excuse me," he mumbled, "beezness, urgent beezness, *sí*," and went as fast as he could stagger through a door under the poop that must lead to his stateroom.

Belinda sighed. "Poor man, he's less a sailor than is yours," she confessed.

"Why have you left in such bad weather, then?" Rupert wondered.

She arched her brows. "Is weather ever good in Northern parts?" Her playfulness faded. "The fact is, we do have some need of haste. My lord foresaw it, wrote his ministry to ask a ship be sent to lie in dock at his disposal. It is well he did." She shrugged. "Oh, I say not our lives were e'er endangered. But since the rebels drove King Charles from Oxford and hunt his scattered army o'er the land, an embassy of a most distant realm, and Catholic, has lowly place or none among sour heretics. Best we depart and speedily report what's happened — Oh!" She saw Rupert's consternation, seized both his hands and inquired anxiously: "What is it, Highness? You look ill."

"I am," he grated. "My King . . . in full retreat . . . already now?"

"You knew not?"

"I was captive until lately," he reminded her, "and since in flight through wild and newsless shires."

"I think that is the underlying reason." Her tone grew ardent. "Sans Rupert's leadership, the Royal cause is in an evil case. . . . Shall we turn back? We can restore you—"

He shook his head. "Nay, I thank you, lady, but I've a mission maybe less forlorn down in those waters whither you are bound."

The duchess glowed. "Then welcome, Rupert!" Softer: "May I call you Rupert, and may I be Belinda on your lips?"

Courtliness had never come naturally to him. Hotfaced, he answered, "You are too kind. I am most fortunate."

"Nay, I am, since our mother sea has brought the gift of this companionship to me on what would else be but a dreary trip. Know you not how we ladies at the court were dazzled into dreaming by your prowess and envied

Mary Villiers, whom you favored—and favored chastely, la!" She tapped his arm in reproof, while smiling and fluttering her lashes, before she took it and urged him into motion. "And now you're mine throughout the voyage. Come, let's go within. We'll see about your quarters and your comfort. And later—oh, we've much to tell each other!"

Dazedly, he accompanied her. The maidservant started to follow. Doña Belinda threw her the tiniest frown and headshake. The girl returned a similar nod, went to the rail and stood looking across the waters.

Will Fairweather sidled to join her. Meanwhile the captain barked commands at officers and crew, who dispersed in their duties.

Will cleared his throat. "Ahem!" he said. "Sine we'd boath better flush this confounded frash air through our lungs awhiale, an' got a longer whiale at zea befoare us —" His gaze admired her. In demure gown and cloak, she was nonetheless a pleasant, plump little brown partridge of a woman. "Mesim I might yet taeke back what hard words I've spoake about tha waters; for ne'er did I await a curve-carved figurehead 'ud come walk 'round on deck. My naeme—"

"I 'eard, sir," she said. " 'Ow you air a soldier weeth the brave preence."

"You've heard no moare than tha beginnin' . . . ah—?"

"Niña Valdes, attendant to 'er Grace." They swapped sidelong glances and simpers.

"Spanish, hey? Well, I ben't prejudiced. A man be what 'a be, zays I, an' a woman be what *she* be, an' thank tha good God for thic."

"Oh no, sir. Not Spanish. Tunisian."

Will, who had left off his helmet, ran fingers through his sandy locks. "I'zooth? Aye, I do miand me, Rupert —I call him Rupert 'tween us, we bein' liake brothers e'er zince a day I'll tell you of if you list—'a did bespeak yonder flag by zome zuch word. But ha'n't I heard Tunis be Moorish? An', comin' to think on't, doan't moast o' yon men have an unchristian look about 'em?"

"A lifetime ago, sir, Don Juan of Austria deed conquair Tunis and es-stab-leesh-ed a keengdom. Most of the subjects air paynim steell, but the rulers air Chreestians of Spanish descent. Eet ees no beeg realm, w'erefore you 'ave not 'eard more of eet—although our Queen Claribel ees daughtair to the royal 'ouse of Napoli—Naples, you say."

"What you do not zay is 'zir' to me." Because her hand rested chubby on the rail, he laid his over it. "Plain Will's planty good, Nina, uh, Niña."

The boatswain came to nudge him. "We've found a place for thee in the foc's'le," he said; doubtless he had once had a berth on an English vessel.

"Tha what?" Will sputtered. "Have a caere o' thy language, fellow. Heare be a gently reared maiden."

"Come see thy hammock," said the boatswain impatiently, "and settle which mess thou'lt be in."

Will folded himself in a bow at Niña. "Mesim 'a wants to feed me," he said, "and I be hungry for sure, even if hamhocks on this queasy riade do indeed zound like a mess—yet not one half zo hungry as I'll be to rejine thee."

"Oo-oo-ooh!" she tittered, and watched him till he had gone below.

XV

A CHANNEL PACKET.

THIS was a broad-beamed craft with high, ugly super-structure and stubby masts. Its sails were furled; paddle-wheels churned on either side, engine puffed and clanked, hull shivered, stack vomited smoke. Elsewhere sunlight fell extravagant over wings of gulls cruising and mewing through blueness, greens and purples and snow-whites of water, other vessels dancing past, chalk cliffs receding astern, castle-crowned above clustered red roofs. Wind frolicked.

Jennifer stood at the rail, looking aft. Beneath the hood of a gray traveling cloak, her face showed pale, though she had regained weight and some life in her eyes. Nearby, in Puritan civil garb, her eight warders poised, paced, or sat on a bench. The area was partly walled off by a cabin and bales of deck cargo.

And now good-by to thee as well, dear Dover, she thought: *dear even if I hardly glimpsed thee more than from a coach or window of my room within our hostel —for I scented salt, spied stocking caps on heads of fishermen, heard honest clogs resound on cobblestones, and English voices, English heartiness; and Cornwall came back to me in a wave. O Rupert, when thou first wast here, a youth, was it but countryside and brilliant court which made thee fall so hard in love with England, or did the English people speak to thee?*

Shy words came as if prompted: "My lady, can't this brightness touch your grief?"

Turning, she saw the young man—hardly more than a boy, nor much taller than she—who had ventured out from among her keepers. "What's that to thee, Sword-of-the-Lord, thou Gerson?" she flung.

He flushed, beneath cropped fair hair, like any scolded child. " 'Tis . . . pain, my lady . . . caged and useless here," he stammered, laying a fist above his heart, "e'en as 'twas joy to watch your health return."

"From what thy brother Righteous did to me." She showed him her back again.

"I pray you . . . he means well . . . though I would never—"

"And having naught to do but sleep and eat while they arranged to bring me captive southward, why should I now grow flesh back on these bones? The restlessness and hunger were inside them."

"My lady, think!" he implored. "You go to expiate —no sin, I swear, no stain on purity—a mere mistake to which a wily fiend lured innocence— You'll win full freedom soon. And meanwhile, here is France ahead of us, a lovely land, they say, and new to see. I've heard how you yourself have blood of France—"

"Ha' done!" snapped his older brother. "Thou'rt here to guard, not mooncalf mope."

"For once, I welcome words of Righteous Gerson," said Jennifer frigidly.

Sword-of-the-Lord slunk aside, under the grins or sniffs of his comrades, sat down on the deck behind a bollard with his own back to everyone else, and hugged knees to chin.

Nobah Barker appeared around the cabinside, in company with another man. The latter might almost have passed for a Cavalier, in long hair, beard and mustachios trimmed to points as exact as that upon his sword, plumed hat held in bejeweled hand: save that his clothes were gaudier yet, and his birthplace was obviously the Midi. In an energetic countenance, politeness fought with boredom.

"Aye, Mounseer d'Artagnan," Barker droned, mangling the name too, "what you have seen of England on your mission for King Lewis, will seem the merest seed in few more years, when we have built the new Jerusalem. Then your own folk, ignited by example, will soak the truth of Puritanism up; and soon, in Christian love, our two great realms will go unscrew the captive Holy Land and scrub it clean in Turkish blood."

"Per'aps," said d'Artagnan skeptically. He became more cheery when his glance fell on Jennifer, who having noticed him in turn could not altogether suppress curiosity. She reddened a little, brushed an amber lock off her brow, and grew interested in the wake of the nearer wheel.

" 'Ow far d'you plan to travel on t'rough France?" he asked.

"To *Mar*-sales," Barker replied. Quickly: "All our papers are in order."

"You stop off in Paris? I could find time"— d'Artagnan made a motion toward the girl which was not precisely a bow, since she wasn't observing, but had the effect of one—"to show your . . . daughter? . . . somezing of ze sights."

"Ah, nay—"

"R-r-respectably, wiz chaperone."

"She's not my daughter! Do I look so old?" (D'Artagnan cocked a brow.) "She is—well, sith 'tis in our documents—" Barker bent close to speak low and confidentially. (D'Artagnan averted his nose as much as possible.) "Her uncle is my friend, a mighty man. Alas, she's lately suffered fits of madness. Close watch is needed lest she harm herself, for while she is most times quite rational, she suddenly may try to flee or fight, accuse the ones who love her best— D'you know? On medical advice, we take her south, in hopes a softer climate may bring cure, or cruises on the pleasant inland sea."

The Frenchman crossed himself. "*Mon Dieu!*" Pity welled in his tone: "So young and fair. Zat twists ze 'eart, e'en in an officer of musketeers. . . . *Adieu, monsieur.* Be sure I'll pray for 'er."

He went rapidly off around the cabin. Barker glowered. "Think'st thou thy Papist chants are aught but noise?" he said under his breath. "Would God that I could shun thy Nineveh!" He squared his shoulders. "Yet I will steel myself, will be a Jonah."

Proceeding to where Jennifer stood, he told her, "That was a most important frog I met."

"And you the lime which made his mouth to pucker," she retorted, still staring outward.

He flushed. "More insolence? Repent, before too late!"

She gave her low-keyed answer some forethought. "I spoke in haste. Nay, you are not the lime they've found will keep men healthy far at sea. You're scurvy."

"Oh, but you will weep for that," he moaned, "when, in the punishment of captured Rupert, you see the error of your willful ways!"

"What makes you think I'll help you track him down?" she said between her teeth. "You took my ring away—"

"Lest you discard it."

"How gladly would I cast it in the sea, or with mine own hand hold it in a fire." Jennifer smote the rail. "You cannot make me wear it for your guide."

"We can," he declared, "and will, once we have reached the South. To slip it on your finger when the wrists are firmly gripped? There's nothing easier. And who will wonder if they see you forced to walk whatever way we prod? You're mad—you're being treated by such exercise—" He took her arm. She shivered and tried to draw away, but he tightened his hold and spoke in a high, hurried voice:

"Believe me, Mistress Jennifer, what woe it is that I must thus give pain to you. How I will cry hosannas when you're healed, your devil driven out by Christian meekness, your grateful tearflow laving this my hand! How I shall welcome you back in the fold! Aye, even —maybe—think you not unworthy, when properly instructed, that I tell Sir Malachi he may betroth you to me." In haste: "No promises thus far! You've leave to hope and strive for betterment; and I will help. I'll preach until my words wear down those doors a demon has made fast within your mind."

He collected air. "But I will not bespeak religion yet," he said. "Let me begin with practicalities. You are a sailor's daughter, I recall. You have known hardship, toil, and friends who drowned. Look o'er the water at our fellow ships"—he gestured grandly—"where men and canvas wrestle wind and tide, then feel this engine striding underfoot and thank the Lord for the progressiveness wherewith our new age is identified, a purifying age of iron men as well as iron instruments— What's that?"

A thump and rattle went through the hull. The paddlewheels chunked to a halt. The stack wheezed forth a few last dismal soot-clouds.

"God damn that pressure gauge!" roared a voice. "All hands on deck! Aloft, you scuts! Set sail ere we collide!"

Jennifer gave Barker a long, sweet smile. "An age of iron men," she murmured, "and wooden brains." Abruptly she giggled, before tossing her head and going from him. Her guards came after.

RUPERT'S CABIN ABOARD SHIP.

Moorish lavishness had largely overcome Spanish austerity throughout the Kingdom of Tunis. Two bunks, with lockers beneath, flanked a thick and colorful carpet. Aft was a built-in, padded seat, before which a table could be folded down. The bulkheads bore paneling inlaid with enamel-and-ivory arabesques. A window stood open to the rush and cluck, the amiable salt breezes of a night sea. A large mellow-shining lantern, hung from the overhead, barely moved.

Rupert sat with a book. His huge frame was attired in shirt of silk, doublet of black velvet trimmed in vair, modish knee breeches and white stockings, pearl-studded kid slippers. At a knock he raised his head and called, "Come in."

Duchess Belinda entered. Silver and rubies glittered in her hair, at throat, on fingers; a low-cut bodice and close-fitting purple gown showed other opulencies. Rupert sprang up. "My lady!" he said. "What brings you here?"

"Shame that you spend your evenings alone," she said merrily.

"I dine and sup each day with you . . . and his Grace, when he feels well—and now, 'tis very late. I thought you'd gone to rest."

"Well, you've not. I hear you talked of as showing lights till every hour. Why can't you sleep?" Her voice was a honeycomb. She came to take his hands and search his eyes. "Do your quarters lack comfort? Surely either of those beds is much too small for you."

"Nay, my lady, a soldier learns how to snore anywhere. 'Tis but that I've less need of sleep then most men. Indeed, I feel guilty that the mates must vacate their room for me."

"La! If they consider themselves not honored to house Prince Rupert of the Rhine, they deserve no more than their hammocks. . . . Place the refreshments, Niña."

The maid, who had followed the duchess in, lowered the table and onto it a tray she carried. Thence she took a decanter, two crystal goblets, sweetmeats in a bowl, and a silk pouch. "Good," said Belinda. "Thou may'st go. I shall not require thee further this night."

Plainly overjoyed, the girl curtsied and hastened out. Her mistress laughed. "Methinks she'll see your Will inside the minute. I've an idea they themselves are skimping on sleep."

"But, my lady—" Rupert floundered, "this—that is—"

"Be not too stiff," she said; "at least, not in respect of propriety. My lord knows where I am and approves, though the voyage has put such strain on him he'd better keep his bed. And see, we leave the door wide open." She went sinuously to hook it. "Yet still we'll have sufficient privacy."

"For what, my lady?"

She slithered back toward him. "For your pride, Rupert. I might well say your haughtiness. First however: I've repeatedly bade you call me by name. We're friends —close friends, I hope—not a pair of titles."

Placing herself on the settee, she gave him no choice but to do likewise. "Will you pour the sherry?" she asked. "We may as well enjoy us, no?"

He obeyed. She raised her goblet. "*A nuestra salud,*" she proposed. A smile stole onto his mouth. They clinked glasses and sipped.

"What were you reading, Rupert?" she asked.

"A Portuguese account of exploration in the northern Americas, which Captain Mena lent me."

"I knew not you read Portuguese."

"Well, when one can follow along in Latin, Spanish, French, Italian—" (She blinked admiringly.) He cleared his throat. "'Tis fascinating, that land about the bay Henry Hudson found. This writer dwells on the fur trade; but more important, I think, are his observations of auroras and the fact that the north magnetic pole must be nearby. Moreover, the natives possess some ingenious artifices we could well adapt, not to speak of most remarkable beliefs and customs."

She leaned cheek on hand. "Ah, Rupert," she sighed, "the whole of creation is the range of your mind."

"*Ach*, no, my lady—Belinda. I'm a mere soldier." He drank deep to hide and ease his confusion. "What business brings you here?"

She pouted. "Another man would wonder what goddess he owes thanks for such a delightful occasion." (Rupert flushed.) She chuckled and stroked his arm. "Nay, I'd not have you be any other man."

Growing serious: "You've told us little about your mission, really only that you were captured at Marston Moor, escaped, and seek something which may aid the Royal cause, somewhere in the waters between Europe and Africa."

"I ought say no more," he answered low. His glance dropped to the ring on his clenched left fist. "If only because 'tis too fantastical and forlorn."

"Well, I'll not urge you 'gainst your will. Yet never forget what friends you have in . . . Carthage. For your own sake as well as that of your King, of kings everywhere, we rejoice at any aid we may lend."

"You are good. I wonder if 'twas altogether chance our courses crossed. I've certain secret allies; their powers are slight— Nay. Proceed, I pray you."

"You were bound for Holland, to ask what help your mother might give." Belinda leaned forward and close. Lantern light moved golden across hair and face; it cast moving shadows in her bodice. Waves whooshed, breezes lulled. The ship moved gently as a rocking cradle. "That would be scant. Nevertheless you chose to fare with us, to arrive sooner near your goal, though you've just a single companion and hardly two shillings to click together."

Rupert shrugged. "The venture's desperate enough that that recks little."

"Your boldness thrills me." She pointed to herself. "See the chill rising on my flesh. . . . Still, you'll not shun assistance, I'm sure." A deep sigh. "Would I could furnish troopers and a frigate! Impossible; my lord's a peaceful man." Her lip lifted a fraction. At once: "After difficulty, I've persuaded him to offer you this purse. The gold should reach some ways along your road."

"Belinda, I—I cannot," Rupert stuttered, half dismayed. "I dare not—"

"Aye, you do!" she said fiercely. "I'd liefer 'twas a gift, but call it a loan if you wish. King Charles can repay us, when you've come down off those crags you're scaling to bring him his crown back from the vultures' nest. Your duty, Rupert. You *may* not refuse."

She caught his right hand in her own and drew it across the table, where her left brought the pouch up against his palm. Slowly, he closed fingers on it. After a few more seconds, she let him withdraw from her clasp and blew him a kiss. "Wise man, in this if in naught else," she sang.

"I have no words to thank you."

"Indeed you do. Words of yourself, Rupert. Your adventures, your achievements—and perhaps you'll draw my portrait, being a master artist?"

"I'd love that."

She turned her head back and forth upon twining neck and rotating shoulders. "Which profile?" she murmured. "What pose? We must try many positions— Oh!"

That last was no cry of joy. Pulling his gaze from her with an almost audible rip, the prince saw Duke Hernán in the doorway. Clad in a nightshirt and robe, leaning on a cane, features sunken and sallow, he gave them a shaky smile.

"Your Grace!" Rupert jumped to greet him and lead him to the table. "What a wonderful surprise. You're feeling better?"

"Better, yes, better." As he settled down next to his wife, Rupert on his other side, the diplomat continued: "Yes, yes, *si*, blessèd be thees calm, though honesty does make me confess 'ow w'en we reach Tunis I've promeesed feefty candles een thanksgeeveeng to San Antonio, that ees St. Anthony, you know, who leeved een the desert very far from water." He blinked benevolently at them. "You 'ave done your beezness?"

She nodded with small enthusiasm.

"My gratitude's unbounded to your Grace," Rupert said. "Here, let me fetch a glass for you."

"No, no," said Hernán. His voice was unsteady. "My stomach ees steel back een that last gale we 'ad, heh, heh, heh. Ah, to be young again! But you two weell find 'ow soon golden youth does flee." He wagged a finger. "So lay up treasure een 'eaven how, because pious self-denials, fasteeng, abstentions, are worth much, much more at your age than they weell be later w'en you must practeece them anyway. Nay, seet down, 'Ighness, seet down. I deed awaken and thought eet would be jolly to join you two young people and, yes, yes, maybe counsel you, geeve you advice from an expeerience wheech ees, eef I may say't, long and—and—varièd? Yes, varièd. Ah, I remember once een Barcelona . . . seexteen 'undred and twenty-nine eet was, or twenty-eight?—I theenk twenty-nine, though per'aps—*bueno*, eet was the feast of the Eleven Thousand Virgeens, I do remember that—"

Rupert made himself comfortable and prepared to exercise the virtue of patience. Belinda interrupted by a touch and a soft remark: "Darling, I'm very happy for you. But have a care. You catch cold so easily. Rupert, would you close the window?"

"Nay," said the duke. "Open, open. Fresh air refreshes. True, I am a beet a-sheever, seence my lady reminds me. . . . 'owever, an old campaigner, heh, heh, heh. You young *caballeros* 'ave 'ad your adventures, yes, yes, you 'ave, I deny eet not, but let me tell you—"

"And you must be starved," Belinda said. "Take a comfit."

She offered him a particularly gooey one. He gulped and waved it away. "No! My stomach. . . . Per'aps a glass of water, a dry beescueet—"

"Ship's biscuits are best left alone on Friday, dear. And Rupert, in spite of what he says, I must insist you

shut the window, no matter how hot, close, and greasy-
smelling it gets. As for thee, my lord, if thou canst rise
(from thy bed, at any rate," Belinda added under her
breath), "I'd be remiss did I not see to't thou receivest
better nourishment than a spoonful of broth or gruel. I'll
have the cook roused at once to prepare thee—let me
think—" She made a pretty gesture of frowning, touching the corner of her mouth, then beaming. "Ah, yes!
Eggplant and onion fried in oil, garlic below and melted
cheese a-bubble above, with lavishness of pepper. Moreover, midnight's not far off, when thou canst lawfully
take a pork chop."

The duke changed color and swallowed several times.
"No," he said feebly.

She did not seem to hear. "Ah, my lord," she asked,
"will it not be delicious, a fat-dripping pork chop and
peppery fried potatoes? Or might these be better cold,
their grease congealed? Nay, the soverign remedy, I've
heard, is the raw white of an egg, let slide down the
throat ere one goes on to fat pork and oozy potatoes."

The duke lurched to his feet. Rupert hastened to as-
sist him.

"Furthermore," Belinda said, "I've heard well recom-
mended the chewing of tobacco. We can buy a good,
strong quid from the slop chest—"

"I . . . feel seeck . . . again," the duke choked
forth.

Rupert took his elbow. "Come, let me help you to
your couch," the Rhinelander urged.

"No, no—stay, *por favor*—" Hernán tried to
straighten. "We . . . del Monte de Gavilanes . . . old
campaigner—" He made what haste he could out the
door and down the passageway.

Rupert stood awhile silent. Belinda sipped her wine.

"You were a trifle injudicious, I fear, my lady," said
Rupert, not looking at her.

"Aforethought, as you can't quite utter? Oh, I knew
what I did," she admitted insouciantly. "Yet think not
ill of me. He has more years than my father who wedded me to him. Shall I not, then, look to his welfare as
might a dutiful daughter? And you know how an ancient
must ofttimes be cosseted, aye, cozened, when weakness

has sapped judgment. I feared he'd overtax what strength the stresses of work and war, followed by this rough journey, have left him."

"Well—"

She beckoned. "Come, sit. You owe me some diversion, did we not agree? Here, take a confection"—she reached it to him—"drain your glass and refill it, and lay aside that earnestness which, I believe, is armor for a heart much too tender."

Inch by inch, he obeyed.

"You learn," she encouraged him. "Next let me start your tongue rolling. I've heard how, after being freed from Linz, you chanced upon the Emperor himself and his huntsmen, threatened by a wild boar, seized a spear and slew it. True?"

"Not wholly." Sherry gurgled into his goblet. "Truth is," he said, growing more at east as he talked, "under the law there, my release could not be final till I'd kissed his hand. Thus I was seeking him, unsure whether he'd allow this ceremony. The boar was not really endangering his life, though 'twas forsooth a gross brute, causing the hunters great trouble. An opportunity. If I, a stranger, helped them, he'd doubtless reach to clasp my hand—"

Belinda listened.

XVI

A ROAD IN FRANCE.

ORLEANAIS rolled subtly parti-colored beneath a cloudless hot heaven: tawny stubblefields, brown hayricks, bleached green pillars of poplar, apple orchards beginning to glow red, vineyards heavy with purple clusters, widely scattered farmsteads whose buildings had walls of gray stucco, roofs of dark thatch or umber tile. Peasants at work wore faded blue smocks and plain sabots; their ox-drawn wagons and donkey carts were gaily painted. They were a stocky, sturdy folk, who would let go sickles or spades to hail passers-by, throw a jest at a neighbor, gulp some wine from a clay jug.

There went a smell of earth and summer, but it was nearly lost in the dust thrown up by hoofs and wheels. A coach was rattling southward behind four horses. Baggage made a hillock on the roof. One black-clad, tall-hatted man drove, another clung behind. Six more fared in saddles, their leader riding postilion, the rest strung on either side. Though likewise in civil array, except for allowable swords, they had the seat of cavalrymen.

Jennifer leaned out a window. Sweat stained her gown and channeled the grime on her features. "What do you want?" demanded Nobah Barker, who sat across from her. He was still more wilted by the heat, battered by the incessant jounce and sway, then she was; his reddened eyes resented her.

"A breath of breeze," she snapped through rattle and creak. "Is that forbidden?"

" 'Tis immodest, Mistress Alayne, thus to thrust one's maiden self upon the public view."

She grinned in unfriendly wise. "Wherefore you stay within, Reverend? Well, let me be entirely lost to shame. Let me take a horse, not suffocate here."

"Nay. How couldst thou receive instruction? Thou. Hear, I must chide thee as I would a child."

"Why, then I'll address thee as I would a dog."

"Peace!" he yelped. "Oh, if I might chastise thee with stripes, flog forth the scornful devil which possesses thee! How thou wouldst weep thereafter, and beg my forgiveness for this insolence wherewith thou tormentest mine every waking hour!"

"I'll strike a bargain," said Jennifer. "Spend no more of thy waking hours in my presence, and thou'lt get never a bad word from me."

"Nay. Thy guardian did charge me most strictly to have a care of thy soul and strive unremittingly to mend its illness. Methinks he was mistaken in forbidding corporal punition; 'twould surely have eased the anguish inflicted on me. However, I comply, I submit. Unto the task of recapturing the wayward lamb do I screw myself. Come within. Sit and hearken. That's an order."

Jennifer ignored it. Leaning as far as possible, she waved at a peasant girl tending a flock of geese which cropped the ditch. "Hallo, sister, hallo!" she cried. *"Je suis ta soeur*—see, I learned some French o' my dad— little sister, free sister, pray for me in my prison. *Prie pour moi."*

"Wanton! Papist! In, I told thee!" Barker stormed. He threw arms around her waist and dragged.

She swung about in his clasp to rake nails across his cheek. He let her go. They both sat back, breathing hard, he dabbling at the blood-beaded scratches. After a moment she said like stones falling: "This time I warned you, Barker. Seize me again, and 'twill cost you an eyeball at least."

"I . . . violence . . . wildness . . . thou'rt truly afflicted—" He stiffened into a sort of calm. "Thine uncle did authorize what force might be needful to carry out my task. I hold that that may include the compelling of thy body."

Jennifer sighed. "Liefer than have thee touch me more, I'll stay quiet."

Barker struggled to smile. "My child, I pity thee. Indeed, the pain I endure on thine account will earn me palaces in heaven. So fair without, so foul within—and yet, beneath that filth which wizard Rupert conjured into thee, may still abide a soul as pure as the driven snow."

"Aye, cold enough, and driven where it would not be."

"Cold? In this weather?" He lifted a bottle. "Here, behold how I return good for evil and offer thee water."

"Not from a neck *your* lips have sucked."

"Thou hurtest me, Jennifer, woundest me here." He laid palm on breast.

"Aye, thou painest me too." She touched her rump.

It passed him by. Shaking the container, he said, "Maybe as well thou refusest. 'Tis nigh empty. Preaching's thirsty work. Therefore, in God's cause I'll finish it."

He did, set it on the floor, inflated his lungs, and stated: "I shall continue my discourse which was thus rudely interrupted. It is, thou wilt recall, upon the eighteenth chapter of Leviticus, having to do with unlawful lusts, and we had reached the twenty-third verse, which closes: '. . . *it is confusion.*' A veritable sign from heaven, that I should be at this exact passage when thou didst cry out unto the goose girl—because that showed forth how thou dost commit confusions, albeit not those specified in the chapter, I hope. Worst, of course, is that thou didst ask for a Papist prayer—horror, horror—but thou hast also a worldly miscomprehension. That thou couldst call yon person free, captive as she is in both flesh and spirit, demonstrates how thou'rt wholly ignorant of matters political—indeed, of the very definition of freedom."

Jennifer stared out the window.

"A moment, ere I explicate." His black coat cut off her view as he himself leaned forth to call: "Throckmorton! Dost see a sheltered spot ahead?"

"A hedge, sir, a mile hence," the driver answered.

"Well, whip up the horses, and make halt there. The Lord's business does not wait." Barker sat down again, crossing his thighs rather tightly. "Where was I? Ah, yes. I have been inquiring and studying of the French situation, from that military envoy I met on the steamer and in Calais from the English consul whilst our transportation was being purchased. Industry, Jennifer, industry and an open mind are the sure eastern and western pole stars whereby we steer toward truth—worldly truth, that is, the divine sort being always a matter of revelation and special grace. Uh-h'm! Know, then, the new King Lewis is a mere child, and the true ruler of the land is an Italian cardinal. How can France be free if she wears the collar of a Roman cleric?"

Jennifer could not forbear to say, "Though 'tis a Catholic land, they tolerate Protestants."

"Ah-ha! A Catholic land. That means they tolerate Catholics too, does it not? Wherein lies freedom there? Nay, those who would die to scorch error from their country are forced, cruelly forced to live in very earshot of its preachments. Furthermore, where's a Parliament of godly men, responsive to the people, such as has sat in London, unchanged by any dissent, these four unbroken years, and will sit as long as is necessary to reform every citizen? France groans beneath feudal monarchy. Archaic laws and usages bind her natural leaders hand, foot, and mouth. In consequence, progress languishes. Behold for thyself, child. See how yonder old cottage stands just where 'twould be advantageous to pass a railway. Hast thou observed a single smokestack or enclosure? The time lost each year in holidays and festivals is a national disgrace. . . . Throckmorton, hurry along, I told thee!"

"We're well-nigh there, master," came the reply.

"I'll give you this," Jennifer said: "that to judge by all the stops we've been making, the French cannot prepare food—or is it drink?— that agrees with your English constitution."

" 'Tis the work of Satan, seeking to hinder me," Barker stated, "and that thou art spared the flux is an ominous token." Hopefully: "Or hast thou need to go this time, after me?"

"Nay, heaven hast not yet vouchsafed me that sign of its feelings which it considers appropriate to you. But I will step out whilst you're busy and rest me by the waters of Babylon."

The coach halted. The footman flung wide its door and extended a handful of hayballs. Barker seized them and made for the hedge as fast as he could waddle.

Jennifer followed, more stiffly than she was wont after this long, cramped ride. She almost gave the footman a word of sympathy; he might have been a statue in gritty plaster, save for his woeful sneezes and snuffles. But he was Rupert's enemy. Standing in what shade the vehicle cast, she stretched herself, muscle by muscle, while she looked widely and wistfully outward.

Boots scrunched hard-baked earth. Sword-of-the-Lord Gerson had dismounted. Holding his steed by the reins, he approached to within a yard of her, stopped, shifted from foot to foot, made a timid salute when she noticed him. His downy cheeks were redder than even the summer day would warrant.

"How are you, Mistress Alayne?" (She could barely hear him.) "Can I help you in aught?"

"I am weary unto death," she answered. "And . . . let me think . . . aye, thou canst do me a great kindness."

"Anything, my lady."

"Hold," growled Righteous Gerson from his saddle. "The witch will have thee pledge a treachery."

"Oh, nay," said the girl. "This would be a boon not to me alone, but to our whole merry band of pilgrims. Take Nobah Barker's tongue and stuff it down his throat."

Three Roundheads laughed. Another slapped his thigh and remarked, "A pretty notion; but, lack-a-day, 'tis too long to fit and too waggly to seize."

Righteous Gerson frowned. "Show respect," he ordered. "He's our minister. Who else would hold divine service for us in this land of Belial?"

Jennifer wandered to the roadside, sat down on her heels, and ran fingers among its wildflowers. "Good day, you blossoms blowing here in France," she murmured. "I bring you greetings from your English cousins, and thank you for your messages to me—O poppies bold as freedom's blood and banner, and bindweed white as Rupert's lofty plume."

Again she heard feet shuffle close, and rose to meet Sword-of-the-Lord. His head hung, he bit his lip and said miserably, "Can you . . . not name . . . a proper task for me? I'd give these eyes to see you happy, mistress."

Her mouth softened. "Thou'rt kind," she said low.

"Who could be else, to you?" He smote fist in gauntlet. "I know. Myself, I can't believe that you're possessed. The fiends may well fly mothlike tow'rd your soul, but char and shrivel in its radiance." (She smiled at his wavering words, half touched, half amused.) "You're lion-loyal, though it be misguided. Can I not find for you one lonely comfort? I'd cherish that beside me when I sleep."

"I've marked how thou dost ever wish me well, despite the gall I ladle from the heart," she replied slowly. " 'Tis time I give forgiveness—and ask it." After a moment: "I'd like a drink of water from thy flask."

"At once! If only 'twere ambrosia!" He unslung the leather bottle at his belt, dropped it, picked it up, wiped it clean with shaky hands and his neckerchief, and nearly fell to the ground himself when he tried to bow as he passed it over. She swallowed thirstily. After she gave it back, he stared at it for a while, then, as if charging a rampart, raised it for a quick swallow of his own. When he lowered and stoppered it, a look was upon his face as if he had received communion.

Barker emerged from behind the hedge. Now he walked easily, rubbing his hands. "Well, brethren, shall we be upon our way?" he called. "Or shall we take a rest for half an hour? Methinks we should, that ye may likewise hear my discourse to our straying lamb."

"O God," Jennifer said skyward, "if Thou'st forsaken me, I understand."

Sword-of-the-Lord breathed, aghast, "You're being driven mad—to blasphemy?" He clapped free hand on weapon hilt and marched to stand before Barker. His led horse loomed behind him like a wall. "Ha' done!" he cried. "Can you not see what harm you wreak? 'Tis bad enough that she must be a captive and made the means of what she thinks betrayal. To hear you drone

and rant and whine all day could make her feel that hell
will be relief."

His brother spurred close, shouting, "Thou whelp,
leave off thine insolence!"

Sword-of-the-Lord held his ground and said in desperate stubborness: " 'Tis not. Hark. There are . . .
there are ways and ways to preach. Theology will
scare the savage off who'd gladly hear Christ's simple words of love, while Joshua's more fitting for a soldier, and— Well, this lady's altogether steadfast; to batter her with God won't break that down; it will but force
her to repel the Name."

"What eloquence," Righteous fleered. "Art thou in
holy orders?"

Jennifer came to take the boy's arm. "Nay, he is
merely showing common sense," she told them. "Is it
too rare for ye to recognize? Why blame him if he look
on me as human instead of as an object? From such lips
I might hear words that did not seal mine ears."

Barker swelled with indignation. "Thou darest,
shameless hussy—" he began, spraying the neighborhood.

"Hold, good sir," broke in Righteous. "I know my
brother . . . and her somewhat, too. Maybe— Let's
talk o' this in confidence."

He vaulted from his stirrups and drew Barker aside.
They whispered together. The remaining Roundheads
stared in their various fashions at youth and maiden.
Sword-of-the-Lord shrank into himself, overwhelmed by
what he had done. Jennifer breathed something which
caused him to straighten, fiery-visaged, dry-mouthed,
and resolute as a Maccabee.

Nobah Barker and Righteous Gerson returned. The
minister cleared his throat. "We will essay it, then, in
these next days," he said, "until we come to Mar-sales
and our work. If this our charge is cursed with such
poor taste a homily grits her teeth, and can't digest it,
then we must give her soul a coarser fare and hope that
that may prove her heavenly fodder." To Sword-of-the-
Lord: "My boy, we'll let thee try to be her mentor. She
favors thee, as nearest to her age. We'll even let her ride
a horse by thee, a ways apart from us. Descant thy best.

We'll see if mildness of this kind may melt the ice of her, that logic failed to break. If thou shouldst bring her to repentance, lad, I'd say that God has called thee to the Church, and I myself will teach thee how to preach. But if thou fail'st—"

"Why, matters won't be worse," Jennifer said. "O God"—through tears—"Thy pardon! Thou dost not forsake." Laughter burst forth. She skipped on the road and caroled:

"A weary age
That felt the rage—"

"Has this released thy madness, ravening?" sputtered Barker. "Stop or be bound!"

She obeyed instantly. "I'm very sorry, sir," she said, folding hands and casting eyes downward. "Hereafter I will strive to mend my ways."

"It woo-woo-works," marveled Sword-of-the-Lord. "The cure's begun . . . already."

"We'll see as we continue on our road." Barker sounded less than ecstatic. "Each man of you will lend his horse in turn and join me in the coach"—he brightened—"and we will talk. Wilt thou be first, good Sergeant Righteous Gerson? Thou canst then hear me practice my next sermon."

Jennifer and Sword-of-the-Lord didn't notice. They were looking too deeply at each other.

THE GUN DECK OF THE TUNISIAN PINNACE.

Cannon were drawn back and lashed down behind their ports. Likewise shut was a door in a forward bulkhead. A screen erected aft marked where the junior officers' quarters began. The time was sunset, but light still came down through ventilation gratings to tinge deck planks violet and make brazen snouts sheen amidst shadows. There was no real wind; the ship ghosted along with barely a sound or surge.

Rupert paced from the stern. His head was bent till the hair hid most of his face. His fists clamped and unclamped. Amidships, his regard fell on one of the guns. He stopped. Seeking distraction, he ran knowledgeable hands across its sleekness and stooped to heft a ball from the rack beside it.

A thud brought him alert. A hatch cover was tilting off the deck. *Who's that in the powder magazine?* he thought, and crouched to peer from the carriage.

Will Fairweather's head poked up, swiveled around, flashed a smile through gloom. "Nobody about," he said most quietly. "Liake I reckoned. Let's leap to it, though."

He slid the cover aside, scrambled forth, stood to buckle his belt. Niña the maidservant came after, her hair and gown rumpled. "Fasten thy girdle, ninny," he reminded her. She tittered.

Rupert rose and trod forward. *"Buenas tardes,"* he said.

Niña squealed. Will jumped, before he emitted a rackety laugh. "Ah, my loard. Thou'st lost no skill at reconnaissance. Nor lost caere for tha needs o' thy poor zoldiers, I trust." To the dismayed girl: "Fear not. 'A can keep a tactical zecret. Do thou taeke caere liakewise, my little messenger pigeon, to let nothin' drop. Now, fly along, preen thyself ere thou must attend thy mistress, an' in thy miand rehearse our next coup."

He slapped her on the behind. She cast a glance half apprehensive, half roguish at Rupert's looming form and pattered off. Will replaced the hatch cover.

The prince sighed and shook his head. "How dost thou do it?" he wondered.

"In the usual way, zir," answered the dragoon. "Or if thou'd'st know how I persuade 'em, when I'm no beauty, why, zir, 'tis a girt fallacy that women caere for looks in a man as men caere for looks in a woman. Attention, my general, attention's what they wish, shy at first for to show respect, brash laeter for to show interest; an' then, o' coua'se, 'tis tha good acts which recall us to tha staege." He bowed. "Not that faeme, high birth, an' handsomeness ben't useful, zir, moare or less in thic order. But by themzelves tha' just zit there, doin' naught. Tha general could 'a royalized half England had 'a obzarved tha zignal flags flyin' everywhere around him."

"Enough prating." Rupert turned harsh. "How long hast thou been at this?"

"Longer than moast, zir, she tells me. However, there's another zuperstition, that meare zize—"

"In time, thou dolt!" Rupert sighed and spread his hands. "Oh, no matter." Stern again: "I'm chiefly shocked to find a soldier of mine using for his lechery a . . . a powder magazine."

Will snickered. "Art afeared we'll touch it off? Zooth, she's planty hot. We did zeek tha hoalds first. Zir, I can repoart no woman aliave'll keep that mood after a dozen cockroaches ha' run ticklefoot across her belly. Well, Tunis be at peace an' no pirates looked for. Thus few zailors come by heare; none poake into yon ammunition locker. An', zir, I can liakewise repoart the smell o' gunpowder works on women like catnip."

Rupert gave up an unequal contest. As a Parthian shot, he said, "Thou'st loaded a single breech under sea conditions, and yet durst generalize?"

"I know who'd love bein' generalized," Will guffawed, "as well as boarded, berthed, oaverhauled—"

With an open-handed blow, Rupert knocked him sprawling. "Get out of here before I kick thee hence!" the prince roared.

Will clutched his ringing ear. "Foargive me," he whispered. "I forgot thine honor, loard." He crept to his feet and went unsteadily aft, beyond the screens toward the ladders.

Rupert remained among the guns.

I'm sorry, mine old friend, went through him. *Forgive thou me. I stoned a harmless rook because he cawed and chanced to sound like words which flayed a nerve.* He paced. *Oh, I'm no pup; I've winded it myself: and Mary was a scentless butterfly whose tints I only dimly can remember.* He stopped. *Belinda—Jennifer—this quest of mine will likely end in that this pulsing flesh lies quiet, meat for dogs, or that these ribs provide a white cathedral for the fish.—.—. Of course, there's heaven, Euclid-perfect heaven.* His fist beat the cannon beside which he stood, up and down, up and down. *Or Jennifer—devoted, chaste, bucolic, betrothed to me by hurried heathen rites I scarce recall—a maid from those romances Cervantes laughed into oblivion. . . . And then this ring. I own 'tis served me well. But to what*

*final end? The Devil's wares, or simple Faerie gold, go
off like leaves in sudden killing frost and midnight wind,
which leave mere skeletons against the sky.___.___. What
is this ring, and what is she who gave it? Belinda is entirely of our earth. But likewise is Hernán—more
woundable—who gave me refuge in a bitter hour—
Argh! I must cease this childish whimpering. Is common decency so burdensome?* He regarded his hand
with astonishment. *Why, look, I've hammered blood
from out my fist. I'd best invent a likely accident.*

XVII

THE MARSEILLES WATERFRONT.

STIFF under a mid-afternoon sun, Jennifer walked between Nobah Barker and Sword-of-the-Lord. The clergyman was on her left. He gripped her wrist in such a manner that the ring on her third finger lay always in his view. The youth simply gave her his arm. His face showed more torment than hers, which was frozen. Behind them, in Puritan civil garb as before, paced the rest of the escort, and a hired interpreter.

Frenchmen—mariners, dock wallopers, ferriers, hawkers, chandlers—bustling between high buildings and bare masts, stared at the party but did not interfere. There was too much else to do; here odors of salt and tar blent with those of spices, corn, lumber, dried fish and fruit, all the produce of the Midworld lands. The hot air racketed.

Abruptly Barker exclaimed, then Jennifer screamed. He dropped his hold as if burnt by an incandescence of her ring. Its colors fountained and coruscated, brighter than day. Shouts and callings upon God lifted from the other men.

The girl whirled and ran. Barker yelped an incoherent order and hastened after her. She could outdistance him, but not the four soldiers who collected their wits and pounded in pursuit. Indignation boiled from people thrust aside. In yards, the Englishmen were caught up to Jennifer.

Hands clamped. She wailed like a wildcat, writhed, tugged till cloth ripped beneath fingers. When she could not break free, she turned around to claw, kick, and bite. The Roundheads lost blood here and there before they got her down on the paving.

Their companions arrived, having made a way through the crowd. Most formed a circle, as much to hide what went on as to keep off the French. Sword-of-the-Lord flung himself on his knees beside Jennifer. She had gone limp, half conscious. Barker knelt likewise, to blurt a quick prayer and take her left arm. The jewel had dimmed a little. He moved her hand around. The brilliance heightened afresh. As it chanced, no ship was tied up at this immediate spot; but not far out, one lay anchored. When pointed straight that way, the ring fairly flamed.

It was no more intense than the triumph on Barker's countenance. Nevertheless he was careful to tuck the hand with the sigil under a fold of her skirt, before he got up to treat with the guards who approached.

A CABIN IN THE TUNISIAN SHIP.

It was considerably larger and more luxurious than the one assigned Rupert: furnished almost like a chamber ashore, save for brass chains to secure chairs, and with an inner door now shut. Long light from the west filtered past curtains to where Duchess Belinda paced.

The opening of the outer door brought her to a halt. Niña Valdes entered "*?La señora*—" the maid began.

Belinda interrupted. "Nay, speak English, and speak low. Make fast that latch; come hither, nigh to me." (Niña did.) "I've summoned thee to talk in confidence, and would not risk some sailor overhears."

"*El duque*—" the girl began. "Ees my lord the Duke—"

"Asleep." Belinda's nod toward the adjacent room held scorn.

"Ah, so." The maid waited with a docility her eyes belied.

Belinda started pacing again. "However steep the cliff of rank between us, Niña, Eve's our common mother. I've always found thee trusty, and I hope thou hast in turn found me appreciative."

"My lady ees most sweet and generous." The tone anticipated.

"Unlike too many, I have never sought to regulate my servants' private lives. That's for their consciences and their confessors. Yet I'm not blind. Thou art a woman grown, albeit young; there's Moorish blood in thee; thou seekest places where I dare not go, to find adventures I may merely dream; and . . . well, it is no decorous example . . . but am I right, suspecting thou hast means, besides plain chastity, to keep thee slender?"

The girl hesitated only a blink before answering, "Some Casbah traders do sell theengs, your Grace."

"Love philters?" broke from the duchess.

Not altogether surprised, Niña still maintained, "I would not know of such."

"Oh, come!" Belinda stopped before her, though she must muster will to continue: "Nay, I mean no insult to thee. Thou art quite charming, and most times I grant that thou wilt have no need of artifice. And yet—I am not blind—I saw in England, there where they like their women tall, slim, blond, and thou wert but another servant wench, and foreign and a Catholic to boot . . . I saw how thou mad'st conquest after conquest. Thou'rt going home with a substantial nest-egg, garnered from thine admirers, even though the English are a cold and stingy race." In haste: "Mistake me not! I make no accusation. I do not speak of witchcraft or the like, but simply wonder if . . . perchance . . . devices . . . as lawful as perfume or talc or rouge—"

Niña smiled, and began to trail the hook which had been baited by the fish. "*Bueno*—but oh, eet ees eemposseeble my lovely lady would 'ave call for more than nature 'as so bountifully geeven."

"The duke is old," Belinda said.

"I understand, your Grace. And . . . eet would be a Chreestian deed, not so, to 'elp 'eem to a son by 'ees last wife?"

"A well-rewarded deed, I promise thee."

"I know my lady would be kind. Alas! I 'ave no mageec I can offer 'er. When strength ees gone—"

"Desire upraises strength."

The maid nodded. "There ees a musk the Casbah grannies make. Eet ees not mageec . . . but eet steemulates." She lowered her lashes. " 'Ow strong eet steemulates, I dare not say. Eet weell not by eetseelf turn men to bulls. But eef, m-m, there ees any lust to start weeth—'eld back by weariness or . . . een'eebeetion—"

Belinda seized her arms. "What then, what then?"

Having gotten the hook in, Niña played it. "I cannot promeese aught. 'Ees Grace eendeed ees vairy old and tired." Deliberately: "Of course, a younger, stronger man, 'eld back by an exaggerated sense of honor—a man in 'oom desire 'as been aroused by celibacy and by . . . weetnesseeng—'oo, left to nature, would re-seest forever—aye, such a man, eef caught all unsuspect-eeng, might fine 'ees senses overw'elm 'ees sense." She drove the hook firmly home. "But such ees not 'ees Grace the Duke."

"I know," Belinda said. "And yet my wifely duty is to try."

Niña grinned and pulled the line in. "True, true, my lady. I weell stay deescreet *w'ataiver* 'appens."

"Then you have a philter?" Belinda cried.

This time it was the younger woman who cautioned quietness. "A musk, weeth subtle 'erbs and flower juices. Maybe some spells were said o'er eet as well. Eet ees a strong perfume the woman wears." She sighed. "Alas, 'tees vairy, vairy costly, too. I only 'ave a leetle of eet left and am not sure I aiver can find more."

"I'd make it worth thy while," Belinda whispered, "especially if it succeeds."

"Pray, let me theenk on eet. I am not sure I should, my lady, though of course your weesh ees my command."

Belinda nodded. "Aye, go. We'd best not closet us o'erlong like this."

The maid curtsied and departed. When the door had closed again behind her, the duchess added to herself: "But soon I'll deal for one poor dram of bliss."

AN INN ROOM, UPSTAIRS.

Eventide filled a glassless window, wherein a roof op-posite stood black against the darkening greenish sky. Scant light entered the chamber. It was tiny, bare planks and mildewed plaster enclosing no more than a bed, a chair, and a washstand. From the courtyard beneath came a clash of hoofs, rumble of wheels, weary day's-end voices.

The door opened. A hand shoved Jennifer through. "Get in there with thee, witch, and bide the night!" Nobah Barker shrilled. She stumbled, nearly falling.

"Sir, we've no need for roughness," protested Sword-of-the-Lord. His companions in the hallway shifted their feet and muttered.

"Haven't we?" Barker replied. "Thou saw'st her struggle when her ring flared bright—the ring that hell bestowed—upon the wharf." Louder: "No supper for thee, witch! Unruliness, if not a demon, may be fasted out."

Head high, she showed them her back.

"Oh, sir, I pray you, let me speak with her," Sword-of-the-Lord said. "It may be I can ease her once again."

"Thou boasted thou hadst tamed her—till today," Barker sniffed. "Well, try it if thou wilt. The rest of us will go to supper and well-earned repose."

"Do thou stand guard outside the door, Uriah," ordered Righteous Gerson. "When we have eaten, Increase will relieve thee. And best we post a sentry in the courtyard. Who knows but what she might get help that way? Jashubilehem first; I'll be next. . . . Be sure, my brother, that thou tak'st the ring along when thou'st despaired."

"Why not at once?" Barker inquired.

"She'll fight and scream, sir, 'less someone persuade her," Righteous opined. "Belike he can. These Frenchies of Marseilles are mulish anti-Protestants, I've seen, and might make tumult an excuse to plague us."

Barker's head jerked assent. Sword-of-the-Lord stepped into the room. The door clapped shut. Boots thudded in departure.

Jennifer stood at the window. He came behind her and said in misery, "Oh, did they hurt thee very much, my lady? Why didst thou try to break away from them? It only earned thee cruel blows and wrenchings. I strove to make them kinder . . . but the fear when suddenly the jewel was a beacon, there on the waterfront, did madden them."

"What happened afterward?" she replied in a small, parched voice, not looking at him. In shadowiness, against a torn and stained dark gown, only her hair, which had fallen loose, and the ring had any real light to them; and the asp stone showed now no special brilliance.

"Thou didst not see? Ah, nay. I saw thee on the cobblestones, alone beneath a hundred Frenchmen's eyes, except for me and . . . and thy pain and grief."

She nodded. "I didn't really hear what happened next."

"How art thou?"

"I'm recovered in the flesh. If thou wouldst give a little balm, speak on."

"Well—" He plunged into it. "Nobah Barker mightily exulted. This was the very thing for which he'd hoped, the ring to point a trail to our great prey. That's why we walked the dockside, for a clue of the same kind that Rupert might well seek. If help for him lies southward in the sea—

"Our leader reasoned that the ship nearby in some wise must be fateful for the search. 'Twas a . . . chebeck . . . not docked, but out at anchor, its tender solely moored against the pier, to save a wharfage fee, as we discovered. When we had satisfied the French police that thou hadst had an epileptic fit, and all the people 'round us had dispersed—through our interpreter, we found the captain. Meanwhile thou lay all mute where we had borne thee—"

The sound of his hurt on her account forced Jennifer to admit, "I mostly was malingering, to spare myself from being further used. Tell on."

"I did not voice my hope that was the case," he said, a shade less unhappily. "The captain is the owner too, a scoundrel quite willing to hire out at no large sum despite not being told what we intend. That seems an omen to inspirit us. For Barker's learned, from English factors here who have connection to Sir Malachi, that naught has yet been seen or heard of Rupert. Therefore he scarcely can have raised a troop, and we're enough to take him, scandal-free," he ended in a rush.

"Speak for thyself," she said bitterly. " 'Tis no good sign for me."

"Oh, Jennifer," he pleaded, "have I not told thee how we are no monsters, simple common men who love their land too much to let it rot?"

"Thou'st spoken better sense, in brighter words, than thy companions: even made me smile," she agreed. "I was right thankful for a beam of light that fell when sunniness passed overhead—but couldn't climb out of my pit thereon. And now the very stars are being snuffed." She leaned palms on windowsill, face into the air. The yard below was becoming a pool of murk. "There may well be some rightness in thy cause. It was mine own, I thought until of late, and many of its folk are dear to me. It hurts to hurt them by my stubbornness. I'm ignorant, the merest fisher lass, quite lost among the ins and outs of this. What may the will of God be? I can't say."

She turned, regarded his twilit countenance, and finished contritely: "I'm sorry that my heart has run away."

Her hands reached to give his a brief embrace. And the ring exploded into light.

He lurched back with a cry. A lifted arm sought to shield his eyes. And yet the many-colored radiance which poured forth was not fiery. It filled the room like a benediction spoken in rainbows.

"The kindled sign—O Rupert, art thou nigh?" Even as she whispered, Jennifer muffled it in a fold of her dress. Fearfully she scanned out the opening. If anyone stood beneath, the flash had been too short to notice. She hastened into a far corner. "Keep silent, friend, dear friend, call not for help."

He had drawn blade. "The sigil's come awake," he said wildly. "What may it mean?"

"No harm. Thou suffered'st none today. Not so?" A quaking went through her. She fought it down, lifted her head and beckoned. "Come hither to me, Sword-of-the-Lord," she said in a strange tone. "Fear not."

He let his steel sink and walked stiff-legged. She spread her skirt to screen off the glow. Her ankles shocked him out of his first dread of witchcraft. Slowly, her left arm rose. When she pointed straight at him, the jewel rioted.

"*Thou* art my luck," she said. "The fire-gem shines for thee. I'll lay it on my breast beside thy name."

Cautiously she slipped the ring off her finger and down the front of her dress. The least light seeped out through cloth, up past bosom, to make throat, eyes, tumbled tawny hair stand forth against a dusk which seemed to have become nearly full night though sunset tarried still above roofs.

"I—thy fortune?" His weapon clattered to the floor. "How? I've tried and failed. I'd spend this penny life of mine to buy the gold of one hour's joy for Jennifer, but thou'rt too steadfast in thine angry grief."

"I think the ring's reflecting from thy soul," she said. This time she took his hands. They lay big and helpless in hers. "And here at last a chance has come for thee."

"To do what thing, my lady?" His voice cracked across.

"Set me free."

"Nay!" He seemed to make an effort to break loose. She held him. "That's impossible. Mine oath, my duty—"

Then she did let him go. "Indeed." Her words grew regretful, almost caressing. "I ought to understand a pledge. Believe me that I do, and care for thee, and merely wish that we might both have stood on one side of the wall they've built between us. Good night, dear Sword-of-the-Lord. Remember me."

"What dost thou mean?" he asked, terrified.

"Thou, being loyal, must know loyalty," she explained as if to a well-loved child. "Wouldst thou be gladly made into a thing that hunts its master down the selfsame link of plighted faith which binds them? Nor will I."

"What canst thou do?"

"This world has many doors, and resolution is their single key." (He uttered a noise.) "A sudden leap o'erboard, with emptied lungs; a poniard snatched for briefest borrowing; self-strangulation on a bit of food" —Jennifer smiled—"though that's not pretty—better, some dark night, to bite my tongue in two and then wait quiet. . . .Should one way fail, there's hundreds more to try."

He stood appalled. She stroked his cheek. "Do not think ill of me for this, my sweet," she said. "Someday, when thou hast had thy fill of earth, it may be we shall meet in Paradise and shake our heads and share a moment's laughter, half jesting and half sad, at this night's youth."

"No heaven for self-murderers, but hell," wrenched from him.

"I think not in this case—"

"Thou'rt wrong, forever!"

"Where'er the door may lead, I'll open it." Jennifer sighed. " 'Tis true, the key is cold and hard to lift. Therefore goodnight. Go. Leave me here to pray."

"To pray for strength in sin? I could not stir."

She said like a slap: "If thou must cumber me, at least keep still." In a few steps she crossed to the narrow cot and knelt beside it. Straw ticking rustled at her touch.

He stood for a moment, stumbled about for a moment, until he cried: "Nay, cease it, stop this horror, Jennifer! I'll aid thee—oh, I will, I will, I will!" He fell likewise to his knees, buried face in hands, and wept with unpracticed roughness.

She came to him, drew his head onto her breast, smoothed his hair, and murmured. He clung to her. "I knew thou wouldst," she said after a while, "less from the ring than thee."

"It is . . . the lesser sin . . . to save thy soul," he hiccoughed.

"Speak soft," she warned.

He withdrew to hunker before her and ask forlornly, "How can I bring thee past the watch?"

Her speech flew sharp. "I've thought on this, as prisoners are wont. Go out and tell the sentry that it seems I'm near repentance—'twill explain thy tears—and thou wouldst fetch thy Bible for its power. Bring back as well, though hidden, from thy chest a suit of thine own clothes; I'm near thy size. I'll don it. Then—oh, quickly, ere the moonrise!—let me down from this window to the court. Its guard, I've seen, stands not below the house but at the portal. Given ample gloom, I can be lowered nigh invisibly. But hasten!"

His mind set, he sprang up. "In thy service, lady mine." The words were bombast; the readiness wherewith he took back his sword and left the room were not.

.From the floor, Jennifer gazed after him. The ringlight glinted off tears of her own. "Oh, hard it is to use him heartlessly," she mourned, "and from its grave call forth knight-errantry."

Bells began pealing. She started. *The Angelus,* she thought. *Here in thy land of France wilt thou hear my confession, Mother Mary?*

She bowed head over close-locked hands. "I marked him for mine own. I know not how. Some fisher lads who paid some timid calls, a London 'prentice winking in the street: what more knew I of men, or they of me? I thought I saw a glint in Rupert's glance, then dared not think it of the prince, the prince. But this poor chick— My skill affrighted me. I widened eyes at his vast earnestness, then shyly fluttered them, and sighed a bit; let fingers linger when he helped dismount; drew breath and held it for to flush my cheek and swell my bosom . . . whilst I crouched alert. Tonight the ring has said there is a chance, and so I hauled him in, struck home the gaff, and mean to leave him gasping on the strand. . . . Is it a deadly sin if done for Rupert? I fear it is. My sin, my sin, not his."

She crossed herself, and remained for a time huddled silent.

The door opened. She glimpsed her guard outside, then Sword-of-the-Lord closed it again. His lungs labored but he moved fast. A moment he took to kiss the Book he bore and lay it on the bed. Jennifer had jumped erect. "I wear two suits of clothes, one 'neath the next," he told her. "Be not alarmed when I take off the first."

She had to giggle.

After he had removed shoes—drawing from his wallet a pair for her—and the outer tunic, shirt, breeches, stockings: he swung about and threw an arm across his eyes as if this were a game of hide-and-seek. "Upon mine honor, lady, I'll not look," he said, hoarse with embarrassment.

She laughed low and touched lips to his, which almost felled him. "Why, in this darkness I'm a simple blob," she said. He held his stance.

As she undressed and reclad herself behind his back, she continued: "I've bethought me of thy safety—"

"Will I not join thee?" he asked, dismayed.

" 'Tis better not. Truly. We'd have to set a rendezvous, and who knows how I must dodge about? Besides, thy disappearance—ye men share a room, don't ye?—'twould rouse quick suspicion and chase. Nay, come forth churned—thou'rt no actor—to say I refused thy ministrations after all, as if my possessor had twinned. Take to thy bed as if in sorrow o'er it. They'll question thee in the morning, of course. Say what thou wilt—the truth may be best—but declare I bewitched thee till none could ha' known what went on. They like thee well, I've marked, no matter how they bait thee. Fain'll they believe, and take the blame themselves for leaving an innocent boy thus alone with a sorceress."

"I more than half believe the thing myself," he mumbled.

Me too, she thought. *I ne'er have felt this giddiness, this swerve and swoop upon a tingling wind, save when with Rupert, and mayhap not then. Is't but I have no time to be afraid?*

"I can't let thee flee alone!" he said. "Where'lt thou go? Who'll protect thee?"

"I've thought of the English consulate. Belike 'tis Royalist, especially here in Marseilles. If not, there'll be Royalists elsewhere about. Remember, I know a bit o' French, to ask my way and— Curse whoever made men's clothes! Every single button in the wrong place. Wilt thou help? . . . Nay, don't tremble. I'm learning how. . . .Ah. Behold thy boy companion, Sword-of-the-Lord."

Jennifer moved to the window, where some light remained. The first stars were twinkling forth. He could see that his clothes hung baggy on her, which served to hide the curves beneath. A shining caught his eye.

"Thy hair," he said frantically. "I couldn't well bring a hat along, indoors, and forgot—"

"I didn't. Thou has thy steel. I've never doubted thou keepest the edge keen."

"What? Oh, nay, I beg thee!"

"Haggle these locks off short. They'll grow back on a live scalp. 'Tis false what's said about corpses: anyhow, if they fried at the stake."

He winced, took up the blade he had removed with his outer garb, and obeyed her. Then he stood dumb by starlight, holding the tresses to him.

She grinned from beneath the ragged cut. "So at last thou'st made a Roundhead of me," she said. "I ought to stroll right by their man in the gateway, if he doesn't converse." With a glance at the rooftop opposite, and its chimney starting to show silver: "That's if I'm begone in the next few minutes. Full moon this night."

"And what abroad beneath it?" He shuddered.

"Merely me. And . . . aye, thy love. Let it not live too long. Thou hast a life before thee, dear." She gave him a real kiss on the mouth. "Farewell."

In a single movement he dropped her shorn hair, caught her wrists, upheld her as she wriggled onto the sill, and lowered her down the wall. She had less than a yard to go when he released her. Already the blackness had taken her from his sight. Hanging out the window, he heard soles hit stones. Was a word blown upward to him? He couldn't tell. She was gone. He dragged himself back to stand alone in the room.

xviii

THE MARSEILLES WATERFRONT.

THE moon had lately cleared steep eastern hills. It tinged roofs, towers of forts and churches, masts of ships; westward the bay had begun to sparkle above darkness; the sky was more purple than black, stars few and small. Shadows reached thick from buildings along the docks. A breeze slid out of the north, stirring up odors of tar and fish; hawsers creaked, wavelets clucked on hulls.

A squad of the watch tramped from around one side of a warehouse. Lantern light bobbed before them, shimmered off pikes and armor. It touched a slight figure in somber, ill-fitting garments that had just turned the opposite corner.

"*Halte-là!*" barked the leader. The person froze. Dark-blond hair, white countenance and collar, made a blur in gloom. The guardsmen quick-stepped ahead. "*Qui va là?*"

"*Un anglais,*" said a high, faltering voice, "*du groupe qui a loué aujourd'hui ce bateau là.*" An arm pointed to a chebeck which lay some ways off, a lamp betokening sailors left on board against thieves.

"*Ah, oui.*" The leader gestured his men to slow down. "*Je m'en souviens. Les parpaillots.*" Contempt tinged his indifference: "*Ca va, passe, garçon!*"

Jennifer proceeded openly to cast loose the jollyboat's painter and climb down into its hull. The patrol had no reason to suppose she had any other errand than some business on the vessel to which it belonged. They soon tramped out of sight. Meanwhile, most softly, she rowed from the wharf.

When well away, she stopped and peeked in her wallet. Luminousness cascaded forth. *The ring is shining yet,* she gloried. *'Tis as I guessed. This boat's my luck*

. . . *aye, see, an unstepped mast, and wind to bear me southward where I'd seek. Where Rupert is! This night is day for me.*

Having hidden the sigil again, she got to work, deftly fitting rudder in brackets, lowering leeboard, raising and staying mast, unfurling lugsail and hoisting it on its yard. That was not an unduly hard task; the craft was quite small. Her thoughts ran on: *Poor trusting Sword-of-the-Lord, I'm truly sorry I left thee here behind to bear the brunt, and halfway lied to thee about my plan. But thou wouldst ne'er have let me put to sea, and least of all to steer in search of him. . . . My Rupert. . . . I can't help that I am glad.*

The sail flapped, filled, and bellied out. The boat swished forward. Jennifer settled herself at the tiller. *No food aboard nor water—and no fear,* she thought. *The ring will not betray me to my death. I may well suffer somewhat on the trip. What matter? I'm no longer starved for freedom, and I will drink me drunk upon salt air.*

She sobbed in her joy. Presently she felt it safe to place the circlet back on her finger. *It has not quieted its radiance. If anything, 'tis burning brighter yet, to show, I'm sure, that I have now begun a voyage leading me unto my love, and even to the triumph of the cause as dear to me as him because of him. Then be my compass, old enchanted ring.* She cocked her head and smiled into its light. *I wonder, wouldst thou care to hear me sing?*

THE QUARTERDECK OF THE TUNISIAN PINNACE.

The ship rode at anchor. To starboard was land, hills and city a-dream, minarets and moonlight making the sight into something akin to a winter forest hung with many-shaped icicles. But the air was warm, still, spiced by fragrances. To port sheened ebony sea, across which the moon cast a shivering bridge. Although high aloft, that disc seemed big, drowned most stars, flooded the deck, turned wan the lanterns hung overside.

Rupert stood by the landward rail. A racked lifeboat

screened him from view of lookouts who, in this safe resting place, were probably dozing anyway. He stared before him, shoulders hunched, knuckles on hips.

And so tonight we've come to Tunis town, he thought. *We only wait for morn to harbor there. Then what? Why did the oracle I've worn commence to burn so brightly as we neared, I thought 'twould best lie hidden in my purse: if not to tell me here I'll find my hope? But in what shape? A borrowed ducal ship whereon to seek the isle, with this for guide? I might have trouble in arranging that. The superstitions of their paynim subjects have made these Spaniards strictest Catholics. If I, a Protestant, play sorcerer—*

A suggestive silken rustle brought his attention around. Belinda came to his side. She had cast her shawl back off a gown cut outrageously low. From her hair and skin lifted an aroma of roses and—something else, disturbing, arousing—or was it simply an older moon-magic than rested in Rupert's wallet which had made her not patrician any more, but elven?

"Why . . . greeting," he said, his voice pitched to the silence. "I . . . I thought thee long abed. And here thou'rt festive clad."

"To celebrate our journey's end? Well, in a certain way." Her eyes searched his. "I must pretend to gaiety at that—aye, to myself I must—that we've come home and I shall be no more a traveler but once again a very proper duchess."

"I may not yet proclaim myself a prince." He shrugged. "But then, I've not been one in aught than name since infancy."

She took his arm. "Thou dost deserve it, Rupert. Nay, more than that. The empire of the world!"

Even in this witchy glow, he could be seen to flush. "Thou art too kind," he said. "Thou hast been ever kind. For me, our voyage was a timeless time of peace and . . . pleasure . . . in thy company."

"And I—what can I say?" She hugged his arm to her. "Must thou go on in hardship and in peril of thy life?" A slim hand curved toward shore. "There's sanctuary, where thou art beloved."

He shook his head; the black locks flew. "My King —my quest—"

"What is't thou seekest, Rupert?" She leaned against him. "*Querido,* thou canst tell me if none else." She brought his arm around her waist.

His tone harshened: "Can I tell any soul?"

"Not even me?" she asked sadly. "It hurts to stand untrusted, thrust aside, and see the hollowness within thy heart which I would gladly fill to overflowing."

He sought to move from her, but she came along like the air itself. He almost made to pluck her off by force, then let his free hand drop. She reached across him to take it.

"Thou'st helped me past all reckoning, Belinda—"

"And in return, ask merely to help more. Nor will I pry into thy privacies. Yet think: without some tiny sign of thanks, the will must wilt, and thou must fare unaided."

She pressed nearer. Fists clamped at sides, he kept his look rigid above her head and stated, "He's not alone whose honor rides along." Sweat stood forth on his face. "I warn thee, nay, I beg thee, tempt no further."

Her laughter blew breeze-soft. "Then by my gallant knight I'm spurned, to boot? Well, I'm the duchess here and do forbid."

"Belinda, leave me be! They call me rash, but that lies many leagues from lunacy."

"*La luna.* . . . 'Tis a moonstruck night in truth, our last when we may simply be ourselves." She brought her body against his. "Cast off thy heaviness. It is so light, so soaring light, so drenched with light, this night." Waving around: "It chimes with moonlight in each bell of dew, it tones and trembles clear across the sea, it rings off stars, it hushes over us like finest fall of rain in blossom time." Her fingers returned to pass through his locks. "Our flesh is spun of moonbeams and the air; the dawn of death will strew its frailty; but on this night it dances under heaven. Awake to joyousness in what thou art, a fleeting trick of moonlight in the dark. How long the moon has waited to wax full, how soon again 'twill be a haggard crescent, and afterward a dream to haunt the new! Our tide is at the flood, my dearest dear."

Neither could tell who started the kiss.

"I thought the siege I laid would never end," she said finally, rapturously.

His answer was thick: "Old Adam plays me false—"

"No conscience pangs," she scolded in tenderness, touching his lips. "If thou must imitate a Puritan, why, think of earning goodwill for thy cause."

"I'd liefer think of lovely thee. And . . . well, why should a heathen rite keep me fast bound against the need my King is in for help? It could be but a marsh-light that I bear—"

She nuzzled him. "Enough of babblement. Let's to thy room. The pagan who has conquered thee is Cupid." Fresh laughter. "He says to render up thy sword to me."

Like a blind man, he followed her below.

THE LION GULF.

No land was in sight. The jollyboat bounded on long quick-silver seas, beneath a moon which had passed its height and begun to sink. Jennifer's beacon made a Joseph's coat of its canvas. Not sleepy, though a little cold, she kept the helm and sang:

> *A sailor fares a lonely way.*
> *His lass is lonely too.*
> *She yearns horizonward by day,*
> *Where there is only blue,*
> *Or only gulls are winging white,*
> *Like sails across the sky.*
> *She hears alone, alone at night*
> *The wind's 'Ahoy!' go by.*
>
> *"The sun will come, the sun will go,*
> *The year will have no rest,*
> *The blood will ebb, the blood will flow*
> *Within the maiden's breast,*
> *Till springtime blows from oversea*
> *To gust against the shore,*
> *And spindrift green across a tree*
> *Says he'll come back once more.*
>
> *He will—"*

Her ditty broke in a scream. The serpent stone had gone out. A moment later, the draught lost steadiness, veered around and around, faded toward dead calm. Helpless, a sliver in the middle of wet nothing, the boat drifted.

XIX

A LIBRARY.

THE room was Moorish, ogive windows full of night, gilt arabesque friezes dimly picked out of shadow by the flames in a single candelabrum. Everywhere loomed shelves piled high with scrolls and codices. Dust was upon them, cobwebs joined them, rats went scuttering behind. The robe and white beard of the caretaker who dozed on a stool in a corner seemed nearly as overlaid by time's grime.

The light came from a table where Rupert sat. Works lay stacked and strewn across it. He wore slippers, hose, a shirt with sleeves rolled up and open halfway down his chest because of the heat. Sweat muddied the scholarly dirt which had rubbed off on him; he reeked of it. Unshaven, uncombed, eyes red and sunken, he skimmed book after musty book, shoved one aside and started the next. An occasional line arrested him; he would trace each word, mutter the sentences, most often shake his head and swear.

Will Fairweather shuffled in. His lankiness was also skimpily clad in European style, save for cavalry boots and saber. He bore a tray of meat, soft flat bread, carafes of wine and water, two goblets. "General," he said. "General, it be me."

Rupert remained unaware till the man's great nose virtually thrust itself between him and his text. At that he blinked, leaned back, and said in a vague tone, "Oh. Will. What's this?"

"This," was the firm reply as the tray came down on Ovid's *Metamorphoses,* "be food. In case tha general ha' forgotten, food be good to eat. Tha' zay it be a meal in itzelf. Eat, zir, an' drink. Thic be an order."

Rupert shook his head. "I have no hunger." He bridled. "And who'rt thou to give me orders?"

Will folded himself into a chair across the table, laid shank over thigh, and flapped an expansive gesture. "Zir, God an' tha laws o' war ha' commanded zartin rights an' zartin duties for overloard an' underlin' boath. I knows my plaece. It be not for me to speak o' strategy —nor tactics, though o' coua'se, in carryin' out of a command, a plain man-at-arms may fiand it wisest if 'a doan't bespeak small changes made for, hm, practical reasons what wouldn't interest a general. Zo, if my measter will stay buried in this heare li-berry o' tha duke's, bloody-be-damn ever zince we landed this mornin', an' snarl at tha duchess when she come bid him taeke zome rest, till she went off in tears . . . why, 'a could court-martial me did I *pro*-test."

He launched into his peroration. "But grub, now, grub, zir, thic's by God's grant tha common zoldier's lawful conzern; nor man nor angel may zircumspect his riaght of free speech where't regards his belly; I make no doubt Joshua's troops entered tha Promised Land complainin' o' tha bad milk an' worse honey what war issued them. Thus, I can zay what I liake on feedin', an' what I zay be that if tha general doan't taeke this heare charge an' ram it down his muzzle, 'a's false to them what ha' need o' his fiere."

A reluctant smile twitched Rupert's lips. "'Tis late indeed."

"Past midnight. Should'a heard tha butler when I kicked him out o' bed! Not that I followed his speech, but 'a opened tha spigot for sure. I 'splained what I wanted in zign language, includin' tha flat o' my blaede 'cross his hindquarters, an' . . . here it be, measter. For everybody's zake, eat," Will pleaded.

Rupert rubbed his eyes. "A sound idea, no doubt. Lord knows thou makest abundant sound about it."

"An' afterward go to sleep."

"Nay. Although my search is proving so barren I might almost as well."

"What dost thou zeek?" Will filled a goblet with wine and water and thrust it into Rupert's grasp.

The prince drank, scarcely noticing. "Our goal: since in my folly I cast away the compass given by a hand which trusted me." His voice was rough and stiff.

Will nodded at the ring and its ordinary-looking jewel. "I thought as much. Last night—tha duchess, ha?—aye, tha zigns war plain on her today. An' what's wrong in thic, pray tell?"

Rupert stared into darkness. "I told myself at the time," rattled from him, "insofar's I thought in any wise through that sudden torrent of lust . . . I told myself my pledge of faith to Jennifer Alayne was meaningless, no proper betrothal, no Christian oath; rather, the whole thing could be a snare of hell, and I skirting damnation. But when at last, near dawn, Belinda slunk from me, back to my befriender I'd cuckolded—" He covered his face. "I saw this darkness in the stone, and my soul had become a stone as dead."

"Oh, General! Talk zense, I beg thee!" Will leaned over the table to clasp a bowed shoulder. "Maybe thou didst maeke a mistaeke. Well, art thou zo unchristianly proud as to think human stumbles o' thine be few an' terrible enough that heaven quaekes? Bezides, 'twould not surprise me if tha duchess used a love potion to o'ercome thee in the end; I've heard o' zuch things in theezam parts. Though as for parts . . . why, thou'rt young an' full-blooded. Thou'd'st been a monk for I know not how long ere we zet north, whereafter thou wert zoon an' always kept aware o' mine own artillery at work, click o' tha cockin', snap o' tha hammerfall, thump an' bang o' tha flyin' balls. No moare magic than this miaght've been needful, an' small wonder if at last thou didst fall; though't might be better I bespeak a girt wonder which did ariase. Liake I heard a learned man zay once, abstinence maekes tha font grow harder."

"Spare me," Rupert said. "Leave me alone to do what little I can toward repairing the disaster."

"*If* thou'lt stoake thyzelf."

Rupert nodded, rolled bread around a slab of meat, and chewed. "Thic's better," Will said. "Uh, if we've lost use of our guide, can we carry on?"

Rupert winced. "I can try . . . to seek my goal—Prospero's isle—by mortal means. The odds are less than poor for finding it and, should I find it, gaining aught thereby. Yet what else can I do?"

"We, my loard."

"Thanks for fidelity too deep to need thanks."

Whether because of nourishment or encouragement, the prince's manner regained some of its iron: "My reasoning goes thus. Six decades ago, Duke Prospero of Milan and his infant daughter were made captive by his usurping brother. He had them taken secretly to sea— *'some leagues,'* says the Historian—and there put into a derelict, *'a rotten carcass of a butt, not rigged, nor tackle, sail, nor mast; the very rats instinctively have quit it.'* Now this must have been a ship, not large, but not a boat either. We have the description, as well's the fact there was stowage for the arcane books and other goods which kindly Gonzalo managed to give the duke along. Nonetheless, it must have drifted at mercy of wind and wave, slowly sinking. What minor magics Prospero could wield at that time no doubt aided him to strand safely. However, considering the starting point and the condition of the vessel, the island he found must lie somewhere between Italy and Spain."

"H'm." Will rubbed his bristles, which made a scratchy noise across the snores of the old librarian. "Thou'st skimped talk o' this to me. But than, we'd thin time for talk till we boarded for our own v'yage; an' thic —Ne' miand. What happened laeter?"

"Oh, Prospero and Miranda dwelt there till he had by his studies become a mighty wizard and she was a young lady. At last his false brother chanced nigh. He'd been with the party which married Claribel, the daughter of his overlord the King of Naples, to the King of Tunis— she who's dowager queen here. By his arts and the aid of a servant spirit, Prospero caused the ship to be driven to his shore, and played such tricks as taught repentance. Finally, when all could be forgiven, he returned to rule again in Milan, while his daughter married the crown prince of Naples—aye, they're the same King Ferdinand and Queen Miranda who reign there still. Prospero practiced no more sorceries for the rest of his life, being mainly concerned with preparing himself for the next one. In fact, he'd abandoned his magical articles on the island." Rupert paused before finishing: "Oberon's thought was that we might recover and use them."

Will shivered despite the heat. "An uncanny quest forzooth. Well, I've aye found All Hallows Eve good for rangin', sine gaemekeepers stay indoors throughout thic night. Know'st thou where this plaece may be?"

"Hardly closer than I've said. Islands are not plentiful in the western Mediterranean Sea. However, Oberon's people failed to find it. Therefore I think it has a magic of its own, including a girdle of invisibility. Mariners espy naught save empty waves, unless by sheer chance they come within a certain close distance. That may well have happened from time to time, men may actually have made landings, though they could never quite find it again, given their primitive navigation in earlier ages. I wonder if it may once have been Calypso's isle, or Circe's—" Rupert's words trailed off.

"An' thou'rt ranzackin' tha records for mentions what might pw'int tow'rd it?" Will asked. (Rupert nodded.) "Winnin' scant booty, zeems liake. How much longer'll thou taeke?"

"A week should exhaust this library."

"An' thee, 'speci'lly if thou'lt not eat. Chomp, measter! What's thy scheame afterward?"

"I'll buy a boat." Rupert's fingernails whitened where he clutched the table edge. "Belinda's money; my penance." Decisive again: "A small craft, which two can man. We'll need no more, in this sea and season. Why add risk of betrayal, when word of my coming here must soon reach agents of our enemies? We'll crisscross the area of possibility, starting at the likeliest parts, until—" He bit savagely into the food.

"Till tha year grows too oald; or King Charles be beaten; or zomething drags us under," Will said. "An' liake thou toald, our odds be none I caere to waeger a clipped farthin' on. Well, Oberon an' Titania loaded tha dice in our faevor, last time. Maybe now tha' can hit on a way for shufflin' that spots around. If not—" He shrugged. "There be no other gaeme, hey?"

THE JOLLYBOAT.

It rocked to a slow swell beneath a cloudless sky.
Apart from that motion, the water might have been
green and blue glass. Westward heaven stood gray-violet
around a sinking moon, eastward whitened by a sun not
yet risen. The air was cool, but barely gave steerage
way; the sail hung more slack than taut, often flapping
as the yard slatted about.

Jennifer half sat, half sprawled in the sternsheets. Her
hands were raw on tiller and cordage, the lips in her
burnt face had cracked open to the dry blood, eyes
smoldered emptily beneath swollen lids.

A night at sea, a day, another night, she thought, *and
here's another dawn. Will I see dusk? How long till
thirst will free me from itself?* Her neck let go. As chin
struck chest she gasped back to consciousness. *I must
not sleep! Impossible at best to tack along that course
the ring once pointed . . . through shifty winds or none,
and unknown currents, by sun, moon, stars unlike the
stars of home, observed through haze of weariness and
scorch . . . impossible surely if I fall asleep.*

She cleated the line she held and scratched in salt-
stiffened hair. *My skull's quite hollow— Nay, there is
much sand within the shriveled kernel of my brain.
Have I gone mad? Am I indeed possessed? This scow's
not even very good at tacking. I know no longer where I
am, or why. I ought to make for shore, where'er 'tis
nearest—whichever way that is, unless too late—not
plod eternally to seek a Dutchman whose own witch-pi-
lot somehow must have died.*

She raised her head, though it went slowly. *Why,
there's my reason! How could I forget for e'en a minute? If the spell has failed, he too may be bewildered
and beset. With God all things are possible, they say, although, of course, the most of them unlikely; thus it may
be I'll find him—help him—find him— If not, I died in
trying, like a soldier.*

She turned the helm a trifle, seeking the most use out
of what breeze she had.

A swirl in the water drew her look. *Why, 'tis a dolphin,* she realized. Aloud, a croak forced from leathery

mouth and tongue: "Greeting, Master Dolphin! Good
morrow to thee. Come, I bid thee welcome. The antics
of thy kind beside this hull, the liquid lightning beauty
of their pace, have helped me keep my reason and my
life. God loves the world; He gave it dolphins— Oh!"

That was a parched scream. For the swimmer had
drawn alongside, arced up in a cataract of spray, caught
the first sunbeams on spear-bright flanks, and shimmered into something else.

Jennifer shrank back. The one who perched on the
middle thwart laughed. The sound was like bells, heard
far away across summer meadows through dawn-dreams
when she was a child; and he sang more than spoke:

"I thank thee for thine invitation, lady, and do accept
with pleasure. Pardon me if I surprised thee when I
doffed my cloak. I have no few of them—as this—"

Abruptly a dragonfly hovered, the absoluteness of
blue. "Or this," it said, and a dove preened an iridescent
breast. "Or this"—a young man, brown, golden-curled,
in a brief white tunic, strumming a lyre, wings on his
cap and sandals—"or this"—a vortex of radiance, not
unlike what had come from the ring before it faded, but
whirling, whirling—"or this," the being said, and returned to the first shape taken aboard, "or many more."

"What sending art thou," Jennifer's words dragged,
"and from where, and why?"

"Am I so terrifying in thy sight?" he teased. "I can
become a gorgon if thou'd'st liefer."

Her breathing began to slow. Certainly his aspect
could in itself only charm: a boy of seven or eight years,
slenderness clad in breechclout and a lily garland across
the fair locks, eyes big and cornflower-colored in a
countenance dusted with freckles—but less than a foot
tall, and winged like a butterfly which had been pat-
terned on a tiger in a field of gillyvor.

No matter his minuteness, she could easily hear him,
and read the concern which crossed his features: "Wait.
Thou hast sailed too near the edge, I see. No babe has
drained thee, but a red-hot vampire, and thou art more
a mummy than a mother. Abide a moment."

He was gone. She stared, opened and closed her
mouth, could get forth no noise. Untended, the rudder

waggled idle, the yard-arm rattled, and the sail spilled its wind.

A footman appeared before her. "Milady, tea is served," he intoned, set a tray on the after thwart, and became the boy-spirit, perched gleefuly in the bows.

She gaped. A pot of China ware steamed upon the brass, next to an eggshell-thin cup; there were plates of cheese, raisins, cakes; beside a pitcher of milk stood one of water, both bedewed from their coldness, and an honest clay mug to pour full.

"Quaff slowly, nibble, till thou'rt wont to life," he warned.

"I know," she answered, "but know not how to thank thee. . . . Oh, thou'st naught against a prayer?"

"Nay, I'll join."

Reassured, she knelt for minute, as he did in the foresheets. Meanwhile the sun had come wholly in flight and the sea lay a-flash.

With wondering care, Jennifer started to drink and eat. Her rescuer found a comfortable position against the gunwale, kicked his heels, and said:

"No doubt thou'rt curious about this business. Well, I am Ariel, the airy spirit who once served Prospero upon that isle which thou'st been dogging, till he slipped me free." Her stupefaction sent him into a gale of mirth. "I read thy mind. Fear not. 'Tis very pure." He grew solemn. "And thus I learned how Faerie's faring ill. I've kept myself too long in isolation—lost track of time, mine island is so pleasant. Now must I help thy cause and Oberon's. Else might erelong the foe bestride my holm, his iron passionlessly ravish her, then flense the daisies from her dying flesh and on her bones erect a countinghouse."

"As has been happening in England," she said between cautious, marveling sips. "Rupert—"

"What's in a name?" Ariel scoffed. "Well, names can be important. They should have made him Ernest. Ah, no matter. He clumps well-meaning, if on heavy hoofs. Myself, I like thee better, Jennifer."

"Speak never ill of him!" she flared.

"That's what I like," nodded Ariel.

"But . . . he's alive and hale?"

"Aye."

"God be praised." Were she not desiccated, she would have wept.

After a while, during which he conjured a sparkling ball into existence, bounced it on his fingertips, and dismissed it, Ariel went on: "Thou know'st our Faerie powers are but slight—illusions, apparitions, some few tricks, forecastings which the stream of time may drown, a whisper of ambiguous advice. Outside mine eyot, I'm a spy, no more. Not only would I not have known of thee, I could not aid thee as I'm doing now hadst thou not by thyself come near my home. Nor can I resurrect those mighty things whereby Duke Prospero first saved, then bound me. I can but show thee where he sank them down, and mortal muscles which may help thee—"

"Rupert?"

Ariel grimaced. "Nay, he sits deep inside a shell of books. I have no strength to winkle him from them, for that whole palace has an iron frame to fence off magic, which its builders feared." Seeing her crestfallen: "However, by himself he'll soon creep forth. Meanwhile, I know how it has fretted thee about the lad who cut thy chains in twain and thus did leave his sword unscabbarded. Well, he is in no danger. His companions agree thou didst bewitch his innocence, and anyway, have too much else to think of." He grinned. "The owner of this boat demands its price of them—a sum left float to bloat, I'm sure—since watchmen state a Puritan did steal it, and furthermore insists on partial rental, although 'tis clear they'll never use his ship. He threatens lawsuit; whilst they speak no French!" He beat the thwart and whooped.

"How dost thou know these things?" Jennifer wondered.

"The span of time I took to fetch you rations, was enough to follow up the clues within thy mind." Ariel began to sing: *"Where the eaves drop, there drop I—"* but broke off in apology. "Ah, nay, I pray thy delicacy pardon each single second sere and useless here within this furnace hole of movelessness. I'll bring an oil which heals all burns at once." His words rose to a cry. "Now from the deeps for thee let whirl a wind, lass!"

He flung an arm aloft. The air brawled to life, the waters beneath it. Sail suddenly filled, the boat sprang forward.

XX

THE ISLAND.

HILLS lifted high from wide white beaches and intimate coves. They were bedecked with forest—here pine and juniper, there tall hardwoods—or meadows star-sky full of flowers. Springs gave rise to brooks which tumbled over moss-softened cobbles and rang down cliffsides. Odors of growth, blossom, sun-warmed resin drenched the air. It was always singing, for wings were overhead in the thousands: chirrup, trill, carol, and chant.

Ariel's medicines had already brought Jennifer close to full recovery. She followed an upward trail. Cathedral coolness dwelt beneath the branches which vaulted it. Sunbeams dissolved into green and gold in those leaves, or reached the earth and minted coins among the shadows. The sprite flitted around and around her. Occasionally he zipped aside to startle a ladybird, play tag with a robin, or drain the dew lingering in an orchid cup.

"And have I died," she asked at last in a sleepwalker's voice, "to find this Paradise?"

"Nay, it is earthly, though thou well hast earned it." Ariel descended to perch on her shoulder. "Is not the whole wide world itself an Eden, and man himself its snake and fiery guardian? The first and foremost miracle thou'lt find, here too as elsewhere, is thy living flesh. That it may get its due, I'm guiding thee toward the cell that Prospero had carved from out a bluff, to house him and his girl. We'll quickly sweep and garnish it for thee, and heap sweet boughs and grasses for thy bed."

He quivered his wings as he went eagerly on: "Thou'lt find the island fare we bring not simple. Each well we tap has its own icy tang, each honeycomb's uniquely from one field, each grape's most subtly blent of sun, earth, rain, while truffles taste of treasures buried deep and mushrumps have the smack of shade and damp, to emphasize the cunning of an herb or quench the acrid ardor of a leek as apple tartness is made soft by pears. That's but to name a few of many plants. Our crabs and lobsters clack self-praise enough; the oysters rightly feel they need no boast. Soon hazelnuts and quinces will be ripe, and I could hymn what hymeneal things occur when they are introduced to trout. I think I shall—"

"A moment, pray, kind sir," Jennifer interrupted. She was coming out of her daze. "Thou speak'st of 'we.' Who else dwells hereabouts?"

Ariel arched his brows. "Who dost thou think? . . . And here he comes to meet me."

Jennifer cried aloud in shock.

The being which shambled around a bend in the path seemed twice hideous against woods, birds, and elf. He was roughly manlike, somewhat beneath her in height. That was partly due to the shortness of his bowlegs, partly to his hunched stance, for the shoulders were broad. Arms dangled past knees; like the splay feet, they ended in black-rimmed unclipped nails. A matted white shock of hair disguised, at first, how small his head was. It had no brow or chin; the eyes crouched deep in great caverns of bone, the face was mostly muzzle, flat nose and gash of a mouth. His skin, sallow and brown-spotted, was covered by nothing save a filthy loincloth.

"Be not affrighted," said Ariel: "neither one of ye."

The creature's jaw dropped, showing tushes which must once have been fearsome but were now a few yellow snags. "What is?" he asked hoarsely. "What fetch is this thou fetched—" Abruptly he bawled *"Miranda!"* and cast himself forward and down.

Jennifer braced body and spirit. The monster groveled at her ankles. Through his head and his clasping arms she was shaken by his weeping.

"'Tis merely Caliban," Ariel told her through the ragged sobs, "these many years quite harmless, or at least in check to me. I do confess his outburst's a surprise."

"Who's Caliban?" Her nose wrinkled at the animal rankness rising about her.

"He's a foul witch's whelp, that Prospero did find when small, and taught to speak a tongue thou hear'st as English here—and raised to be a servant unto him. A nasty, surly, sneaky one he was, who at the end sought to betray his lord, but soon got tipsy, reeled through foolishness, and later ululated his regret. When Prospero released me and went home, he left this hulk behind as well. What use a Caliban in Italy, except to be such butt of japes and bait of dogs as to ignite his flimsy wits in rage, and make him pluck someone apart, and hang? So he's grown old alone upon the isle, save now and then when I, in quest of sport or in an idle kindliness, pay calls and make mirages for his entertainment."

"Miranda, oh, Miranda," grated the monster, and lifted his wet visage toward Jennifer's.

Ariel fluttered off to regard her. "Nay, thou'rt not," he deemed. "Aside from clothes, cropped hair, and all the rest, thou'rt fairer than she was, more tall— Ah, well. She was the only maid he ever saw, and in the many years between, though begged, I never thought it proper to bring back the darling semblance in a show for him." He pondered what appeared to be a new thought. "So ghosts do age and change in mortal wise?"

Shuddering still, Caliban got up. He flung arms widely and wildly, drummed his breast, broke off at every few words to give a bark of pain. "Thou art not a Miranda? But thou art! This must be a Miranda, Ariel. Thou'rt clever in the tinting of the air, but never has thou wrought a dream like this. Behold how sweetly curved, how finely carved! Thou hast no skill to melt and mold a moonbeam and taper it to make those hands of hers. Couldst thou invent that vein within her throat, as blue as shadow on a sunlit cloud? What melody of thine could sing her walk? And—oh, I'm sorry for thee, Ariel!—thou hast no nose like mine, to drink the breeze that she perfumes; thou knowest common roses, while I could drowse a million happy years within the summer meadow of her breath. Her cheeks are soft as sleep. . . . Lie not to me! I've not forgotten what Mirandas are, and this Miranda's real—is real—is real!"

He began to hop about, chattering, slavering, baring what was left of his teeth at the sprite. "Thou shalt not take away this new Miranda!" he screamed. "Thou squirrel, raven, thievish heartless mocker, hast thou not hoarded up bright gauds enough that I may keep one realness of mine own? Come down, thou insect! See, my gape stands wide and bids thee enter—though 'twill spit thee out to make a meal for blowflies!"

"Caliban," said Ariel sternly, "thou'rt overheated as of yore." To Jennifer, who had backed off in alarm: "I'll quench him."

A whine whirled over the path. Ariel became a tiny thunderhead through which leaped needles of toy light-ning. Caliban yammered, raised arms for shield, and crouched. Rain and hail flogged him, bolts jagged into his skin. It was a harmless punishment, to judge by the lack of wounds, but painful, to judge by how he jerked and wailed.

"Don't hurt him more," Jennifer pleaded after a min-ute. "His hair's too white for this."

Ariel resumed his usual shape. Caliban lay snuffling. "Why, it was mild," said the sprite. "I've felt much worse than it myself when riding on the rampant gales." As Caliban dared look at him: "Methinks this is the first of any time thou hast been pitied, since thou wast a pup. Thou might give thanks for that."

The creature crawled back to his feet. Jennifer saw how he winced, not at the chastisement he had taken, but at the ache of age within his bones. "I do, I do," he rumbled abjectly. "Aye, sweetness goes with being a Mi-randa." He tugged his forelock and attempted a bow in her direction. "Be not afraid. 'Tis I'm afraid of thee. When I was young, and with the first Miranda, I own I terrified her tenderness, but none had taught me better how to be. The thoughts do drop and trickle very slow through this thick bone that sits atop my chine. Nathe-less I've had a deal of years to brood on how 'tis best Mirandas be adored. I'll clean thy place each day, and bring it flowers, and chop thee plenty firewood, scrub the pots, lie watchdog at thy feet, and if thou wilt, show thee a secret berry patch I have. Or anything, Miranda. Only tell."

"Come," said Ariel. "Let us go prepare for her that cell."

A BOAT AT SEA.

It was a tartane, sharp-snouted and bowspritted, rigged with a jib and a lateen mainsail. That made it less handy than the Dutch jachts Rupert knew; but a boom would have crashed onto an outsize crate near the middle of the mostly open hull. Boxes and casks of supplies left scant room for two men to stretch their mattresses. This was a noontide of white-streaked violet waves beneath a thrumming breeze and overwhelming sun.

Will Fairweather had the helm. At the port rail, feet braced wide apart, Rupert wielded an astrolabe. A sudden yaw nearly threw him. Canvas banged. "The Devil snatch thee bald!" he roared. "Three days o' this, and still thou canst not hold her steady as she goes whilst I take a sight?"

"She be navigated to start with," Will answered sullenly, "aye, gaited liake tha drunkest navvy thou e'er didst meet. There be none o' thic black magic thou maekest in thy tools an' charts an' almanacs an' scrubbin' o' logarhymes—there be none of it goin' to do moare'n show us where we war. No tellin' where this slut'll *be*."

"The fault, brute steersman, lies not in her spars but in thyself." Rupert sighed. "However, I admit to a less than masterly job of placing us. Was there no modern equipment anywhere in Tunis? Had I even a decent timepiece, let alone one of those new-invented sextants—"

"What? General, I doubt anybody's invented aught new in thic line zince Zodom an' Gomorrah." Will wiped the sweat from his forehead. "Three days we been faerin'? Three liafetimes, moare like."

"I'd spend them if necessary—and if we had them. As 'tis, we can take perhaps a month casting about, nigh sure to be futile, before the fall storms force us ashore."

"Aye, zo thou'st zaid. An' than we return to fiaght, eh? From what tha English ambassador's butler toald me, our King's cause won't zelebrate another Christmas. Which means nobody can. How be liafe in Holland?"

"They're tolerant of religion, if not of whatever might stand in the way of their merchants' profits." Rupert spoke absently, while taking the sun's altitude and recording it together with clock time and compass bearing. "On that account, I fear the machines will overwhelm their land within few years."

"Well, I hear it be flat, open, an' even wetter nor England. I listened once to zome Dutchmen talk. Why be it tha French be called frogs? I swear nobody can hoot, hawk, an' gargle thic language what ha'n't got a built-in coald in his throat. Thus, small loss, a country-zide what never held any magic."

"But it did," Rupert said low. "It does to this day. The sorcerers bear names like Frans Hals or Rembrandt van Rijn—"

"Hoy!" Will shouted. The instruments clattered from Rupert's grasp.

A flash overhead had become a boy, tiny but perfect, who skimmed on butterfly wings and chimed forth laughter.

Will let go the helm and grabbed for his sword. Rupert waved him to stay seated. It blazed from the prince: "What apparition art thou, and from whence? No angel, surely—we're not worthy that—but know, if demon, we are Christian men. Yet if a messenger from Faerie land"—he lifted his arms—"behold the ruined lodestar which I bear. I freely own my fault, and to thee, elf, plead for my King alone, not for myself."

"Art thou indeed Prince Rupert of the Rhine?" the sprite teased. "She called thee taciturn, a warrior. So dost thou boom like this for want of cannon?"

Rupert let his hands drop, empty, and said wonderingly into the wind: "She?"

"Jennifer Alayne—" the figure seemed to enjoy seeing them thunderstruck, but went on in a brisk tone: "who asked I seek thee when thou wert safely far from other folk, and bring thee to the island where she is. I'm Ariel, who once served Prospero."

"Her?" Rupert choked. "Jennifer?"

The fullness of wonder was more quick to break upon Will. "Thy luck ha' turned at last—turned zouthward, for she's ever been thy luck." He sprang to slap his master's roughly-clad back. "Let's uptails all—whate'er one does on boats, liake bilge tha strakes, belay tha mast, rake yards, bound mains, whate'er will maeke this damn thing move! If zuch a girl awaited me, I'd faere on bugle winds, wi' sheets o' flaeme for zails."

"Aye," said Rupert. "Oh, aye. . . .But we must render thanks to God."

"First set my course and get well under weigh," Ariel advised. "I'll reappear from time to time to guide thee, although the zephyr's fair and will improve. Tomorrow late thou'lt come unto the isle and Jennifer." Pointedly: "Why dost thou never smile?"

"How came she here? I thought her safe, I swear!"

"I promised ere I soared into the air, no other lips than hers would tell thee this." Ariel gave Rupert a long and thoughtful regard before he added: "A very unpretending kind of kiss." Cometlike, he rushed high and ahead, pointing. "Steer yonderwards!" he cried. "This time thou shalt not miss!"

THE ISLAND.

A bay faced west to where the sea burned and shimmered with eventide. It was as if the forest behind the beach drank down those level beams and gave them back in a glow of its own. The heights further on were tinged lilac. Woodbine fragrances passed through salt freshness. Little save drowsy bird-voices broke the quiet. High overhead went a flight of wild swans.

Rupert's boat could not be drawn ashore as readily as Jennifer's. He cast anchor in the shallows, leaped overside and waded to her. Save for the mangled hair, she had cast off the marks of her journey. The boy's garb was scrubbed clean, its darkness relieved by a wreath of marigold. Her hands were crossed before her and silent tears ran down her face.

Neither of them heeded hovering Ariel or squatting Caliban. Rupert strode to tower above her and whisper in his helplessness: "Why dost thou weep, most dear?"

"For pain of joy," she said as softly and unevenly. "Too much of joy is riving me apart and kindling every fragment that it strews, to make me into stars and crown thy brow."

"Nay, thou'rt my queen, and I a beggar come to ask

thy healing touch, here where I kneel"—he sank before her—"in tatters of buffoonery and pride. If thou wilt cure me of my faithlessness, and then bestow the customary coin—thou canst well spare it, for thy treasury strikes endless burnished ones like it each day, and 'Honor' is the stamp—why, I will then begin to understand what's royalty."

"O Rupert, raise thy heart!" She stroked his bent head, over and over. " 'Tis no more right that thou be humbled than the sun. Arise."

"That burnt-out ring upon thy finger there burns me into the brain," he mumbled.

"Pray, pray do not make me rip loose and cast away thy sign! The hand itself would come off easier." She tried hard to laugh. "Though if thou must in truth reclaim this ring, why, take the hand therewith—and all things else."

Then he summoned courage to stand and offer her his embrace.

Caliban growled. "Go easy," Ariel warned. "She's not for the likes of thee."

The monster slumped. "I know." Shyly: "She touched mine arm this afternoon. Right here it was. I'd brought her oranges. She smiled and thanked me, and she touched me here. I went away and bellowed for an hour. Yet . . . nay. I'm old and ugly and foul-humored. That is the strangest thing, this being trapped—not in this body or the rot o' years—that doesn't matter much; but in my soul."

Will's disembarkation took his mind elsewhere. "Ha, ha, I'm not the only freak around!" he hooted. "Who'rt thou that walkest thin as sparrowgrass behind yon red cucumber of a nose?"

"Well, not a mildew-spotted calabash," drawled the Englishman. "I think I know thee from my measter's taele. Now come an' sniff mine own."

Caliban edged toward him, stiff-legged and bristling. "Be careful, cur. I'll haul thy bowels forth to make thy leash."

"What kiand o' hospitality be this?" Will complained to Ariel. "I need zome help in shiftin' stuff ashoare"— he winked—"liake, zay, a brandy cask we got along."

"What? Brandy?" Caliban stopped and gaped. "Uh
. . . a fiery juice like sack? I do recall—Stephano—
Trinculo— My welcome, welcome friend, of course I'll
help!" Hugging Will: "My tongue is rough, till brandy
wash the sand off. Forgive my jest about thy splendid
nose. 'Tis lovely, like a mountain peak, a sunset!"

Ariel sighed. "Well, do your singing here upon the
beach," he ordered, "that only whales and screech owls
need to flee." He cast a glance at Rupert and Jennifer,
who were starting hand in hand on the upward trail. "I
wonder if those two would ever notice."

PROSPERO'S CELL.

Clay lamps in fanciful shapes stood on shelves to illu-
minate rough-hewn, crystal-sparkling walls behind them,
floor strewn with rushes, a few plain wooden utensils and
articles of furniture, a pair of beds made from juniper
branches and hay. A bast curtain hung in the entrance
conserved warmth. Rupert's voice drifted through:

"Aye, we have well-nigh talked the night away. King
Charles's Wain goes wheeling tow'rd the morn."

"I hope that is a sign," Jennifer answered. "Although
the chill—"

"Both come about this hour. Let's back inside. The
time is overpast for thee to sleep."

"Oh, I've been whirling in ecstatic dreams. Must I already waken into slumber?"

They passed by the curtain, which rustled. Rupert
had to stoop beneath the ceiling. Jennifer led him to a
spot where more green branches had been stacked for a
backrest. They sat down, she leaning against him. He
laid an arm around her, but instead of sharing her smile,
he stared somberly before him.

"Unknowing hast thou flicked a whip of truth," he
said. "What holds thee is mere sin-corrupted flesh.
Dream-Rupert rises from thyself alone like dawn-mists
off an alpine lake."

She caressed him. "Do hush! How often must I say
that Ariel has found a magic potion worked on thee?"

"But there were hankerings that worked with it."

"And what of that? Thou'rt no mere piece of sculpture. A statue does not fall, but never strides, nor yearns, nor plucks a springtime bunch of may to give a girl that it may care about." Hastily: "Wound me no longer with this wound of thine. If thou hast any debt at all to me, repay it now by speaking of tomorrow."

"Tomorrow—well—" He squared his shoulders and forced crispness into his tone. "Thou'st shown the broken staff of Prospero, which Caliban dug up, at Ariel's direction and thy wish, from the deep grave where he had rooted it. Know'st thou how it may be made whole again?"

He did not see how she must swallow disappointment before replying: "The trick of that may lie within his book, says Ariel, who's told me where it rests. When faring as a lantern-gaudy fish, he's seen it open on the offshore sand, and cold green currents idly turn the leaves that the incurious octopus might read. It is too heavy for his strength to raise, the grains beneath too diamond-cutting sharp for him to burrow through and pass a rope, the depth too thick for Caliban to dive."

Rupert nodded. " *'And deeper than did ever plummet sound I'll drown my book,'* the wizard vowed, and did. I've memorized most of that chronicle. And pondering, I may have hit on means whereby we can recover the lost word."

"Thou'rt thinking solely of thy duty now?" Jennifer's tone was wistful. "Teach me to love it as I love thyself."

"As I love thee—" His attention plunged back to her. "Dear Jennifer, I do."

"God, God, I dared not hope!" she whispered, fists crammed against breast as if to keep the heart from breaking out. "When thou didst say thou . . . hast regard for me . . . and called me darling—the whole world turned to waves and roared around. And yet I thought, 'Belike he's being kind. He's friendly to me, brotherly, no more.' "

"I did not really know it till today," his words plodded; "or else I did, but shrank from owning to it because my spirit is less brave than thine." He held her close. "If thou wilt wed me—morganatic, maybe—"

Flinging his head up: "Nay, before heaven! Thou shalt mother kings!"

"What matter, if the children just be ours?" she answered through tears.

The kiss went on. Lamp-flames guttered, dusks drew close, a breeze twittered in the doorway.

Rising at last with her, he said, shaken by delight: "Now best we sleep, to strengthen us by day, though every day beyond when thou art by will strengthen me. Goodnight, my morning star."

She blinked her eyes. "Why, where'd'st thou go?"

"Outside—"

"Thy bed is here." She pointed.

Fiery-cheeked, he backed off.

She regarded him seriously and tenderly for a while before saying, "I'm thine forever, any time thou wilt."

He shook his head. "It is my nearest hope that from this hour I may do naught but right by Jennifer. I'll often fail; but never willingly."

Her lips brushed his, her fingers ruffled his hair. Laughing a little, she told him: "Oh, very well, I'll spare thy modesty. We can blow out the lights ere we disrobe, and here are blankets left from Prospero beneath which we may sleep and later dress. And there's a yard between our beds, thou seest—a mile, a league, a polar continent— Still, I can reach across to clasp thy hand."

After a space he nodded, having likewise begun to smile. "I yield me on those honorable terms."

She let him go and moved around the chamber. One by one the flames vanished. "I do confess I suddenly am tired," she said, "as tired as death . . . a happy, happy death which, undeserving, knows what heaven waits."

Rupert's eyes followed her about. " 'Our revels now are ended,' " he murmured: " 'these our actors—as I foretold you—were all spirits and are melted into air, into thin air; and like the baseless fabric of this vision the cloud-capped towers, the gorgeous palaces, the solemn temples, the great globe itself, yea, all which it inherit, shall dissolve and like this insubstantial pageant faded leave not a rack behind: we are such stuff as dreams are made on, and our little life is rounded with a sleep.' "

She had stopped, amazed. "What words are those?"
"Old Prospero's."

"So grave, so beautiful. Their kind has never chimed
upon mine ears."

"Nor ever will, save when thou hearest read the
chronicles of the Historian. We're born into a sad and
lowly age, whose very language limps; we can but croak
like crows on lark-forsaken winter fields." Rupert hesitated. "I only speak of me. Thou art a hawk, as once I
thought, who writes her eloquence upon the wind. I
worship thy fleet shadow."

"If thou'rt swart-feathered, Rupert, so am I!"

His moodiness broke first in a chuckle, afterward in
an honest yawn. "Ah, well, beloved, let's to our repose.
The world and time have also need for crows."

OFFSHORE.

The day lay totally quiet. The island was emerald
upon glass and silver, set against lapis lazuli. The single
liveliness was Ariel's, where he zoomed about on his
wings. The others worked, but were slow in their care.
Sweat made their skins shiny.

The tartane lay at rest, sails furled, no anchor needed.
A stout pole had been secured to the bottom of the
mast. Ropes ran from its free end to a block and tackle
at the peak; thence lines led downward for hauling and
control, to make the whole a cargo boom. From it hung
a curious object: a huge barrel, bottomless and heavily
tarred, hooks inside the lower edge holding bags of
sand. That weight canted the boat far over.

"Halt!" Ariel called. "Halt! Suspend the thing exactly there. Nay, ye have overshot. Come back . . .
come back . . . a grass-blade width—aye, stop. It dan-
gles right. Mine self-sight and my sense for current flow
confirm that it will sink around our goal." He returned
to perch on a thwart. His mien grew troubled. "Yet I've
no eye to scan the future, friend. I cannot say if thou
wilt overstrain those hoops and staves, or thine own
lungs and ribs, and well below five fathom lie en-
tombed."

Kindled by excitement, Rupert responded, "I'm traveling in goodly company: my Lord, my lady's prayers; what need I fear?"

His frame clad simply in breeches, knife at belt, he swept Jennifer to him for a kiss. "I'll soon be back, the book beneath mine arm," he said, "and maybe have a pearl for thee besides."

"Thyself—I want no more— Fare ever well," she could barely reply.

Rupert eased himself over the rail. "Lower away."

"Measter, I beg thee, let me go," Will said. "Tha King ha' need o' thee."

"He needs commanders who'll not let men do what they'd not do themselves." Rupert's tone came sharp from where he trod water. "Lower away, I ordered."

Will bit his lip and obeyed. Caliban helping, he brought the barrel down to the surface on its creaky ropes. Rupert swam thither. For an instant he paused, to wave at Jennifer, then ducked within.

"Let go tha gear," Will rasped. "Tha zooner 'a's off, tha zooner we'll know if 'a's comin' back."

The boat lurched. Cordage whined through sheaves, slapped loose and went under, where the black cylinder had already plunged from sight.

Jennifer leaned over the gunwale, staring and staring until the last ripple died. "Now I may weep," she said, and sank to the bottom of the boat.

Ariel flitted to console her. "He should survive the trip," the sprite said. "Duke Prospero did not really bear away his book to the middle sea, above abysses. He feared there'd be a risk of theft en route. Our friend can stand this depth."

"Thou'lt swear it?"

"Nay," he admitted.

Caliban made his own rough attempt at patting her head. Will grabbed his arm and snapped, "Come away, mudbrain. Has she not grief aplenty without smellin' thee?"

"Aye. I know not how to help the Miranda, do I?" Caliban slouched aft and sat down by the tiller next to the dragoon. "If I did! If I did!"

"If I knew how to help my prince—" Will shook himself. "Ah, well, good mooncalf, we're in the zaeme boat. Let's dull tha edge o' this waitin' as best's we can."

Caliban brightened. "Brandy?"

"Nay, not yet. We may need our moast, not our fullest strength an' wits. Tonight, however, after 'a's returned, aye, liake tha heathen we'll zacrifice a cask! An' if 'a doan't return—" He stared across unmerciful brightness. "We'll drink."

Caliban scratched his mane, dislodging fleas. "I still can't understand what this is about. Thou callest that thing a diving bell. Not once did I hear it go dingdong."

Will cuffed him. "From tha shaepe, as I miaght liaken thee to a midden. As for a clapper, Rupert himzelf, crashed back an' foarth till— Nay!" He drew a ragged breath. "Hark'ee," he said fast. "My prince learned in Tunis how yon book had been zunk, but tha water'd not damage zo magic a thing. Were't damageable, thou zeest, Prospero could'a got rid of it in easier ways nor this. Well, my general thereon had a cooper in Tunis maeke him the bell, which be another new-fangled invention. Gaunt though our hoape zeemed o' fiandin' tha spot, 'a knew we'd need means o' goin' down if zomehow we did get heare. I'll 'splain tha principality. Tha zandbags drag it under, tha tar zeals in air to breathe. Thic air thickens, 'a zays, squeezed by water; yet a bubble should remain for him. When on tha bottom, 'a'll fiand what 'a zeeks by feel, then cut loose them weights whilst hangin' onto a stanchion inzide. Tha barrel should fair leap tow'rd tha zun."

"And the Miranda." Caliban scowled. Hopefully: "He's taking a long time, right?"

"Who knows? We can't tell how deep it be, how coald an' dark down yonder, an' naught zave tha bell, that book, an' his life's one candle—"

Jennifer cried out. Ariel rocketed aloft. Will scrambled to his feet. Caliban yelped. In a roar and white gush of cloven water, the device had returned.

It nearly flew free before it splashed back down. It and the boat rocked toward quiescence.

"Rupert, Rupert!" Jennifer screamed after part of a minute. "Why comes he not forth? I'll to him—" She tore at her clothes.

"Nay, hoald. *Be*-hoald," Will said. "There!" (Rupert's head appeared from underneath the barrel.) Sudden dismay: " 'A zeems death-paele. . . .Be 'a movin'? —Measter, canst grip this?" He snatched a boathook and held it over the side.

Rupert caught it feebly with his free hand. The other clasped to his side a huge volume bound in brass and scaly leather. Will drew him close, leaned out, let go the staff, and held him by the hair.

"Get that book ere he loses it," Jennifer snapped. " 'Tis what he was hurt for." She herself was the one who did. Meanwhile Will and, after profane orders, Caliban hauled Rupert aboard.

The prince lay doubled over in the bilge. "Pain, pain in every limb," he groaned. "I scarce can stir—"

Ariel darted to land beside him and pass quick fingers across the contorted body. "Aye, too much air within," the elf said. "He rose too fast. I blame myself that I did not foresee. A miracle of strength that he could move enough to save himself. There's fate in him."

At once, flashing a smile to Jennifer, who knelt frantic: "Nay, be at ease. A spirit of the air knows how to charm these humors out of him and mend whatever ruptures they have caused. Thereafter he'll need but a few days' rest to raise anew the tempest of his health. Now draw aside and let me sing my spell."

In awe, she and the others went astern. Will took her right hand, Caliban her left, and the three of them waited.

XXI

OUTSIDE PROSPERO'S CELL.

A gibbous moon hung above its cliff, turning hoar the treetops. Otherwise they stood black against a sky of hurried thin clouds and flickering stars. The earth below was a well of night, save where a fire burned at the cave mouth. Wind rushed cold and noisy. Sometimes an owl hooted.

The flames leaped, streamed, whirled off in red and yellow rags. Whenever a dry stick popped, sparks torrented. That light picked five uneasily out of shadow. Rupert stood sword at hip, holding the book; furrows gouged his mouth and brows. Beside him Jennifer held a staff taller than she was, its broken halves spliced together by withes tied in an intricate knot. Phosphorescence from the capital, which was carved into a lotus, fell across her widened eyes, half-parted lips, the teeth behind and the pallor around. Ariel poised on a boulder, fingers dug into its moss, wings folded but fluttered at the edges by the wind. Caliban hunkered, a lump; Will Fairweather reared above him, a scaffold; neither could down every sign of dread.

Rupert spoke slowly: "Now we have said our prayers, to ask that God bestow His blessing on the deeds we do and keep our usage lawful of these powers that we have gained from reading gramarie."

"An' please doan't let 'em run away from us," Will added. To his chieftain: "Prince, art thou altogether sure 'tis wiase? Thou'st oanly had zome days, a week or two, however long 'tis been, to zearch them words. Oald taeles agree that magic's liake a stallion, 'twill throw his riader, be 'a ne'er zo pious, unless 'a know just what tha hell 'a's doin'."

"Hell," Caliban shuddered, "hu, hu, what's chillier than hell?"

Rupert frowned at his man. "How often must I tell thee, I well know how little I have learned in this short while of poring over text arcane, complex, beset with ancient words and secret signs? By that same token, I cannot do much in those few spells deciphered—raise clairvoyance, call forth the simple spirits of a land, transport us quickly—that is all I know, if I know even that. Well, who can guess if he has read aright, unless he try? Tonight's our first attempt, a minor one which, if done wrongly, should at least prove harmless. Ask Ariel. He's helped me in my work, whilst Jennifer sustained me, and thou boused."

"He's right," said the elf. "But hurry. We must have the moonlight."

Rupert opened the book. Jennifer shivered. "My darling, art thou frightened?" he asked.

She raised her chin. "Not near thee."

"Then hold the staff aloft while I read forth, and give it to me when I reach for it."

Rupert began chanting: "Ye beings quick and unseen, yet as bright as this our fire of oak and ash and thorn, by smoke of herbs and mushrumps rising thence, wherein ye do delight, be drawn to me, and by these words inscribed in pentacle upon the dust from which my flesh has sprung, be bound to strict obedience, under God." Jennifer passed him the staff. He wrote with its bronze ferrule while voicing: *"Adam Te Dageram, Amrtet Algar Algastna—"*

The conjuration took a few minutes. At their end, Rupert closed the book, gave it to Jennifer, and called: "This is the task I lay on you: three visions, clear to our sight and hearing, as commanded. First show us in an overview that field in England, from which Ariel lately came to say a battle had begun there. *Aleph.*"

The fire roared and lifted, became a tree-tall column, split into a ring wildly spinning through lurid reds and blues. Within its vast circle, as if through a window, appeared a scene.

It was the same night, beneath the same moon; perhaps even the wind was the same which drove clouds and whistled over acres. Water gleamed across the darkness of the land, canals, ponds, a river that lapped three

sides of a conical height, tiered and skewed by nature,
crowned by man with a tower now ruined, which rose
sharply above neighbor hills and the flats beyond. Nearby bulked walls, roofs, steeples of a minor town. A few
windows still glowed lonely. Brighter were the campfires
of an army, two or three miles outside. There guns could
be seen, wagons, animals, tents of officers, gleams which
must be off the pikes and armor of sentries.

"Oh, Glastonbury!" Will cried. "Oh, naught but
Glastonbury! Aye, look: tha elven-haunted Tor—tha
abbey—Wearyall Hill, where grows tha thorn o' Joseph
—Mine own hoame lies off yonderwards—my Nell—
My Nell an' every kid of ours, my loves, has war come
by, an' me not there for help?" He sank to his knees,
buried face in knobbly hands, and wept like a barking
seal.

The view swept nearer, as if the watchers swooped.
Over ravaged leagues the revelation flew. Now it drew
close to linger a moment, now fled from what it found.

Jennifer bit her fist, not to whimper with the agony of
those sights, and huddled inside Rupert's free arm. Caliban squatted slack-jawed, sometimes lifting a paw as if
to poke, never quite venturing it. Ariel escaped aloft and
fluttered bat-fashion in the blast.

A heap of dead stiffened ashen under the moon. A
drummer boy lay by himself in his own tangled entrails;
the wind ruffled his fair locks, while ants marched over
his eyeballs to his tongue. A horse kept screaming, the
remnant of a man kept begging for water that there was
none to give; neither could die. A cannon yawned uselessly, spiked; among the balls it had never fired was a
shorn-off human head. Someone's Bible lay in the mud,
open but covered with blood and vomit. A cripple
crawled along, trailing a shattered leg he had rudely
bound up; the cold had gotten to him, his teeth clapped
and frost was in his beard. The wind and the wounded
sang Miserere.

"What has man done," Ariel asked heaven, "that he
deserves himself?"

" 'Tis war, thus cruel," Rupert told Jennifer, "though
one can die worse, or live worse yet, a slave—Hold on!
What's here? The image closes on an army, camped—"

Several men sat around a fire, perhaps on call, perhaps too exhausted for sleep. Grimy, unshaven, a couple of them bandaged, they held palms toward coals and exchanged low words. They were outfitted in buff coats and heads were close-cropped.

"They're Parliament," Rupert said starkly. "Our foe then holds the field."

The ring contracted to a pillar, which sank to a common blaze. Jennifer uttered a cry, Caliban grunted in surprise, Will lifted his wet countenance, Ariel flew downward.

Rupert had stayed moveless. "So ends the vision, murky as our hopes," he stated. "Well, we have two to go. Let's on with it."

The hovering sprite regarded him through red glow and shifty shadows. "Thou hast a hardy soul," Ariel declared at length.

"I am a soldier." Rupert raised the staff. "Next show our chiefest enemies in council," he ordered, "most recently, if not this instant. *Beth.*"

Again they looked into a fiery circle. The Puritan camp appeared—evidently earlier in time, for some embers of sunset smoldered and the moon hunched low. Sight rushed past guards to a pavilion, and through its canvas. There it steadied.

Two men sat by lamplight, in conversation over a small table strewn with maps, dispatches, notes. One was a Roundhead officer, to judge from his bearing and russet coat: a strong-built person whose homely features grew mustache, chin-tuft, and warts. The other wore civil black, tall hat on knees, and appeared older though remaining trim. His skull was domed and bald; grayish eyes blinked in the sharp face.

Jennifer cried out again. "Mine uncle—guardian—"

"Shelgrave!" Rupert snarled. He recovered himself. "Fear him not. He's far away; and thou'rt no more his care but mine, forever after." He waved his companions to silence. "Hush. They speak."

The officer—he looked like such an ordinary squire —said: "Of course you're welcome, Sir Malachi. The service your manufactures and railroads have done our cause do more than overbalance the escape of that prisoner." He made a stern smile. "Anyhow, naught having happened yet about him, I suspect Hot Rupert lies long since cooled in a ditch, his throat cut by some fellow rogue—which, to be frank, spares us considerable trouble. . . . Well, what brings you here, this far west and south, and on the day of battle?"

Shelgrave must have rehearsed his speech, for he got it out crisply. "What I have to say, General Cromwell, may sound feverish, yea, verging on heresy. Nonetheless, I beg you, remember from when we both sat in Parliament." He leaned forward. "I'll freely explain everything in fullest particulars, and confirm it by a clergyman of unquestionable reputation, who was directly concerned himself. He accompanied me hither, though at present he's unfortunately carriage-sick. Together we'll testify what witchcraft is Rupert's. You know he was called a wizard, who kept familiars and—Well, 'tis true, and more than true."

"Go on," said Cromwell quietly when he paused.

"We'll give you circumstantial accounts, General, of how Rupert ensorcelled my niece, my ward, into setting him free; how they received hex-rings from woodland demons; how Rupert and a confederate crossed this island, eluded hounds, and vanished; how they reappeared in Tunis, the guests of Papist nobles; and how again they've left, after commissioning equipment of unknown purpose but ill foreboding."

Cromwell touched the Bible among his papers. Otherwise he stayed imperturbable. "Go on," he repeated.

"We'll further relate how I caught my deluded niece with the wicked sign on her finger; how we extracted confession from her; how we sent her south under the clergyman's guidance, accompanied by soldiers, in the hope of intercepting Rupert; how she in her turn enchanted one unfortunate young lamb to helplessness, escaped, and has doubtless rejoined her diabolic paramour. 'Tis a long tale, and time is at our heels—yours also, General. Will you take this for a promissory note, and credit what I really wish to say?"

"I'll hear you out."

"This news has but lately reached me, when the woman's warders returned and mine agents brought post-haste word from Africa. Meanwhile, freed of Rupert's cursed presence, our armies have gone from victory to victory over the forces of Satan—"

"Speak not thus," Cromwell rapped. "Charles remains my King."

Shelgrave was taken aback. "But . . . forgive me, General . . . was Charles Stuart not himself in command of the host which this day you met and broke? Hasn't he withdrawn behind those walls, and don't you propose to storm them on the morrow?"

Cromwell's fist lay heavy on a map. "His evil geniuses are one thing," he said. "The king's own person—" After a second; "Parliament must decide that. As for my immediate task, here's the last Royalist muster of any consequence. And it was mostly patched together from such rags as blew in on every wind, from every other battle lost. A final onslaught, and England will have peace." Prophecy flickered out of him. "Say on, Sir Malachi."

"Does it not strike you strange, General, that they should come to this precise country for their last stand? 'Tis flat, save for the Tor and a few lower hills; open; hard to defend. Why not the Mendip range—or, better, Wales?"

"We've questioned captured officers. They wonder too. 'Twas the King's express wish, they relate." Cromwell rubbed his massive jaw. "I've thought he thought, being no military expert, here's a famous old town in the midst of strongly Royalist countryside, with communications southward. Faulty reasoning, of course."

"I wonder too what put that thought in him." Shelgrave spoke low. "Glastonbury . . . the heart of ancient Britain . . . where Christendom first came unto this isle, say High Church legends, though in eldritch guise, when Joseph of Arimathea brought the Grail and thornwood staff which flowers yet each Christmas . . . its abbey ruins where folk swear they see, of moonlit nights, the phantom monks hold Mass. . . . Glastonbury, which was Druid ere 'twas Christian, and Celtic Christian ere 'twas even Roman, and which some say was Arthur's Avalon . . . its hinterland aflit with Faerie folk, who still are given secret offerings. . . . Is it not strange the

King's last stand is here, two days before the night of equinox?"

Cromwell scowled. "Make plain your meaning."

"I am trying, sir." Shelgrave's reply was as harsh. "I tell you from experience, Prince Rupert is Lucifer's own agent, sent by him to halt us in our scouring from this land idolatry and mystery and hell. Now I have learned that he's alive, at large. What darkling legions is he leading hither?" He seized Cromwell's shirtcuff. "This is the word I came to give you: Strike! Send forth Jehovah's lightnings from your guns; smash, scatter, and ride down Philistia; leave in this place of trolls no King, no priest, no soldier, wizard, witch, or stone on stone to greet Hell-Rupert and afford him aid! Then must he skulk back to his smoky den"—Shelgrave's voice broke, his face writhed—"he and his bitch who was mine own pure maid—" Controlled again: "And England will be safe. But don't delay."

Cromwell stayed unshaken. "That's not my wont. Nor is it to stampede. 'Twas a stiff battle, and my men need rest. Tomorrow, aye, we move upon the town. And as for fiends and sorcerers, what reck their bolts men armored well in righteousness?"

The vision ended.

Will Fairweather cackled laughter. "Our darklin' legions, hey?" he cried. "Liake Caliban? Nay, 'a an' Ariel 'ull stay behiand. I doubt my measter's magic has tha strength to lift them from this plaece where tha' belong. Zo lead thy hoast to victory, my loard: one row-foot hoa'seman, lackin' but a hoa'se; one wench clad liake an out-at-elbows boy!"

"No talk," said Rupert, who had stood as if cast in metal. "We have one seeing more to come." The staff rose like a wan beacon above the sinking red fire, toward stars, white-rimmed cloud wrack, moon in frantic flight. "Show me my King. My final fiat. *Gimel.*"

As if with their last might, the flames formed the ring. It enclosed an upstairs room, well-furnished, not too brightly lamplit for an open window to reveal, across roofs, a view of Glastonbury Tor. Several men sat around a table, some in faded finery, some in soiled soldier's garb, all drained by weariness.

Rupert started at sight of the largest. "My brother . . . *ach*, Maurice!" he whispered. Then toward the smallest: "His Majesty." For Charles was a tiny man, though he bore himself so erect, even now his dark handsomeness was so neatly groomed, that the fact did not stand forth. Rupert recognized others. *Goring the villain, Digby the conniver,* he thought flashingly, *Eythin the greedy: what fine Cavaliers. I'd liefer have a bluff and honest Cromwell. No matter what one's side in any strife, some allies would make better enemies. . . . Well, there are dear Maurice and good Will Legge and my beloved ever-kindly kinsman—*

"Is that thy brother?" Jennifer asked. "He looks fine indeed."

He silenced her with a gesture which was the sole gentle thing about him. Voices rolled.

"Make never doubt, tomorrow they'll attack," Maurice was saying dully. "They'll batter down our pitiful defense, as they have done to city after city. Thus Glastonbury will soon be sunk in fire, like any ship that flies the Stuart flag when pounced on by the Navy that was yours. They've cannon for't—including most of ours."

"*Why* did your Majesty insist we meet and rally hereabouts, upon a plain as flat as we've been beaten?" lamented Eythin.

Charles overlooked the insolence; it was born of desperation. "I know not," he answered.

They stared at him. He gave them the least of smiles. "I had a thought . . . a dream . . . a sense . . . a murmur . . . a feeling here was right, and our last hope," he said.

"A witch did brew that dream, your Majesty," Digby mumbled.

Charles shook his head. "Nay, Puritans abhor the mildest magic, and any magic flees away from them, who will not own God also made the elves. Was it a sprite who sang within my sleep? I venture not to think it was a saint."

"Whate'er it was, it lured us to our doom," said Goring.

"Now, wait, that is not fair," objected Legge. "Remember, sirs, we did hold council more than once between us, agreeing Somerset might not be best, but any other place was nigh as bad, so sorely are we hurt since Marston Moor. What have we truly lost by coming here?"

"The war," snapped Eythin.

Goring formed a gallows laugh. "'Twas lost already. We are spooks hallooing 'round awhile before the dawn —the winter dawn, our graves more snug than it."

"What shall we do?" King Charles asked. "I hate to yield my sword, but more would hate to see this fine old town bombarded, fired, and plundered, uselessly."

"Worse would be yielding up your royal person," Maurice said.

The King winced. "How much more anguish is this carcass worth?"

"Whilst you're alive and free, the cause is too," Maurice declared. "How well I know, whose mother is your sister!"

"You are no walking rack to hang a crown on," Legge added, "but the embodiment of countless hopes."

Maurice glanced around the table. "If we've lost England, we've not lost the world," he said. "We may yet get our King across the Channel. For that, we can't stay in this rat-trap burgh. Let's move, before the enemy can act"—he pointed at night and height—"to yonder hill. Dug in upon its crest, we can cast back a hundredfold assault."

"Then lie besieged," snorted Eythin. "They'll thirst and starve us out."

Maurice nodded. "Aye. But we will have bought those days, you know—mayhap to smuggle him away disguised; mayhap to raise the peasants in our aid and cut a seaward road like Xenophon; mayhap—I cannot tell. We'll likely fail. But surely we will fail, attempting naught."

Their eyes went to the King. For a space he stared at his fingers locked on the table before him. At last he sighed: "The prince has right. Ridiculous it is. Yet for the sake of folk who've trusted us, if God allow, we'll raise our exile banner, that they may dream defeat will have an end."

He rose, went to the window, stood gazing out with

hands clasped behind his back. Most softly he spoke. "There will be other times, my comrades. There will be a day of trumpets. This we must believe. Now when all flags guide corpses to the sea, and ships lie hollow on a smoking shore, broken of bone, and windy shadows weave a dark about tall widows turning whore to feed gashed children, I must say that more days shall remain than hobnailed victors thieve. And if our iron's broken, there's still ore—stones of our sharded cities lying free to sharpen it—and if you should perceive rust and the dimness in us, do it silently."

The vision guttered out, and the fire beneath.

Rupert shouted into night: "We must away to England ere too late!"

"Too late for what?" fluted Ariel.

"To help, or die for him."

xxii

THE ISLAND.

AGAIN it was night, but calm and warmer than before. The moon had just cleared the heights, yellow, an edge bitten out by that murk which lay everywhere on land. The bay and the waters beyond glimmered. Five stood by that boat which had brought Jennifer. While it was still beached, its mast had been raised and sail unfurled.

"Here is the hour when we may start our flight," Rupert said. "Let us embark. This day was long to wait."

" 'Twas far too short for me, that breath of peace, belike our last, we shared in beauty's home," the girl replied.

Hope jumped in him. "Thou'lt stay behind in safety, as I wish?"

"And let thee go?" She summoned a laugh. "Thou art a darling blockhead."

"I fear she really must accompany," Ariel said. "What feeble spells thou'st learnt can barely serve when there are moonbeams to uphold this craft she came here in, diminutive though 'tis. Thou'd'st not get far ere morning brought thee down, save that the presence of a virgin maid has always strengthened magic."

"Well I know!" Rupert snapped. "Stop babbling—" His tone changed. "Nay, I'm sorry, Ariel."

"I would that I could help thee further, Prince." The elf's wings quivered, glow and glitter against forest blackness. "But far from home—surrounded by cold iron—"

"Thou'st aided us beyond our giving thanks." With infinite care, Rupert bent over and clasped the minute hand in his enormous one.

"Because 'tis for the Old Way thou hast drawn thy sword: the wholeness of the living world. Farewell."

"Farewell."—"Farewell."—"God keep thee well."

Words went caressing among them. Ariel fluttered aloft to touch Will's brow and brush lips across Jennifer's.

"Good-by," the dragoon said gruffly to Caliban. "Enjoy tha brandy I've bequeathed."

The monster didn't hear. His shaggy head never stirred from staring at the maiden, though the rest of him shook with pain. "Thou never wilt come back again, Miranda?" he rasped.

"Only in dreams, I fear," she answered. Moonlight caught sudden tears. "But always, always I will remember thee, dear Caliban."

She ran forward, kissed him, and fled to the boat. Rupert and Will had already boarded. The prince stood holding Prospero's staff on high, the book laid open across his other arm. As Jennifer sprang into the hull, he called: "Our spell is cast; the unseen tides now flow to bear us off. *Zain.* I conjure thee, rise!"

Silently, smoothly, the vessel lifted. Will looked downward, gulped, squeezed his eyes tight shut, and folded himself as small as possible in the bottom. Jennifer gasped once, then leaned out and waved as long as she had sight of the island. Rupert stood before the mast, staff aimed at the North Star.

Awhile Ariel followed. When he returned, Caliban had not moved on the beach. "What, art thou petrified?" the flyer asked. His japery trembled.

"She kissed me," the monster whispered.

"Aye. Her sweetness breathes across the whole horizon."

"Thou dost not understand. She kissed me. Me." Caliban shook mane and shoulder. "She did. She does. She will. It cannot die until I do. What need I more than this? How wonderful the world is, Ariel."

"Ah, well, I'm glad for thee." The spirit clapped him on the back. "Come to thy rest. I'll sing thee lullabies of Jennifer."

Ariel flitting, Caliban trudging, they went on into the woods.

THE BOAT.

It scudded before a breeze which was part of the en-
chantment. Nonetheless a hush dwelt in heaven, only
deepened by a low thrum in the lines. This far aloft, air
was so keen that breath smoked white as the few drifting
clouds. Earth rolled vast and vague beneath. Forward,
aft, overhead, and right, a purple-black ocean was
crowded with stars; to left went the westering moon. Radiance ran down the sail until it lapped the gunwales.

Jennifer had the helm. Rupert stood at a rail, peering
over. Will sat in the middle of the midmost thwart, holding on. The prince pointed to a thread which twisted
and gleamed below. "There's the Dordogne," he said.
His voice was nearly lost in immensity. "We'll raise our
goal ere dawn."

"How canst thou tell?" the other man inquired.

"I've pored o'er many maps. How strange to see the
lands themselves like that. They have no borders. . . ."

"Me, I'll buss tha swile, although it be a barnyard
where we zettle." Will flickered an uneasy glance. "No
disrespect to any Powers, o' coua'se. But zea or sky, this
messin' around in boats just ben't for me. Oh, nothin'
liake it, true! Tha which I thank God's goodness for,
amen."

"When we are down—unarmored, since the spell can
scarcely lift more iron than our blades—maybe thou'lt
think thou didst enjoy this ride." Rupert gave a sardonic
chuckle. "We chatter thus, while miracles go on. Perhaps the saints can pass eternity enrapt in solemn bliss;
but we are mortal."

He stepped astern and lowered himself beside Jennifer. "Shall I take o'er thy watch?" he asked. "How dost
thou fare?"

"Most marvelously, since it is with thee." She gave
him a smile which, in the strong subtlety of bone and
flesh, under huge eyes and moon-frosted hair, was elven
as Ariel's. Gesturing out: "And many of mine oldest
friends are here. The Wains are homeward bound the
same as us; to ringing of the Lyre, the Swan takes wing
across a river clangorous with light; near Pegasus, the

Princess waits her hero; and from the sunrise quadrant comes Orion, who will bestride the heavens—art thou he?"

Rupert was still before he answered harshly: "Nay, I'm the Scorpion. Thou canst not see where I am on my peril-poisoned path. How could I bring thee . . . even for my King?"

"I'm frankly tired of hearing I'm too fine!" she flared. At once she grinned. "Though true it is, thou'st ground me down between the millstones of thy duty and thy conscience. When we are wed— Oh, grant me this last flight, for afterward the blueness of new seas for me will only lie in children's eyes, and melodies from Faerie in their mirth, and high adventure in their growing tall — When we are wed, the foremost task for me will be to tease thy moodiness from thee."

He hugged her to him. His voice trembled. "Thou'rt far too good for me. But so's the sun. God gives with spendthrift hand. His will be done."

The boat flew on through moonlight.

A MEADOW.

Grass was almost as dark as trees, under clouds blown off a rapidly nearing storm-wall. Wind droned, the first-flung raindrops stung, like cold hornets. Stars had been swallowed, but a last few lunar beams touched the boat. It staggered down from the sky, thumped, and lay. The sail flapped wild.

Rupert's call tore across that noise: "Art thou hurt, Jennifer?"

"Nay, save . . . save for rattled teeth," she answered shakily.

"I had to land fast." He groped to help her out; the gloom thickened each second. "Else we'd been trapped above the overcast, and the moon that bears us is going down."

"Where be we?" came Will's voice.

"South of Glastonbury," Rupert told him. "I can't say closer."

"Who can, in this weather? Blacker'n tha Devil's gut —there went tha moon—heare comes tha rain. Welcome hoame to England."

"Can we find shelter?" asked the girl as sluices opened above her.

"Not by stumbling blind," Rupert replied through a wet roar. They could barely see the shadow-form of him point. "Yonder's north, our direction. We'll walk cross-country till we strike a road bound the same way. There ought to be houses near it, though we'd better take care who's inside."

"Friends to us, if I know my Somerset folk," Will assured him.

"Aye, but have the victors begun quartering troops on them? Come, march."

"Thou'rt riaght, as always. Damnable bad habit o' thiane, Rupert, bein' right. For how I wish I could zee tha farmer hereawa, when 'a fiands a zailboat in his pasture!"

A ROAD.

The storm had ended soon after sunrise. Wind kept on, sharp and shrill from the north, driving a smoke of scud beneath a low iron-hued heaven. Rupert, Jennifer, and Will leaned into it, heads down, hands mottled blue, as they tramped along the mud. Water from their garments fell into ruffled puddles. On either side of them ran a hedge, and fields beyond it flat, brown or gray with autumn, the occasional trees begun to go sere and let leaves be whipped off their boughs. A flight of rooks went by, grating forth lamentations.

"A bitter, early zeason," Will said at last. His nose was the sole spot of brightness in the landscape, save for the drip from it. "I doan't recall no worse."

"Was ever year more weird than this?" Jennifer replied. She attempted a smile. "See here's Prospero's wand my walking staff."

"An' his book weights down tha bottom o' my scrip, underneath food from his island." Will touched a bag slung around his shoulder. "Anybody caere for a bite?

Nay? Well, I too 'ud swap theeazam pears an' pomp-
granites for a zingle bowl o' hot oatmeal topped wi'
cream an' honey; an' this zaber o' miane 'ud liefer carve
a Cheddar cheese than a trail to glory."

"Or the freedom and safety of thy household?" Rupert rapped.

Will's lips drew thin. "Pray doan't bespeak thic, zir. It
be hard enough for me aloane to keep myzelf from fret-
tin' thus. 'Fear not,' I tell me, though it doan't do no
good for long; 'fear not for wife an' kids,' I zays, 'only
for thine own hiade, an' for whatever Roundhead regiment might anger Nell.' She's a big woman, zir; when
she milks, tha whoale cow shaekes; an' as for temper,
why, if instead o' his wretched powder kegs, Guy Fawkes
had had my Nell—"

"Hold!" Rupert lifted a hand. "Around yon bend
ahead of us—horsemen— Enemy!" His sword flew
from its sheath.

They were five who came. One was a fat, middle-aged
peasant in long brown coat, baggy trousers, mucky
shoes, greasy hat, mounted on an ambling cob. The rest
were unmistakable Ironsides. When they saw Rupert's
party, their yells blew down the wind: "Stray Cavaliers
—a Puritan boy their captive— Save him! At them!"

"Get backs against this hedge," Rupert ordered.
"Stand fast. Behind me, Jennifer."

Earth boomed, mud-water splashed, hoofs broke into
gallop. Will did not draw steel. Instead, he removed his
loaded scrip and whirled it by the strap. Rupert gave
him a puzzled look but had no time to say more. The
leading Roundhead was on him.

"Yield thee or be cut down!" the man bawled.

Rupert stood firm. The horse reared to a halt. A
blade whined from above. Rupert's met it in mid-stroke.
Metal screamed, sparks spurted. Sheer violence tore the
rider's weapon loose, sent it spinning free. Before he
could skitter off, Rupert's left hand had him around the
jackboot. A heave, and he was out of his seat, entangled
in one stirrup. His charger whinnied and bolted, dragging him through the mire.

Will had let fly the bag. It struck the second cavalry-
man in his jerkin. He whoofed out air and slumped

across his saddlebow. Now Will unscabbarded sword.

He and Rupert came in on either side of the third trooper. The fourth tugged pistol from belt. Jennifer sped his way. "Aye, to me, good lad!" he encouraged her.

"Indeed to thee," she said. "Accept my staff." She gave it to him across his wrist. He yelped and dropped his firearm. She whacked him in the nose. He bellowed and clutched at red ruin.

Rupert and Will got their quarry disarmed and dismounted. The prince soared into the saddle. He went after the first horse, which had slowed, caught its bridle, released its erstwhile master, and led the animal back for his friend. Together they rode at the remaining two. Dazed, Jennifer's victim offered no resistance when Rupert relieved him of weapons and commanded him to earth. The man of the book recovered sufficiently to spur his own beast into headlong southward flight. No one bothered to pursue.

"O Jennifer!" Rupert cried. While he rode about rounding up prisoners, he kept blowing her kisses. She clutched Prospero's emblem and glowed.

"One escaeped but three captured," Will said. "Not a bad bag."

The peasant had sat open-mouthed. Will cantered to him, reined in, and exclaimed: "Why, it be my neighbor, Robin Sledge!"

The other must swallow several times before he got out: "Will Fairweather . . . back from tha dead?"

"Not yet. However, quick ere I bogie thee, how's my house?"

"Tha last I heard or zaw, unharmed. Ye be lucky, dwellin' offzide as ye do."

Will wiped his forehead, albeit he said merely, "Foarezighted, Robin, foarezighted. When I war after a croft to rent, an' zaw how thic 'un zits vizzy-vizz tha coney runs— Well. How'd'st thou fall in 'mongst theeazam bad companions?" He jerked a thumb at the muddy, bloody, and disconsolate Parliamentary soldiers.

"Scouts, wantin' of a guide; not that there be aught left for Croom'll to fear, or war till you three caeme."

"Thou'd'st help them cantin' rebels, Robin? Thou?"

"I'd scant choice when asked," Sledge said bitterly. "Two zons o' miane, Tom an' Ned, be 'listed under tha King. I'd better do what I can to win mercy for 'em, do tha' live."

Rupert had trotted up, stopped, and listened. "How goes the war?" he inquired.

"It rocks tow'rd an end, zir," Sledge sighed. "Tha last o' tha loyal pulled out o' Glastonbury an' onto tha Tor. Thic should'a been better to defend: but him Croom'll —rebel commander— Well, I zoldiered a bit whan I war young, an' zince ha' downed many a pint along o' veterans what ben't all witless bags o' brag; but never have I zeen or heard o' one liake Croom'll. 'A must be wiald to catch tha King; for 'a's drawn in everything 'a got, ne' miand hoaldin' that countryzide peaceful; 'a's laid 'em 'round tha hill tighter'n Jack Ketch's noose; an' his guns only stop hammerin' whan they crunch cloaser inward. From what I zeen, zir, I doan't give tha King three days, nor *no* chance to slip free."

Rupert and Will exchanged a look more bleak than the wind.

Abruptly the prince said, "Thanks for thy word, goodman. Thou might'st as well play safe by conducting these fellows further, after I've interrogated them about dispositions and so forth. 'Tis not thy fault they were overpowered." He laughed, not blithely. "True, they'll have to fare afoot. We've need of three horses, also of buff coats and the rest. Well, let them walk, and in their natural buff. They'll doubtless be grateful for such help in mortifying the flesh and bringing down sinful pride."

He turned back toward Jennifer.

Sledge stared after him. "Who be thic wight?"

"An acrobat," Will said.

"A what?"

"One what treads a tightroape 'bove hell. Come, let's away an' talk as long's we can."

XXIII

GLASTONBURY TOR.

CROMWELL'S army had started well up the staggered flanks of it. Few men were readily seen on either side. Taking what lee they could in dug trenches or behind trees, bushes, boulders, bluffs, they lay waiting for their officers' call to make the next advance or the next resistance. Musket fire crackled only irregularly. This was the hour of the cannon.

Those roared steadily, in masses, from the Roundhead stations. Muzzles flashed, missiles rumbled through air, solid shot hammered down and canister burst in shrieking thousandfold, over and over and over. Smoke hung in a bitter blue haze. For the wind had died with afternoon. A pallid sun glimmered, vanished, struck through again, out of slowly dissipating chill gray. Given such calm, the attackers employed a lately invented device: two hot-air balloons they had brought, tethered to float higher than the hilltop, observers in the baskets using telescopes and surveyors' instruments to spot for the artillery to which they wigwagged down their signals—grotesqueries hanging above town and land like the future itself.

The Royal positions made slight reply. Riding, Rupert said to Will and Jennifer: "The guns are plainly few which our people could drag to the top of this mount. No doubt they're equally poor in ammunition. They'd've been overrun erenow, were it not such labor hauling ordnance uphill against fire."

"It costs, thic," said Will. (A dead man sprawled in withered grass.) "Why not just lay ziege?"

"We are the reason." Rupert's grin writhed. "Inadequate; quite likely soon refuted."

"Too laete, I think we should'a cut our hair short, thee an' me."

"With Occam's razor? Nay, not every Parliamentarian goes polled, the more so after weeks of dispute. I think best I be quickly recognizable at need. Meanwhile, wear thine Ironside outfit as if it belonged to thee."

"Thine plainly does not," Jennifer murmured.

"Well, I hate seeing a soldier sloppy-unlaced as myself," Rupert admitted. "However, we mustn't act apologetic, or timid, or unsure in any way. That's death—or capture, which could be worse. Behave as if we own the place." His neck stiffened. "We do."

Jennifer's fingers tightened on Prospero's staff. " 'Twould be too cruel if thou . . . any of us got killed by a loyal sharpshooter."

"Aye, we've a gap to win across, and must build our bridge with whatever wreckage we find— Hold!" Rupert drew rein. "I spy. . . . Follow my lead, say naught, obey any command on the instant."

A trio of fieldpieces—one sacar, two lighter falconets —had appeared as the riders passed a thicket. Shot and bags of powder lay heaped around; wagons and horses must have gone on elsewhere, for none but the crews were in view. Two men to a weapon, they swabbed, loaded, corrected aim, touched match to fuse, swabbed, loaded. . . . An ensign squinted through his glass at the balloon which was visible from here, notepad held ready for a calculation of how best to lay the next barrage.

Rupert cantered toward them. Discharge crashed; his ears hurt, smoke rankled in his nostrils, echoes tolled. Despite the weather, some soldiers had stripped to the waist. Sweat shone through the dirt on them. *These men who man this post of guns court deafness,* he thought. *How bloodshot glare their eyes from powder soot; how weary must they be from hour on hour, unknowing when they may be blown apart—yet still bombard their King in honest effort, methodical, indomitable, English.*

"Halt!" challenged the ensign. "Who comes hither? To your muskets, boys!"

"Why, 'a's no ancient," Will muttered; "hear his voice go squeak."

Rupert stopped. No matter his disarray, in the saddle he towered overwhelmingly above them. "Three scouts sent forth to probe the area," he announced. "The aerostats have spied what well may be the founding of an enemy emplacement. Cease firing whilst we dash on high to look; stand ready, though, to cover our retreat."

"Aye, sir." The youth saluted. "You're valiant, risking—"

Jennifer. Rupert smote fist in palm. "I'll take the lead, and Will the rear," he said. "Ride on!"

He spurred his animal.

Up over the rough ground he went, a jarring gallop where sparks flew from stones and the breath of the beast came hoarse through boom of more distant cannon. Ahead loomed a wall of brush and scrub woods. Who loured behind? *Dear God,* he prayed, *if Royal lead must bring me down, let it be me indeed, not her, not her! . . . I know, I hope our friends will hold their fire, astonished, curious, at this lonesome three. . . . Well, if they don't—O Jesus, keep her safe.*

"Shoot not at us, King Charles's men!" he shouted out of full lungs. "Stand by! It is Prince Rupert of the Rhine come back!"

He unbuckled the morion which sat so badly on his too-big head and cast it aside. Cut from a shirt and tied underneath was a white cockade, his olden sign. Down spilled the black locks, around that face which many should remember.

A bullet buzzed near. The artillerymen had realized something was amiss. But at extreme range, and they not trained musketeers—He crashed through leafage. Withes whipped horse and rider, drawing blood.

Then suddenly men surrounded him, no different from their enemies to see, but crying aloud: "It is Prince Rupert! Rupert has returned! Protect him with your bodies, him and these! Bring him at once, the prince before the King!"

WITHIN THE TOWER.

Nothing else remained of the Chapel of St. Michael on the Tor. Its roof was gone and holes were more broad than empty windows, where shots had battered through. Cloud-shuttered sunlight entered more weakly than did the gun-grumble. Yet those olden walls were the sole shield there was for the sovereign of Britain.

He stood like a miniature, or like a much larger man seen through the wrong end of a telescope, in front of his captains and councilors. They were grim and be-grimed, their backbones slumped, the rags which clung to them soured by the sweat of days. Charles was no less gaunt and sunken-eyed. But his little body kept erect; dust seemed almost an ornament upon combed hair, trim beard, lace and plum velvet of Cavalier garb; and the bandage across his brow might well have been a crown.

Guards at the doorway stamped pike butts on floor-stones. Rupert entered, Jennifer and Will shyly behind, among a tumult of men who shouted their tidings. Down on one knee before his uncle, the warrior still was close to overtopping him.

"Your Majesty, I am come home to serve you," he said.

Charles's tranquility broke asunder. He shook as he embraced the other. "Be welcome, welcome, triply welcome, Rupert! Arise. Thou spokest truth. Here is thy home." To those around: "Make free, his friends! Rejoice while still ye can."

Some held back, stating formalities. Even today, when nothing seemed left for their losing, they had no love for the meteor which had shaken their military firmament. Lord Eythin bustled to the doorway, rattling: "Out, out, ye rabble! Cram not in. Go back where ye belong, upon the firing line," and got several sergeants to help him enforce this. Meanwhile, the rest swarmed around Rupert. Maurice cast himself into his brother's arms. They pounded backs, swore sulfurous Dutch, German, French, Bohemian oaths, and scarcely heard William Legge say, "We thought thee dead. If heaven has kept stored the prayers for thee, already thou'rt a saint."

"You're prating like a Papist, Legge," Eythin growled. He windmilled his arms at Rupert's companions. "Forth! Out!"

"Not those, my two beloved followers." Rupert elbowed aside the Scot, who stood speechless in his indignation. Turning to King Charles, Rupert went on, above diminishing voices and confusion:

"Your Majesty, without the pair of them, I'd lie in chains or headforeshortened coffin. Not only did they pluck me freedom's flower as a free gift of love and loyalty, but fearlessly fared far and far away to stare down strangeness in its inmost lair. The weapons they've brought back to fight for you belike have scanty power in this world; but in your heart, my lord, the Royal standard will fly eternally victorious through knowing you have subjects such as these."

Jennifer clung to his arm. "Oh, Rupert, nay," she whispered. "We were two sparks at most, struck from thy flint and steel."

Will shuffled his feet. "Doan't puff us up," he added. "We'd bust liake bladders flailed against a zword."

Maurice scratched his head. "What cookery of metaphors is this?"

Silence fell over the gathered noblemen and soldiers. The bombardment sounded unreal. Charles held out his hand. "If such they be," he told his nephew, "I crave of thee the honor of learning what their names and stations are."

His courtly reserve cracked again when the smaller one curtsied. Rupert had to smile. "This is no lad you see before you, sir," the prince explained. "She is a maid hight Jennifer Alayne, and she will be my bride if God allows that we outlive this war." Defiantly: "A commoner, 'tis true, but worthy to be made a princess. Likewise Will Fairweather, a humble crofter, could supply heart" —his gaze raked his rivals—"to fifty thousand dukes."

Charles stood thoughtful a moment before he also smiled, in grave wise, and addressed the two: "If this be so—and Rupert's ever truthful; as starkly truthful as a battle-ax—why, then, you're welcome, less to these poor quarters than to the throne-room of my regnant soul." He kissed the girl's hand. "My lady, if thou hast no near male kin, may I bestow thee on thy wedding day?" (She burned in bewilderment and glory.) To the man: "And thou . . . art William called Fairweather, right? This is no time to speak of peerages, estates, or any other mortal gift. But if thou wilt swear service to the Crown—'tis but a form, I'm sure thou'lt understand—"

No less confused than Jennifer, Will blurted, " 'Foare God an' Christ, I'll ever zarve my King."

"Then kneel." Will obeyed. Charles drew blade to touch him on shoulders and head. "For our own honor more than thine, here in this hallowed place we make thee knight. Arise and be Sir William Fairweather."

The man reeled to his feet and stood trembling. "Me? Kniaght? Liake thic there Lancelot? Can't be!" His Adam's apple bobbed. "What'll Nell zay whan she do hear o' this? Oh, zir, thou'st maede me blubber liake a baebe."

Rupert, Maurice, Legge, and some others pressed in to congratulate him. They could not take long about it. Jennifer drew him aside and held him as a sister might, while Rupert stood before King and court.

"Lord, I have weeks to tell you of in minutes," the prince said. "I'd fain discuss them privily with you and certain councilors who'll stay discreet— Nay, best we two alone; no jealousies. I'll hope that you'll believe, and not recoil, and reach a calm decision what to do.

"However, gentlemen," he announced to the whole gathering, "I shall reveal: the three of us did not seek here to die, but from a quest abroad where we have won some secret strong instrumentalities. I'll not pretend that they can win the fight. Quite probably there's naught will come of them. Yet if we do not try, we spurn God's grace."

Slowly his voice grew, till it drowned the cannon: "Whatever happens, let's not crouch besieged until those dogs around have dug us up. We're men, I say, not badgers gone to earth. Let's tighten every sinew we have left and sally forth. Mayhap we can break through and find the sea, and ships to save our King. Mayhap at least we'll give the foe a shock that makes him grant us honorable terms by which we may depart alive and free, to amnesty or exile as we choose. Or maybe we'll be shot to nothingness. Well, what of that? If we do naught, we're done; while if we fare and fail, we'll fall together —how better than in battle-brotherhood?"

Maurice cheered. Several men joined in. The younger prince sprang forth, to pace leonine as he responded: "Whate'er thy weapon, Rupert, thou art ours! It was the lack of thee which gutted us. Thou'd'st ne'er have let us creep into a hole; nor, given thee, would we have thought of it. Hear how the troopers shout beyond our tower! The single word of thee is worth a Caesar. And think how it goes flashing down this hill to burst and flame among the enemy. Hell-horrible to him, thy name strikes lame. At dusk, O King, when gunfire's fallen still, I'll take some chosen comrades to the plain. A careful few, who lead hoof-muffled horses, can slip past sentinels, in tricky twilight, who are but plowboys and apprentices stuffed into jerkins. Rupert will recall how he and I, beneath the walls of Breda— No matter now. We'll scatter far and wide, from house to house and moor to hill to forest, and cry the word: 'Prince Rupert has returned! That lump-machine of Cromwell's could not crush him. If ye'd be free, take down your fowling piece, your crossbow, scythe, bill, staff, avenging flail; make haste unto the ancient holy Tor and battle for the right to be yourselves. Though the year falls, the Green Man has returned. The plume of Rupert's flying for the King!' "

Charles himself looked half dismayed; but a spirit had suddenly arisen among his men, and he was borne forth on its wings.

BEFORE THE TOWER OF ST. MICHAEL.

Its ruin lifted like a crag over wan grass, darkling brambles, bushes, and trees. The moon was barely up, to touch with ice the river, the plain, the ditches that vein it and are known as *rhines*, the remote but weirdly near-looking gray-blue Mendips, and that slow surge of hills called the Island of Avalon, which crests in Glastonbury Tor. The town below huddled mostly in darkness; hostile watchfires ringed the heights with red. Lean clouds coursed here and there among stars which flickered as cold as the whittering wind. Cold likewise were the guns, but bitterns boomed afar in the marshes.

A flame sprang up, became a fire, beat red-blue-yellow, and sang its dry, mysterious song. Four stood between it and the vanished chapel, facing the moon. Three had not changed garb. Rupert held Prospero's book, Jennifer—in a skirt improvised from a cloak—his staff, King Charles a Bible; Will stood aside, an empty-handed scarecrow.

"So are we gathered," Rupert spoke into night, "quite alone with God and with what lesser Powers we may raise by casting what small spells we know and dare. I fear they'll be but few and feeble sprites. Yet must we try it for our fellows' sake—"

There went a sound of movement, as quiet as possible, underneath the summit.

"—before we join them in their night attack, Sir William and myself."

"I'll pray," Jennifer said in anguish.

Rupert nodded and looked at the King. "My lord," he asked, "lead us in prayer, ere we draw wand or sword."

XXIV

BEFORE THE TOWER OF ST. MICHAEL.

RUPERT ended his incantation, closed the book, held high the staff, and said into the wind: "Thus be ye summoned, spirits of the land. It is your King who calls you to his aid. If there be meaning in the holy bond between the King, the people, and the land, if there be sacredness in reverence for what is old and good and deeply loved, arise for him upon this judgment night!"

His words blew away. The fire flared once and sank, making the company mere glimmers of red amidst darkness. A cloud engulfed the moon. The stars were hazing out. Only the wind had speech; and its chill gnawed inward.

After an endless while, Charles said, "Nothing?"

"No stir, no whisper of a help for us," Rupert answered as low.

"Well, 'twas a brave attempt. I must admit some seeming pagan aspects troubled me."

"We'll die like Christians, surely." Rupert straighted. "I'll now go to fetch my horse and harness for the charge we hope in hopelessness may break the ring." To the girl, his voice most soft: "Hark, Jennifer. If I do not return, forget not my last wishes were for thee. Remember what I've planned that thou shouldst do to reach to safety—"

"What's that without thee?" Her words were muffled by her clinging to him.

"Spare me the fear that thou wilt always mourn."

"Nay, wait," said another.

King, prince, and maiden looked about; for that was a somehow eerie sound. "I think we be not finished, us," Will Fairweather went on, and shambled forward till his ungainly shape caught the coal-glow.

"What's this about?" Rupert demanded.

216

Will shook his head. "I really dwish I knew." He spoke in a sleepwalker's tone. "But zudden-liake, a thing ha' come on me . . . nay, through me, liake I war a dudelsack tha wind's about to play a jig for ghosts on."

Jennifer held fist to mouth, free hand straining over her man's. Charles, head of the Protestant Church of England, crossed himself. A minute streamed past before Rupert breathed, "He is transfigured. See. He's more than man—or else more wholly man, more of this earth than we have soul to let us understand. . . . O Will, what have I done to thee, my friend?"

"The spell thou'st cast was but a fleeting spark," Charles said, looked into the commoner's face, and went on his knees. "Yet did it find a waiting torch in him. Because this is his land?"

Will lifted his arms. The fire leaped after them, taller, brighter, till he stood in a beacon radiance. The cloud departed from the moon and the stars grew near and brilliant.

He said forth across night: "I am the land."

For an instant, his human self broke through. "Thou went about it all wrong, General. What do tha land caere for kings or noables or priests or loards protector —any o' thic lot—zave as tha' belong in *it?* Thy brother caeme moare nigh tha mark whan 'a called thee tha Green Man. Be thic, naught else. Lucky 'twar, liake Charlie yonder zaid, zomebody war heare what tha spell could taeke hoald on in tha right way."

Thereafter it was more than he who called:

"I have the right to raise the land I am. In me alone the mightiness indwells, till I bestow it on my messengers that they may bear my wrath across the world. Mine is the outrage, as mine was the love.

"I am the land, by virtue of the bones of my forefathers which have strengthened it, the flesh which they give back to us in harvest, the patience of their plowing centuries, each blossom time when they went two by two, each hunter's moon on woods afire with fall, each winter and each sorrow they outlived till humbly they went down to namelessness. Their gnarled old fingers made me what I am—nor wilderness nor iron desert:

home—the while my skies and seasons worked on them.
Their songs and hearthside tales, my wind and rain,
speak each unto the other of our oneness. Though men
and trees do die and die and die, the blood, the house,
the field, the woods endure, and every babe or lamb or
new-leafed branch says forth the immortality we share.

"Thou shalt not bind me fast in brick and steel, nor
make my people to idolaters of little frantic leaders and
their texts. If mystery and merriment alike be human
rights, I claim them for my folk.

"Mine are the dead, the quick, and the unborn. From
out of time, I call their life to me that it may leap in
those embodiments to which the wonder of the folk gave
birth.

"Come in your love and in your dreadfulness. Ye gar-
landed white maidens of the springs, ye dancers in a
bright midsummer night, ye tricksy elves who are a
household's luck—ye huntsmen who go rushing through
the air, ye tall gray-cloaked who walk the hills in awe,
ye lurkers in the rustling river depths, ye warriors who
sleep by rusted swords that once did bell, 'This country
is our own!'—arise. The hour is gruesome late. Arise.

"I am the land. I bid you come alive."

Higher whirled the flames, until they seemed to min-
gle with stars. Dwarfs were feeding them on wood which
the storms of a hundred years had shaped. An owl went
overhead—two ravens—an eagle.

The Tor groaned and opened. Horns resounded. Out
above the earth rode huge shadows, and troll-hounds
clamored. "There goest the true Wild Hunter, Gwyn ap
Nudd, leading the heathen dead from Annwn forth,"
said Will's throat. "Theirs be the land's unrest and deepest peace."

That which came after brought Rupert's question
wavering: "But what is the magnificence behind, a troop
of riders bannered by the Cross, whose mail and lances
burn as cold as moonlight?"

"King Arthur and his knights from Avalon."

"In God's name, I must follow them. Farewell."

Through one heartbeat, Rupert held Jennifer to him.
Meanwhile a procession of men, robed and hooded,
streamed from the chapel which no longer was. The first

bore a crucifix, the next a chalice, and together they all chanted:

"*Dies irae, dies illa,*
Solvet saeclum in favilla—"

Out on the plain, a stag bugled, a red bull bellowed, and a great white stallion went tramping.

Rupert was gone. Jennifer and Charles sought each other. Side by side, they looked at the balefire and at the form of Will Fairweather. "Oh, see," the King stammered, "those visions in the sparks and smoke—they're surely true—our tattered, splendid men go forth like storm—not only spirits rally to them, but common folk —I am not worthy."

Sight: Prince Rupert is ahorse, armed, armored, on his helmet a white plume. He cries to the cavalry he has gathered, flings saber aloft, and leads their charge. In a shining tide, they stream on down to the enemy guns.

Sight: Prince Maurice, at the head of yeomen, crofters, wrights, herdsmen, diggers of peat and burners of charcoal, a reeve or two, weavers, tanners, fishers, laborers, carters, poachers, vagabonds, whoever wants the freedom to remain himself—hastens to join the army of the King.

Sight: A Puritan trumpet sounds alarm. Men spring from their rest, toward steeds which they have left saddled. Over the sky goes the spectral hunt. Shrieking, they scatter from what to them is a vision of hell.

Sight: A ranking Parliamentary officer, quartered in a Glastonbury house, hears the racket and reaches for his gear. A small brown person appears to the goodwife, nudges her, jerks a thumb. She nods, takes up her rolling pin, and lays the officer flat.

Sight: Rupert's Cavaliers gallop straight at the Roundhead cannon. One gunner has the prince before the muzzle and a lighted match ready to bring to the fuse. Then a damsel stands in front. Save for a wreath, she is nude. Like wind and water, she dances. He gasps, covers his eyes against her laughter, sinks shuddering to earth. The Royal horse thunder on past him.

Sight: A platoon of Puritan musketeers takes stance outside their main force, ready to enfilade the attackers. The monks pass by. Their faces are hidden by cowls, but the tapers they bear burn clear and steady. Their chant goes under and through every noise of the living. Men wail, cast down their arms, start to flee. Their commander brings them to heel and orders them to sing a hymn which may drown out the ghostly Mass. So they hold their ground; but they are no longer in combat, and presently they are taken prisoner.

Sight: Rupert's charge surfs on the adversary host. Off that rock it recoils, in a roar and a rattle. Lances and sabers are too few against pikes and pistols. Shouting, he rallies his followers, re-forms them and heads back across the strewn dead. Now on his flanks go horsemen like steel towers, and at his side one who wears a crown. Overhead, golden-glowing, flies a dragon banner. Those rebels who see know that this is Arthur come home. They remember what blood of Britain is in them too. Their leader casts down his standard and weeps. The King's riders burst through.

Sight: Maurice's people draw near. Roundhead artillery prepares to rip their disorderly mass asunder. The air seems to thicken overhead. All at once there is a cloud, which opens in rain that drenches powder to uselessness. Six feet away, stars gleam clear. The peasants pour onward.

Sight: Couriers have sped to outlying units of the Parliamentary army, bidding them come help. A large band of reinforcements approaches on the far bank of the river. They are almost at a bridge when the waters rise. Brawling, furious, more white than black in the gloom, the river breaks the bridge and sweeps it away. Walled off from their comrades, the soldiers must wait to be beaten in detail—later, when the stream again deigns to let anyone pass.

Sight: Rupert is in the middle of his foes, hewing, slashing, cleaving. But they outnumber his band. Not many of them ever saw the knights, who have departed. Maurice's gang has gotten to the other side of them. A troop of heavy cavalry detaches itself from a wing and canters scornfully to scatter that rabble. Screams and howls rive the air; eyes flash, fangs glisten; wolves and wildcats, unseen for generations, are in among the horses. Those bolt in terror. The peasants hurl themselves full into the fray.

Sight: Heaven burns with meteors. Earth quakes underfoot.

Sight: At the core of his host, Cromwell rides from unit to unit. In the name of his God, and by sheer will, he makes them once more one. Like an iron idol, he looms in the saddle above his infantry, as it stands fast and hurls back assault after assault. There is no breaking that wall. And now it begins to walk. It will retreat in good order, to fight another day and that time win.

But a noise goes through its bones. Looking north, all men alike see what comes, slow, unstoppable, and inhuman. It is the forest.

Oaks on their mighty roots, ash trees swaying, thorns raking with cruel branches—behind, marching fir, skipping laurel, slithering vines, rumble-rolling boulders, a murk of life—the wildwood comes; and terror sighs forth from every leaf.

That brings the end. Though Cromwell cries that here are just other phantoms, his warriors can endure no further. Pan has taken their souls, and they stampede. Barely does Rupert hold his own folk together.

Sight: A few hours afterward, having disarmed and put under guard what rebels are not still in blind flight, he meets Cromwell. Both remain mounted. They exchange a few courtesies. He accepts the sword of the defeated, in the name of their King.

In a cold sunrise, red and green above a suddenly ordinary world, the prince rode back up Glastonbury Tor, saluted, and said, "Your Majesty, you are victorious."

Will Fairweather, who had stood as if locked before the balefire, stirred above its burnt-out coals. "What's happened?" he asked, blinking around; "I war doazin' for a whiale," and sneezed.

XXV

LONDON.

ALL bells were ringing and banners flew from every staff, as the King rode into the City. Among the myriads who lined those streets, no few had worked or fought for Parliament. Yet well-nigh each of them cheered wildly for an end of war and the return to them of brothers. Above tumult and color, the sky was asparkle with sun. Wind in parks and gardens frolicked with leaves gone gaudy.

On Charles's right rode Prince Rupert, on his left Prince Maurice; immediately behind, a gilt carriage bore his family, surrounded by mounted noblemen. After it came one for Jennifer Alayne and Sir William Fairweather. She appeared lost in this spectacle. He did service for both, beaming and waving, especially at pretty girls. In the procession were churchmen, peers, mayors, ambassadors, and other dignitaries. Representatives of the Royal army formed an honor guard, burnished armor, flowing crests and flags, high-stepping horses, crash of boots under pikes. But no full regiment was on hand, and never a gun came along. "We shall not enter as a conqueror into our home," the King had said. "We hope to be a healer."

WHITEHALL.

Amidst peacock pride of lords and great captains, sober garb was before the throne, on the burgesses of England. Some compeers of Scotland and Ireland stood defiantly unmistakable among them.

Light smote through arched windows and shattered on gems as King Charles raised his hand.

"Ye know the most of what we shall proclaim tomor-

row to the people and the world," he said. "Let us, however, in curt courtesy, lay it before you here to think
upon.

"We both, we Crown and commoners, were sent
through a sharp school which birched us in the lesson
Our Lord first offered freely on the Mount. Hereafter
may we do our sums aright!

" 'Tis true high treason cannot be ignored. The unre-
pentant leaders of revolt—as Cromwell, Fairfax, Shelgrave, and the rest—must go from us, their riches con-
fiscate to loyalists who formerly were poor. But they
may fare as exiles where they wish, or, if they like, be
granted ships and help, that in New England they may
found new lives. It can well use such steadfastness as
theirs.

"And to the most, the vast majority, is given
pardon unconditional. Let us be reconciled with one another, rebuild this house we wasted in our rage, then
dwell together in a common love.

"Toward that end, the Crown must do its share. Up-
rising, though unjustified, had causes which partly lay in
King and Church and nobles. Not simply folly and ex-
travagance, but outright tyranny, archaic use a crust
across the growth of a new age, unwillingness to listen or
to change—such things from us; and from the Parliament an arrogance, intolerance, and haste—unholily en-
gendered civil war. Let us instead join better qualities.
Let a new Parliament be called to us, and with us write
new laws which long may stand because they serve the
welfare of our land."

A COTTAGE IN SOMERSET.

It was a low little thing, huddled beneath its thatch as
if for warmth. Smoke blew on a streaking wind, out of a
crude clay chimney, past leafless trees and over bare
earth. The day was clouded to shadowlessness.

Into that gray and brown Sir William Fairweather
came like a fire. A few pigs and chickens, loafing about
the courtyard which house and outbuildings made, scattered from his charger. He sprang onto frozen mud,

flung reins across hitching post, and caroled: "Halloo, my kiddies! Heare be your daddy come!"

Small forms boiled forth, to roil and pipe around him. He hugged them, lifted the two least onto his shoulders, and strutted toward the door.

It opened. A large woman, in drab and patched gown, appeared. For an instant she drew breath; tears started forth. Then at once she put arms akimbo and glared. "Why, good day to thee liakewise, Nell," he said through a weak smile.

"An' what's good about it?" she demanded.

"Look. I be hoame. No hurried visit for to let thee know I war zafe, but hoame from London an' everywhere."

"Until thy next gadabout!" his wife snorted. "What'll thic be? This night a raid on tha coneys? Or a fearless foragin' to tha Boar's Head? Nay, no moare, Will Fairweather! Thou'st filled thy belly planty long in town; an' I'll waeger that ben't all thou'st filled, either. Meanwhale, tha roof went leaky, tha peat undug an' uncarted, I must zell our plowhoa'se for to pay the plowman's waeges —an' dost thou bring hoame another? Nay, behoald yon evil-eyed keffel o' thine! Bring him near any useful work, an' 'a'll shy as fast as thee; or else'll kick tha whippletree to fierewood, though thic'd at least be moare than thou canst bestir thyzelf for to provide. Out o' them fanciments! Lay down thy snickersnee. Take honest smock an' pitchfork, an' get tha barn cleaned. Else never await a bowl o' what mush we can affoard for zupper, scant thanks to thee!"

"But—but—but, my dear," he stuttered, "zee, heare at my belt, a purse full o' goald. We'll dine on beef an' caepon tonight—"

"Not if *thou* ridest to market after them."

"An' as for leaks in tha roof an' zuch, why, we've an estaete comin', zoon's title gets cleared. Doesn't thou understand? I be maede kniaght. I'll be tha new squiare. Let them poachers bewaere!"

"Humf. Indeed? Zo *I* must learn la-de-da manners, have tha vicar's wiafe in weekly for tea, go pass Christmas baskets out 'mongst tha smelly parish poor? 'Tis

fiane for thee to swagger 'round twirlin' thic tomcat
mustache thou'st grown, aye, aye. But woman's work be
never done."

After a moment: "Ah, well," Nell finished, and
spread her arms, " 'twar a drab dworld without thee,
oald gib, an' I'll not ask how many drabs thou didst
fiand in thiane. Come in an' dwarm thee; I've zaved an
evenin's dworth o' yale; go thou ahead, whet on me tha
lies thou'lt forever hence be stickin' to thy bousy
companions. . . .Hoald! Wipe thy web feet, ninny!"

A HIGH PLACE.

Forest stood everywhere around, black save where
gleamed an icicle or the eye of an owl. The hill, though,
rose clear, one glow and glitter of snow under a full
moon and so many stars that darkness itself seemed
crowded out of heaven. Air lay crystalline still and cold.

Tethering their horses, Rupert and Jennifer climbed
to the top. She shivered. He brought an arm and a part
of his cloak around her shoulders. "Art chilly, dearest?"
he asked. His voice was lost in ringing silence.

She snuggled. "Never next to thee."

"I likewise. But let's do this final duty as quickly as
may be, and hasten back to where men dwell. We've
known sufficient strangeness. Now that we have been
wed, I fain would clasp a sweet reality, too good for
dreams."

Rupert raised the staff he bore, she the book. Silver
flashed on their hands. "King Oberon and Queen Titania," he said louder, "this one last time we call you forth
to us. By the moon's witchery, in Yuletide season whose
joyousness foretells a year reborn, come out to claim
what rightfully is yours."

A glow awoke, and the rulers of Faerie stood before
them. A new majesty, or an old one returned, made the
humans bow very deeply.

Yet the queen's words sang mild: "Greeting, good
Rupert, gentle Jennifer. How happy 'tis to welcome you
again."

"More than your kin, the Half-World owes you thanks," Oberon said. "Ye have lit countless candles in a shadow. What luck and love may lie within our gift we promise you, each night ye both do live. And when at last your Father bids you home, ever shall elven songs remember you, ever shall springtime garland your graves in blooms, ever shall fortune follow your children's children, as long as kindly magic does endure. May it not fail before the Judgment Day."

"We thank you too, and most sincerely hope"—Rupert hesitated, shook his head—"though I know not— know not—and cannot know—" Straightening: "It hurts that we must make a severance. But we're too much of flesh, my bride and I, and too much mortal world and work await. These eyes are blind to color by the moon; these heavy ears hear birdsong but are deaf to thin delirious music of the bat; these fingers are too coarse for harvesting of dewdrops or for weaving spider-silk; these nostrils drink no odor from a stone; these tongues can find no taste in thistledown. So we'll no longer tread in Faerie's rings or follow its wild stars beyond the wind. We'll seek what wonder is in common earth."

Jennifer seized the Queen's hand. "I think you also always will be there," the girl said. Titania smiled.

"Take back the serpent sigils that you gave," Rupert told Oberon. "Someday, maybe, you'll find a man with strength to keep that flame—"

"Or with less blood than thine," Jennifer interrupted him. "I'll see thou'lt never wish for more than me!"

Amusement went mercurial across the kingly pair. Rupert continued doggedly; "Likewise take off the book and staff we bear, old Prospero's, to keep where seems you best. Greet Ariel from us."

"And Caliban," Jennifer murmured. "And . . . there's a lad—no cause for jealousy—your Majesties must know whom 'tis I mean—If sometime soon, along some twilit lane, he might meet one who has a heart to swap. . . .And oh, I know so many more besides—"

"Dear girl, we cannot ward the living earth," Oberon answered, grave again and softly, "no more than can the rivers, hills, or sky. That loneliness is laid upon thy race." He and his queen gathered the things of sorcery.

"Fare always well." He raised the staff. "Titania, away!"

They were gone into the radiant winter night.

After a long while, Rupert took Jennifer's arm and said, "Come, darling, let's get home before the day."

Epilogue

THE TAPROOM OF THE OLD PHOENIX.

THEY were many gathered this evening, to sit before the innkeeper's fire, enjoy his food and drink and regale him with their tales. Valeria Matuchek leaned against the bar, a pint in her fist, the better to oversee them. A few she recognized, or thought she did—brown-robed monk at whose feet lay a wolf, gorgeously drunk Chinese from long ago whose calligraphic brush was tracing a poem, rangy fellow nearby whose garb was hard to place but who bore a harp, large affable blond man in high boots and gray leather with an iridescent jewel on his wrist, lean pipe-smoking Victorian and his slightly lame companion, wide-eyed freckle-faced boy and Negro man in tatterdemalion farm clothes, coppery-skinned feather-crowned warrior who held a calumet and a green ear of maize—but of the rest she was unsure. Several were not human.

Being impatient to hear everything that could be spoken and translated before they must depart, she finished her turn rather hastily:

"Yes, I came back through that universe, and spent a while learning how things worked out. Earlier, I'd gone to history books elsewhere, for background. Evidently this had to be the time-line where the romantic reactionaries do better than anywhen else. And . . . *this* Charles the First was either a wise man from the beginning, or chastened by experience."

She shrugged. "I'm not sure how much difference it'll make in the long run. In my history, Prince Rupert—well, he didn't simply help invent the mezzotint, he became a scientist, a sponsor of explorations, a founder of the Royal Society. . . .I don't think that in any cosmos he'll sit smug on his victories. And they've got a new world a-borning there too, the real New World, the ma-

chine—science itself, which matters more; reason triumphant, which matters most—no stopping it, because
along with the bad there's too much good, hope, chal-
lenge, liberation—

"Well." She drained her tankard and held it out for a
refill. "Nothing ever was forever, anyway. Peace never
came natural. The point is, it can sometimes be won for
some years, and they can be lived in.

"Enough. I hope you've enjoyed my story."

THE BEST S—F IN THE UNIVERSE
from
ⒷⒷ BALLANTINE BOOKS

LEST DARKNESS FALL L. Sprague de Camp $1.25

ALPHA 5 Robert Silverberg, Ed. $1.25

STAR TREK LOG TWO Alan Dean Foster $1.25

THE TEXAS-ISRAELI WAR: 1999
  Howard Waldrop & Jake Saunders $1.25

STELLAR 1 Judy-Lynn del Rey, Ed. $1.25

DARK STAR Alan Dean Foster $1.50

THE QUESTOR TAPES
  Dorothy C. Fontana $1.25

THE HOUNDS OF SKAITH (STARK #2)
  Leigh Brackett $1.25

MAJOR OPERATION James White $1.25

▼ Available at your local bookstore or mail the coupon below ▼

SCIENCE FICTION
from